RUSHING TO PARADISE

J. G. BALLARD

RUSHING TO
PARADISE

BALL
c. 1

Picador USA
New York

Picador® is a U.S. registered trademark and is used by St. Martin's Press under license from Pan Books Limited.

ISBN 0-312-13164-X

First published in Great Britain by Flamingo, An Imprint of HarperCollinsPublishers

First Picador USA Edition: May 1995
10 9 8 7 6 5 4 3 2 1

Contents

PART I

Saving the Albatross

'SAVE THE ALBATROSS . . . ! *Stop nuclear testing now . . . !*'

Drenched by the spray, Dr Barbara Rafferty stood in the bows of the rubber inflatable, steadying herself against Neil's shoulder as the craft swayed in the skittish sea. Refilling her strained but still indignant lungs, she pressed the megaphone to her lips and bellowed at the empty beaches of the atoll.

'*Say no to biological warfare . . . ! Save the albatross and save the planet . . . !*'

A passing wave swerved across the prow, and almost struck the megaphone from her hand. She swore at the playful foam, and listened to the echoes of her voice hunting among the rollers. As if bored with themselves, the amplified slogans had faded long before they could reach the shore.

'Shit! Neil, wake up! What's the matter?'

'I'm here, Dr Barbara.'

'That's Saint-Esprit ahead. The albatross island!'

'Saint-Esprit?' Neil stared doubtfully at the deserted coastline, which seemed about to slide off the edge of the Pacific. He tried to muster a show of enthusiasm. 'You really brought us here, doctor.'

'I told you I would. Believe me, we're going to stir things up . . . '

'You always stir everything up . . . ' Neil moved her heavy knee from the small of his back and rested his head against the oil-smeared float. 'Dr Barbara, I need to sleep.'

'Not now! For heaven's sake . . . '

Already irritated by the island, which she had described so

passionately during the three-week voyage from Papeete, Dr Barbara raised two fingers in a vulgar gesture that shocked even Neil. Between the lapels of her orange weather-jacket the salt-water sores on her neck and chest glared like cigarette burns. But her body meant nothing to the forty-year-old physician, as Neil knew. For Dr Barbara the polluted water tanks of the *Bichon*, the antique ketch that had brought them from Papeete, their meagre rations and sodden bunks counted for nothing. Albatross fever was all. If Saint-Esprit, this nondescript atoll six hundred miles south-east of Tahiti, failed to match her expectations it would have to reshape itself into the threatened paradise for which she had campaigned so tirelessly.

'Reef, Dr Barbara! Time for quiet . . . I need to hear the coral.'

Behind them was the Hawaiian helmsman, Kimo, his knees braced against the sides of the inflatable as he worked the double-bladed oar. He sat like a rodeo-rider across the outboard engine, which he had tipped forward to spare the propeller. Neil watched him jockey the craft among the running seas, feinting through the gusts of spray. For a son of the islands, Neil reflected, Kimo was surprisingly hostile to the ocean. The sometime Honolulu police-man seemed to hate every wave, sinking the sharp blades into the swelling bellies of black water like a harpooner opening a dozen wounds in the side of a drowsing whale.

Yet without Kimo they could never have carried out this protest raid on Saint-Esprit. The disused nuclear-test island was a junior and more accessible cousin of the sinister Mururoa, which Dr Barbara had wisely decided to leave alone. Captain Serrou, the Papeete fisherman, was waiting for them in the *Bichon*, two miles out to sea. He had refused to join the run ashore, taking Dr Barbara's talk of chemical warfare agents and imminent nuclear explosions all too literally. Only Kimo had the nerveless skill and brute strength to steer the inflatable through the reef and find an inlet among the deceptive calms that floated a few feet above a Himalaya of teeth.

'We're drifting . . . !' Dr Barbara clambered over Neil and tried to seize the Hawaiian's oar. The inflatable had lost headway, bows wavering as it fell back on the rising sea. 'Kimo – don't give up now . . . !'

'Hang on, Dr Barbara . . . I'll get you to your island.'

As Dr Barbara shielded the megaphone from the spray, Neil gripped the waterproof satchel that held her tools of trade. Needless to say, Dr Barbara travelled without any medical equipment. Instead of the hypodermic syringes and vitamin ampoules that would have cleared the ulcers on their lips, or even a roll of lint to bandage a wounded albatross, there were aerosol paints, a protest banner, a machete, and a video-camera to record the highlights of their raid. The television stations in Honolulu, if not Europe and the United States, might well be intrigued by the filmed material and its emotive message.

'She's coming, Dr Barbara.' Kimo bent his back and drove the craft forward, a mahout of the deeps urging on a reluctant steed. Listening to the spuming air above the coral towers, he had found an inlet through the reef, a narrow gulley which the French engineers had cut with underwater explosives. Wider and less hazardous channels crossed the southern rim of the atoll, the route taken by the naval vessels supplying the military base. But the open lagoon exposed any unwelcome visitors to the soldiers guarding the island, who would be standing on the beach ready to throw them back into the surf, as the anti-nuclear protesters landing on Mururoa had discovered. Here, on the dark north coast, they could slip ashore unseen, giving Dr Barbara time to find the threatened albatross and rally the full force of her indignation.

Oar raised, Kimo ignored a black-tipped shark that veered past them, chasing a small blue-fish. He waited for the next swell, and propelled the inflatable through the whirlpool of foam and coral debris that erupted as the trapped air burst from the gasping walls. The reef fell away, slanting across the cloudy depths like the eroded deck of an aircraft carrier. They entered the quiet inshore waters, and Kimo fired the outboard for the final six-hundred-yard dash to the beach.

'Kimo . . . Kimo . . . ' On her knees in the bows, Dr Barbara murmured the Hawaiian's name, reproving herself for any fears that his commitment might falter. Neil had never doubted Kimo's resolve. During the voyage from Papeete the large, stolid man had kept to himself, sleeping and eating in an empty sail-locker, preparing for the confrontation that lay ahead. He always deferred to Dr Barbara, stoically enduring the ecological harangues with which she greeted every unfamiliar bird in the sky, and clearly regarded the sixteen-year-old Neil Dempsey as little more than her cabin boy. Kimo had sunk his savings into their air-fares from Honolulu and the charter of the *Bichon*, but at times, as he fiddled with the ketch's radio, Neil suspected that he might be a French agent, posing as a defender of the albatross in order to keep watch on this eccentric expedition.

Eight days out of Papeete they passed a fleet of Japanese whalers, escorting a factory ship that left a mile-wide slick of blood and fat on the fouled sea. The spectacle so appalled Dr Barbara that Neil held her around the waist, fearing that the deranged physician would leap into the bloody waves. As they wrestled together, cheeks flushed by the reflected carmine of the sea, the pressure of Neil's hands on her muscular buttocks seemed almost to excite Dr Barbara, distracting her until she pushed him away and shouted a stream of obscenities at the distant Japanese.

Kimo, however, had been eerily calm, soothed by the thousands of sea-birds feasting on the whale debris. During the last days of the voyage he sacrificed his own rations to feed a solitary petrel that followed the ketch, even though Dr Barbara warned him that he was becoming anaemic.

He fed the birds and, Neil liked to think, dreamed their dreams for them. In Kimo's mind the freedom of the albatross to roam the sky deserts of the Pacific had merged with his hopes of an independent Hawaiian kingdom, rid forever of the French and American colonists with their tourist culture, shopping malls, marinas and pollution.

It was Kimo who told Dr Barbara that the French nuclear scientists were returning to Saint-Esprit, which they had abandoned in the 1970s as a possible testing-ground after moving to Mururoa, an atoll in the Gambier Islands safely remote from Tahiti. The two hundred native inhabitants of Saint-Esprit had already been relocated to Moorea, in the Windwards, and the island with its camera-towers and concrete bunkers lay undisturbed during the long years of the nuclear moratorium.

12

However, the threat of a new series of atomic tests had failed to inspire Dr Barbara, a veteran of the protest movements who was helping to run a home for handicapped children in Honolulu. This restless and high-principled English physician was bored by the endless rallies against ozone depletion, global warming, and the slaughter of the minke whale. But Kimo also informed her that the French engineers on Saint-Esprit had extended the military airstrip, destroying an important breeding-ground of the wandering albatross, the largest of the Pacific seabirds.

Saving the albatross, Dr Barbara soon discovered, held far more appeal for the public. The great white bird stirred vague but potent memories of guilt and redemption that played on the imaginations of the University of Hawaii graduate students who formed her protest constituency. Coleridge's poem, she often reminded Neil, was the foundation-text of all animal rights and environmental movements, though she was careful never to quote the familiar verses.

Now that they had arrived at Saint-Esprit, where were the albatross? As they coasted towards the beach a flock of boobies circled the inflatable, a hooligan vortex visible to any French patrol boat five miles away. They mobbed the rubber craft, soaring along the wave troughs, beaks lunging at the open sores on Neil's arms. Dr Barbara thrust the megaphone into their faces, and hopefully scanned the shore for any signs of a hostile reception party. Thriving on opposition, she was always disappointed to be ignored, and aware that she might have to make do with this audience of raucous birds.

The monotonous thudding of the inflatable's bows against the waves had turned Neil's stomach. He retched over the side, leaving a few grains of breakfast oatmeal – an obsession of Dr Barbara's – on the greasy float. Fending off a persistent booby, he wondered why he had joined the protest voyage. Not only were there no nuclear tests, which he had secretly been curious to see, but there were no albatross.

'Neil! You'll be fine when we land.' Dr Barbara wiped the

phlegm from his mouth. 'Try to hang on – I'm as nervous as you are.'

'I'm not nervous. Where are the albatross?'

'They're here, Neil. I'm sure the French haven't killed them.'

'Do we leave if there are no albatross?'

'There are always albatross.' Dr Barbara held his head against her shoulder, a proud smile on her chapped lips. Her fading hair was swept back from her high forehead, as if she were determined to expose her principled brow to the malign and unscrupulous French. 'If you look hard enough you can find them. Now, pull yourself together. We can't film the landing twice.'

Neil tugged wearily at the satchel. 'Seriously, doctor, I feel sick. It could be radiation poisoning . . . '

'Very likely. It's all that talk about Eniwetok and Mururoa. I've never met anyone who dreamed of nuclear islands.'

'Save the atom bomb . . . '

'Save Neil Dempsey.'

Neil allowed her to cuff him. Dr Barbara was able to switch from peremptory schoolmistress to doting mother in a way that always disarmed him. She was forever touching Neil, peering into his eyes and checking his urine as if carrying out a running inventory of his working parts, a calculated appeal to a sixteen-year-old's libido that he could barely resist, whatever its motives. Once, when she hugged him playfully in the galley, a slice of sweet potato between her teeth, he had been tempted to strip naked in front of her.

'Neil, get ready to start the film. I can smell the French . . . '

Neil slipped the camera from its waterproof case. Kimo had cut the engine, and they rolled with the waves towards the shore, where the palms formed a dense palisade above a beach of black volcanic ash. Dr Barbara threw aside her weather-jacket and stood legs apart in the bows, shoulders squared and blonde hair flying like a battle-standard on the wind.

As always, Neil enjoyed filming her in close-up. Through the viewfinder he could see the exposure sores on her face, and her left nipple extruding itself through the wet cotton of her shirt, an eye-catcher for the television news bulletins or the covers of *Quick* and *Paris-Match*. He steadied himself against the float as an overtaking wave eased them from its back, and zoomed in on Dr Barbara's high nose and determined mouth, wondering if she had been plain or beautiful as a medical student in Edinburgh twenty years earlier.

'Take lots of film of the island,' she told him, now directing the documentary of which she was already star and scriptwriter. 'And get as many birds as you can.'

'There are no albatross. Only these boobies.'

'Just film the birds – any birds. Good God . . . !'

Neil sucked his numbed fingers and fumbled with the miniaturized controls of the Japanese camera. He had been working as a part-time projectionist at the film school of the University of Hawaii when Dr Barbara recruited him, and despite everything he said to the contrary she instantly convinced herself that he was a skilled cine-photographer. Fortunately the camera refocused itself, and he began to film a panorama of Saint-Esprit. The atoll was a chain of sand-bars and coral islets, the rim of a submerged volcanic crater that enclosed a lagoon five miles in diameter. The largest of the islands lay to the south-west of the lagoon, a crescent of dense forest and overgrown plantations dominated by a rocky mass that rose to a summit four hundred feet above the beach.

Searching for the threatened sea-birds, the great ocean-wanderers, Neil panned across the cliffs. The fluted cornices of blue lava together resembled the corpse of a mountain dead for millennia, propped into the sky like a cadaver sitting in an open grave. A tenacious vegetation clung to the exposed chimneys, living wreaths feasting on a set of aerial tombs. No albatross had yet appeared, but a steel tower stood on the summit, its cables slanting through the forest canopy.

The slender lattice was too frail to bear the weight of a nuclear device, and Neil assumed that it was an old radio mast. As they rode the last waves towards the beach he fixed the camera lens on the tower, hoping that its rigid vertical would restrain his stomach before it could climb into his throat. Thinking of the newsreels of atomic tests, he imagined a bomb detonated at its apex, releasing a ball of plasma hotter than the sun. For all Dr Barbara's passion for the albatross, the nuclear testing-ground

15

had a stronger claim on his imagination. No bomb had ever exploded on Saint-Esprit, but the atoll, like Eniwetok, Mururoa and Bikini, was a demonstration model of Armageddon, a dream of war and death that lay beyond the reach of any moratorium.

The stern of the inflatable rose as the last breaker swept them towards the beach. Neil stowed the megaphone and camera in the satchel and sealed the waterproof tapes, bracing himself against the centre bench. Dr Barbara crouched like a commando in the bows, fists gripping the mooring line. Two-bladed oar in his huge hands, Kimo stood astride the engine, holding the craft on the curved shoulders of the wave. The rolling wall crumbled in a white rush that hurled the inflatable onto its side and sent the oar windmilling through the spray.

Bludgeoned by the violent surf, they swam through the waist-deep water as the craft broke free from the sea and slewed across the sand. Carrying the satchel over his head, Neil forced himself against the undertow and waded through the slurred foam. Kimo dragged the inflatable onto the narrow shelf below the palms, and calmed the trembling rubber hull with his massive arms. Dr Barbara retrieved the oar, but a wave struck her thighs, knocking her from her feet. She fell to her knees in the seething water, stood up with her shirt around her waist and seized Neil's hands when he pulled her onto the beach.

'Good chap . . . are we all here? Where's the camera?'

'It's safe, Dr Barbara.'

'Hang on to it – the world's watching us through that little lens . . . '

She sat gasping on the sand beside Neil and wiped the water from her salt-roughened cheeks. Snorting the phlegm from her nostrils, she stared back at the sea, openly admiring its aggression. Still breathless, Neil leaned against the coarse sand. After the three-week voyage, the endless yawing and rolling deck, the sheer immobility of the island made him giddy. The black ash was covered with coconut husks, yellowing palm fronds, spurs of pallid driftwood and the shells of rotting crabs. Over everything hung the stench of dead fish. The sun had vanished behind

16

the forest canopy and a cold spray enveloped the island. A few feet away, through the trees behind them, was an insect realm of high-pitched chittering, dank mist and over-ripe vegetation.

'Right . . . time to move on.' Dr Barbara stood up and shook the water from her shirt. 'Kimo, it's up to you to get us out again.'

'We'll make it, doctor. I'll fool the sea for you.' As the foam surged around his feet Kimo worked on the outboard motor, clearing the sand from the air intakes. 'We'll wait for high tide, two hours from now.'

'Two hours? I hope that's enough. The French may be having lunch . . . Now, where's Neil?'

Neil touched her ankle. 'Still here, Dr Barbara, I think . . . '

Dr Barbara squatted beside him, buttoning her shirt from his queasy gaze. 'Of course you're here. Don't lose heart, Neil. I need you now – you're the only one who can work the camera.'

She brushed the damp hair from his eyes and ran her hand over his muscular arms, as if reminding herself that he was still the pugnacious and lazy youth she had met one evening in Waikiki, dreaming of atomic islands and marathon swims. During the voyage from Papeete she had spared him from the more arduous tasks, leaving Kimo to shift the heavy sails and work the bilge pump, and Neil sensed that he was being saved for a more exacting role than that of expedition cameraman.

'How long do we stay on Saint-Esprit?' he asked.

'Long enough to make the film. We can't help the albatross yet, but we can show people what's happening here.'

'Doctor . . . ' Neil gestured at the deserted beach and the clouds of mosquitoes. 'Nothing's happening.'

'Neil!' Dr Barbara forced him to sit up. 'Send some sort of current through that brain of yours. We've almost reached the year 2000 – let's make sure the planet's waiting for us when we get there.'

'That's why I came,' Neil assured her. 'I want to save the albatross, Dr Barbara.'

'I know you do. I wish there were more young men like you. We've got to protect everything here, not just the albatross but every palm and vine and blade of grass.' She waved away the mosquitoes that hovered over Neil's lips. 'We'll even save the mosquito!'

Needless to say, she had forgotten to pack any repellent. Himself the son of a doctor, a London radiologist who had died three years earlier, Neil again wondered if Dr Barbara was a real physician. Through her damp shirt he could see the tattered underwear held together by safety pins, and the zip of her trousers tied into place with fuse wire. He followed her to the inflatable, which Kimo had readied for departure, its bows facing the sea. She sat on the rubber float, a worn hand touching the outboard, and stared in a bleak way at the waves. For all her calls to action, she seemed disoriented by the size of the atoll.

She rallied when Neil raised the camera and began to film her. A low cloud ceiling extended to the horizon, below which lay a grey, marbled air, the perfect film-light. Despite her ragged clothes, the sores on her lips and fraying hair, the camera lens instantly restored Dr Barbara's confidence in herself. As always, Neil found himself drawn to this eccentric woman, and determined at whatever cost to protect her from reality.

Escorted by the mosquitoes, they set out to locate the airstrip, and followed the narrow beach under the overhang of palms. Kimo took the lead, machete in hand, pausing without comment whenever Dr Barbara stopped to rest. Waiting for her, Neil was aware of the radio mast high above the island, its antennae trailing them through the breaks in the forest canopy. A concrete blockhouse sat in a grove of tamarinds, a forgotten totem of the nuclear age that seemed more ancient than any Easter Island statue.

Rainwater leaked down the hillside, seeping between the moss-covered trees. After hiding among the ferns, a small stream fanned into a delta of silk-smooth ash and vented itself into the sea.

Neil bathed his feet in the cool shallows, the first fresh water he had felt on his skin since leaving Papeete. Dr Barbara knelt beside him and washed her arms and face. From a hip pocket she took a leather make-up pouch and combed her hair into damp waves. Dissatisfied with herself, she grimaced into the mirror and sucked the sores on her lips.

'Not very good, but never mind.'

'You look fine.' Neil spoke sincerely, intrigued by the way in which this often scruffy middle-aged woman hovered on the edge of glamour. 'Everyone will be impressed.'

'You're impressed, Neil. But that's not what I meant. I want everyone to see how serious we are.'

'You are serious.' Tempted to tease, he added: 'I'll film you from your best side.'

'Have I got a best side? What a dreadful thought.'

Neil filmed her as she followed Kimo through the forest, feet sinking into the spongy ground. The Hawaiian slashed at the ferns, exposing the rusty steel sections of a small-gauge railway. Everywhere lay the debris of Saint-Esprit's earlier occupations. Wooden huts leaned on their worm-riddled stilts, roofs open to the sky, hibiscus and morning glory flowering between the floorboards. A prayer-shack of corrugated iron stood on a headland above the lagoon, surrounded by the graves of an overgrown cemetery laid out by the Catholic missionaries. The forest had long since reclaimed the modest farm plots. Breadfruit trees, jack and eucalyptus crowded together among the taro plants, wild yams and sweet potatoes.

Imposed on this smothered realm was the refuse left by the French engineers, a moraine of abandoned military equipment. Kimo rested on an empty fuel tank beside the railway line, hacking at the lianas that snared it to the ground. Cloudy wine bottles lay in a wooden crate at his feet, surrounded by truck tyres and coils of telephone wire. A second camera-tower stood among the deep ferns, its window-slits staring at nothing.

They crossed a drainage ditch and stepped through the screen of palms. The airstrip swept past them, freshly surfaced with pulverized coral, its eerie geometry forming the outlines of an immense white altar among the trees. A camouflaged radio-cabin stood in the undergrowth fifty yards from them, aerials pointing to the empty sky. At its southern limit the airstrip ended in a barrier of dunes, where an army bulldozer sat with its scoop sunk in the sand.

Swinging the machete in his hand, Kimo walked to the bulldozer and tapped its metal tracks. An empty beer can rested on the driver's seat. Head raised, he stood stiffly in the strong wind as the sunlight flashed on the machete's blade. Lost in some reverie of his Hawaiian kingdom, he at last turned and gave a dismissive wave, like a travel courier warning a party of visitors from an uninteresting site.

'What is it, Kimo?' Dr Barbara called. 'Can you see anything?'

'Albatross, doctor . . . just albatross.'

'Albatross . . . ?' Dr Barbara seized Neil's arm and hurried him across the runway. 'Neil, the birds are still here! Get the camera ready.'

They reached the dunes and clambered up the slopes of churned sand, sinking to their knees in the black ash. Dr Barbara shielded her eyes from the wind and peered at the sky as Kimo strode down the beach to the headland beside the prayer-shack.

'Kimo! Where are the albatross? I can't see a single one.'

'There are plenty, doctor.' Kimo gestured in an offhand way at the hillocks of sand and beach-grass. 'Every albatross you need.'

'Kimo . . . ?'

'Over there.'

'Dr Barbara . . . ' Neil lowered the camera, unsure whether to film her when she was caught off-guard. 'They're all around us. They're not in the sky any more . . . '

A colony of albatross had nested among the hillocks, taking advantage of the wind that rose from the surface of the dunes. Their nests were little more than hollows in the sand, crudely lined with feathers and grass, but every one of them had been kicked apart. The heel-marks of heavy boots had stamped themselves into the rain-sodden ash. Fragments of broken shell trembled in the cool air, blurs of down quivering on their serrated edges. Dead chicks lay in the crushed grass, smeared with the yellow stomach oil that their parents had vented over them in their panic. Wings outstretched, dozens of the great birds rested at the water's edge, clubbed to death as they tried to escape. The ruffled plumage glared against the black sand like ice-white blossoms thrown into a refuse pit.

'Thirty-eight . . . nine . . . '

20

Kimo wandered among them, a stiff smile masking his face. The machete hung loosely in his hand, as if he were tired after cutting down the sky. Listening to his flat voice, Neil realized that the Hawaiian was counting the dead birds, and that in some way a finite number of fatalities would diminish the atrocity committed against the creatures.

'Kimo . . . why are they killing the birds?'

'They need to extend the runway.' Kimo spoke matter-of-factly. 'On Midway the Air Force killed thirty thousand goonies last year. They get into the jet intakes.'

'What about the French soldiers?' Neil scanned the empty runway, as white as the feathers of the albatross. 'They must be here somewhere.'

'Maybe they're bored. Killing is slow work . . . '

Unable to console the Hawaiian, Neil returned to Dr Barbara. She stood among the dead birds, hair floating from her forehead like threatening vapour above a volcano. As the wind stirred the plumage of the dead birds the beach seemed to shiver under her gaze. But her mouth was set in a curious grimace that was almost a smirk of satisfaction.

'Neil, I want the world to see this. Make sure you include every bird. Especially the chicks.'

'There are too many, doctor.' Reluctantly, Neil raised the camera and searched for the wide-angle button. 'They look like chrysanthemums . . . '

'All of them! They deserve to be remembered. And don't forget Kimo.'

But the Hawaiian had lost interest in the birds, and was walking towards a camera-tower that looked out over the lagoon to the detonation zone four miles away. The iron-grey cement, and the hieroglyph formed by the camera slits, reminded Neil of the gloomy bunkers that he and his father had explored at Utah Beach on the Normandy coast, remnants of the Nazi West Wall that outstared time.

At the northern end of the runway the French engineers had set up their camp. A wooden pier jutted into the lagoon, a cargo lighter moored against its landing stage. Crates filled with signals gear sat under the trees beside a storage shed, from which a set of landing lights and an aluminium water tower had been unloaded. But there was no sign of any nuclear or chemical warfare equipment. Saint-Esprit, Neil guessed with some disappointment, was no more than a refuelling stop on the air-run between Mururoa and Tahiti.

After filming Dr Barbara among the dead birds he wiped the chick entrails from his running shoes and followed her down the airstrip. She strode through the powdered coral, white dust rising at her heels, a dead albatross clasped in her arms. Her chin and forehead were streaked with blood, a warning to the sky to hold its breath. Neil had been unsettled by the fate of the huge birds, but he already realized that he was filming a well-rehearsed scene in the theatre of protest. Kimo climbed the water-tower and hung the banner from its spherical reservoir, while Dr Barbara sprayed her slogans across the green canvas roofs of the three barrack tents, slashing blades of gaudy crimson through the khaki fatigues hanging on a washing line. They posed together, native Hawaiian and English spinster, committed to their shared defence of the threatened Pacific.

Ten minutes later, as he replayed the sound-track to a critical Dr Barbara, Neil became aware that he was not the only person to film this contrived scene. A hundred yards from the airstrip, by the path that led up the hillside to the radio mast, three soldiers in French uniforms were watching the display. While his men waited beside him, smoking their cigarettes, the sergeant took a leisurely series of still photographs with his camera, like a tourist recording a quaint folkloric rite. After replacing the lens shroud, he beckoned his men forward, and together they strolled towards the airstrip.

'They're here! Kimo, take the camera!' Dr Barbara snatched the video-camera from Neil's hands and thrust it against Kimo's chest. 'Neil, climb the ladder and wrap the banner around your shoulders.'

'Dr Barbara . . . shouldn't we wait? The soldiers are armed.'

'Neil, try to help me.' Dr Barbara propelled him towards the ladder and forced his hands onto the metal rungs. For all the excitement, her eyes were calm, as if she had colluded with the French soldiers and was relieved to see them arrive. Before pushing him up the ladder she spoke rapidly to him: 'Neil, there are millions of young people like you all over the world. They won't listen to me but they'll follow you.'

Kimo had dropped his machete to the ground. He knelt on the runway and, with an expertise that surprised Neil, began to film the approaching soldiers. He recorded Dr Barbara shouting into her megaphone, and ended with a close-up of an embarrassed Neil on the ladder, the banner draped across his chest.

'Go, Kimo . . . now!'

Dr Barbara pulled the Hawaiian to his feet. He held her wrists, as if uncertain whether to leave, and then tore himself from her and ran across the airstrip towards the forest, camera in hand. When he reached the prayer-shack he paused among the graves, waiting for Dr Barbara to follow before plunging into the waist-deep ferns.

The French soldiers made no effort to pursue him. As Dr Barbara bellowed at them through the megaphone they put out their cigarettes, amused by this over-excited Englishwoman tripping over the dead bird at her feet. Dragging the banner with him, Neil jumped from the ladder and tried to wipe the blood from her arms.

'Dr Barbara, let's go. They'll arrest us.'

'I'm staying, Neil. I want to see this through. Kimo can show the film to the world.'

'Doctor, the world isn't interested . . . '

He was about to follow Kimo across the airstrip when the French sergeant raised his right hand. He unbuckled the flap of his holster and walked forward, pointing to Neil.

'Arrête-toi! Ne bouge pas!'

Cursing Dr Barbara, Neil sprinted along the airstrip through the trail of bloody feathers. Kimo was running among the trees, retracing the railway line towards the beach with a lightness of foot that Neil had never suspected.

'Kimo . . . wait! Kimo!'

He was still shouting at the Hawaiian when he heard the pistol shot behind him.

2

Protesting Too Much

THE PROTEST RALLY at the University of Hawaii campus had reached a climax, its rhetoric as inflated as the helium balloons, emblazoned with ecological slogans, that rose from their cradles beside the podium. Lying in his bed on the sixth floor of the Nimitz Memorial Hospital, Neil watched the familiar scene on his television set. He turned down the sound as the last speaker, a local basketball commentator turned eco-evangelist, began his address to the student audience.

This aggressive sermon, which Neil now knew by heart, combined religious fervour, high-flown sporting analogies and blatant threats against the French consul in Honolulu and any French tourists daring to defile the beaches of Waikiki. Buying a Citroën or an Hermès scarf was a sin equal to the destruction of ten acres of rain-forest or the murder of a hundred albatross.

The hospital was almost a mile from the rally, but through the open window Neil could hear the amplified voice reflected across the rooftops. Megaphones hectored him in his deepest dreams. Even when he pressed the sound mute on the remote control, his last defence against the protest movements, the repeated slogan 'Save the Albatross' seemed to drum from the loudspeaker. Every mention of the wandering albatross – no specimen of which, an amateur ornithologist in the kidney unit informed him, ever nested in the Hawaiian Islands – produced a spasm of pain in his injured foot.

'Save the frigate bird,' Neil muttered. 'Save the quetzal . . . '

The bullet from the French sergeant's pistol had struck the ball of his right foot, exiting between the metatarsal bones and causing what his doctors termed a partial amputation of the big toe. Six weeks later, Neil moved in a painful, one-legged hobble, a legacy of the infected muscle sheath which the Papeete paramedics had allowed to run out of control while the French authorities tried to resist the world-wide media clamour for his release.

The wound was still leaking when Neil at last flew to Honolulu. But the bloodied bandages on the television newscasts had been a propaganda coup whose impact rivalled the stigmata of a saint. A breathless Dr Barbara embraced him on his stretcher and assured the cameras that these few crimson drops redeemed the ocean of blood shed by the slaughtered birds. Had she aimed the pistol herself, Dr Barbara could not have found a more valuable target.

Even Neil's mother and his step-father, Colonel Stamford, had been impressed by Neil's celebrity. They flew from Atlanta to be with him during his first week at the Nimitz, and sat by his bed surrounded by the huge bouquets that endlessly arrived from well-wishers. Accepting a rose from Neil, his mother gazed at the blood-red petals as if they had been dipped into her son's heart. Neil promised his step-father that he would join them in Atlanta as soon as he was strong enough to walk to the aircraft, but the colonel urged him to remain in Honolulu for at least a further month, perhaps seeing Neil's fame as a therapeutic process in itself that might free the restless boy from his memories of his dead father.

A helium balloon sailed over the hospital car park, bearing the stylized image of an albatross. On the television screen the basketballing evangelist had begun his final peroration. Neil kept his thumb firmly on the sound mute, but the door of his room opened. Nurse Crawford, a keen windsurfer from Cape Town whom he had first met at a beach party in Waikiki, walked over to the set and turned up the sound.

'. . . And let's not forget someone who gave everything in the fight against ecological terrorism – Neil Dempsey, lying at this moment in the Nimitz. That French bullet he took was aimed at every one of us, at every albatross and dolphin and minke whale. We're with you, Neil, lying right next to you in that bed of pain . . .'

25

Nurse Crawford playfully lifted Neil's sheet, rolling her eyes as he shielded his crotch with the remote control.

'Neil, who's lying next to you? I just hope you haven't given everything. We're all waiting for a special treat.'

Neil pulled the sheet from her hands but allowed her to pinch his ribs. 'I'll save some for you, Carole.'

'Hearts are bursting, Neil.' She grimaced at the television screen. 'Now, look who's here. The great lady doctor, still itching to save the world. What do you think of her new hair-do?'

Neil rearranged his get-well telegrams. 'It looks great. Dr Barbara's all right. I like her.'

'Of course you do – she nearly got you killed. Who can compete with that? But you take care, Neil . . . '

'I'll be fine. Don't worry for me, Carole.'

'That's what you said before you left with Kimo.' Still puzzled by Neil despite the weeks spent bathing and feeding him, Nurse Crawford sat on the bed. 'Why did you sail to the island, Neil? You aren't interested in the albatross.'

'Maybe not. Saint-Esprit's a nuclear test-site, like Eniwetok and Kwajalein Atoll. I wanted to see it.'

'Why?'

Neil shrugged. 'I don't know yet. I didn't get a chance to find out. Maybe it's where the future begins.'

'The future? Neil, all that atomic war stuff is over now.'

'Not for me.' Neil aimed the remote control at her and pressed the mute button. 'The point about Saint-Esprit is that they never exploded a bomb there.'

'So?'

'It's still waiting to happen. Life and death, Carole, things they've never heard about in Waikiki.'

'They've heard about life and I'll stick with that any day. It's your lady friend Dr Rafferty I'm not sure about.'

Neil let this pass. 'She wants to save the albatross. Is there something wrong with that?'

'Maybe there is, Neil. Yes, I think there is . . . '

★   ★   ★

When Nurse Crawford had gone Neil returned to the protest rally. Dr Barbara had stepped to the podium, where she received a standing ovation from the action committee – a retired astronaut, two over-earnest academics, a public-spirited car-dealer and three wives of local businessmen. In phrases that Neil had learned to lip-read off the silent screen she saluted the students for their support and cash donations. Her blonde hair floated freely about the well-tailored shoulders of her safari suit, but her modest smile was firmly in place as her level blue eyes, steadied by some internal gyroscope, assessed the size of the audience and the likely take of dollar bills.

'Save the phoenix . . . ' Neil murmured. The rally, for all the balloons and applause, had attracted fewer people than Dr Barbara's previous jamborees. Indignation, even the fierce variety patented by Dr Barbara, had a short shelf life. The albatross was her trademark, that long-winged, ocean-soaring, guilt-bringing bird. But practical results, of the kind achieved by Greenpeace, Amnesty International and the Live Aid concerts of the 1980s, had eluded Dr Barbara. The French government still denied that nuclear testing would resume at Saint-Esprit. For all the footage of graffiti-scrawled camera-towers that Kimo had supplied to the TV networks, an anti-nuclear campaign could no longer bring in the crowds. Too many of the people at Dr Barbara's rallies were tourists, elderly Japanese couples and family groups from Sydney or Vancouver, for whom an ecological protest meeting was an established part of the holiday street scene, along with the fire-breathers, pickpockets and nightclub touts. Dr Barbara was a minor media phenomenon, appearing with her bird-atrocity footage on chat shows and wild-life programmes. She attracted a troupe of dedicated admirers, but failed to enlist the support of the established animal rights groups.

Nonetheless, she was as undeterred as ever, and addressed the rally with all her old fervour. The salt-water ulcers had healed, along with the eye infection that she refused to allow the French doctors to treat with their antibiotics ('tested on animals and third-world volunteers!'). She had put on weight, thanks to a regime of fund-raising dinners, and the micro-climate of TV studios had left her face attractively pale.

Neil remembered how she had cradled him in her arms as he was carried from the plane at Honolulu Airport – so different from the aggressive stance she had taken as he lay bleeding on the runway at Saint-Esprit, when she faced the pistol-waving French sergeant with the triumphant gaze of a huntress guarding her prey. Despite all her efforts, however, her audiences were declining.

'Doctor, you'll have to shoot me in the other foot . . . '

Neil massaged his aching calf, thinking of the bedraggled and eccentric woman he had first seen five months earlier outside a Waikiki hotel, shouting abuse at the doormen exasperated by her high-pitched English voice and the banner she waved in the faces of the guests.

Neil was leaving the hotel after a farewell dinner with his mother and step-father. Having completed his tour of duty in Hawaii, Colonel Stamford was being reassigned to a base in Georgia. Neil's widowed mother had met the colonel soon after her husband's death, while she worked as the catering officer at a U.S. officers'. club in London. Neil liked the amiable Californian, who was forever urging him to enlist in the Marine Corps and find a new compass-bearing in his life, and accepted the colonel's suggestion that he join them in Honolulu.

Neil was still unsettled by the suicide of his father, a radiologist who had diagnosed his own lung cancer and decided to end his life while he could breathe without pain. But suicide was a suggestive act, as a tactless counsellor at the hospital had told Mrs Dempsey, often passing from father to son like a dangerous gene. Trying to distance himself from his memories of his father, Neil gave up any hopes of studying medicine. The vacuum in his life he filled with body-building, judo and long-distance swimming, lapping hundreds of lengths each week at his London pool. He swam the Thames, despite the efforts of the River Police to stop him, from Chelsea Bridge to the first lock at Teddington. Above all, he revelled in long night-swims, when he moved in a deep dream of exhaustion and dark water.

The powerful physique of this moody sixteen-year-old, and his plans to swim the English Channel at night, together appealed to Colonel Stamford, who talked to Neil of the great seas around

Hawaii. Once he arrived, the Waikiki beach world swallowed him whole. He missed his girl-friend Louise, a highly strung but affectionate music student, and sent her video-cassettes of himself surfing near Diamond Head. Bored with his class work, he dropped out of high school and crewed on yachts, worked as a pool attendant and then found a part-time job as a projectionist at the university film school. During his spare time he prepared for the challenge he had set himself, the thirty-mile swim across the Kaiwi Channel from Makapuu Head to the neighbouring island of Molokai.

When his mother and Colonel Stamford told him of their imminent move to Georgia, Neil asked if he could remain in Honolulu for the summer. To his surprise, his mother agreed, but Neil was aware that in her vague way she had begun to reject him. An anxious and easily tired woman, she saw in his square shoulders and boxer's jaw an upsetting reminder of her dead husband. She and the colonel settled Neil into a student rooming house near the university, and celebrated their departure with a last dinner in Waikiki. Afterwards Neil kissed his mother's over-rouged cheek and accepted his step-father's kindly bear-hug. He then walked through the lobby doors and straight into the quixotic and testing world of Dr Barbara Rafferty.

When he first arrived for dinner he had noticed the shabby, middle-aged woman in a threadbare cotton dress. She crouched between two limousines in the car park, unwrapping a paper parcel, and Neil assumed that she was a beggar or down-and-out, hoping to cadge a few dollars from the delegates to a maritime safety convention. Two hours later, when he left, she was still there, hovering around the ornamental fountain that faced the entrance. Seeing Neil emerge from the hotel, she waved a makeshift banner and shouted in a strong English voice:

'Save the albatross! Stop oil pollution now!'

Before she could confront Neil the doormen bundled her away. Handling her roughly, they propelled her into the drive beyond the hotel gates and flung the banner onto the ground. She knelt beside it, skirt around her white thighs, a hand to her bruised chin.

Drawn by her English accent, Neil helped the woman to her feet. She accepted his handkerchief and wiped her tears, flowing from indignation rather than grief.

'Are you one of the delegates?' She frowned at his youthful face. 'If they're sending their midshipmen they really must have something to hide.'

'I'm not a delegate.' Neil tried to calm her trembling shoulders, but she pushed him away. 'I've been saying goodbye to my mother and step-father. He's a colonel in the U.S. Army.'

'The American Army? One of the world's greatest environmental threats.' She brushed the dirt from her hands. 'No use saying goodbye, they said goodbye to us a long time ago. Listen, do you have a car?'

'I came by bus,' Neil lied. The army-surplus jeep he had bought to please his step-father was parked a hundred yards along the beach, but Neil decided to distance himself from this unstable Englishwoman. As he folded the banner he noticed the slogan hand-painted in red ink. '"*Save the Albatross*",' he repeated. 'Do they need saving?'

'They certainly do. Still, I'm glad you've heard of the albatross.'

'Everyone has.' Neil gestured to the evening sky over Diamond Head and its corona of soaring birds. 'They're just a common sea-bird.'

'They'll soon be a lot less common. The French are killing them at Saint-Esprit, poisoning them by the thousand.'

'That's a shame . . . ' Neil tried to seem sympathetic. 'But it's a nuclear test island.'

'You've heard of that, too? I'm impressed.'

A tourist party emerged from the hotel and waited by the limousines, but a dispute between the drivers and the courier left them standing in an uneasy huddle. Seeing her chance, the Englishwoman unwrapped her banner. In an effort to make herself presentable, she brushed the blonde hair from her high forehead and relaxed the muscles of her face, imposing a fierce smile on its warring planes. She pulled a bundle of leaflets from her bag and pressed them into Neil's hands. 'Start giving those out. You can tell the doorman you're a guest at the hotel.'

'Look . . . it's too bad about the albatross, but I have to go.'
Neil was aware that at any moment his mother and the colonel
might leave the hotel and be surprised to find him involved in
this curious demonstration. Hiding his face behind the leaflets, he
noticed that the Save the Albatross Fund invited contributions to
the treasurer and secretary, Barbara Rafferty, at a children's
home in a poorer district of Honolulu.

'Come on, don't look so shy.' The woman seemed amused by
Neil. 'Help me hold the banner – you don't have to think
everything out first. And why are you so muscular? Steroids
aren't good for the testicles. In a few years you won't be any use
to your girl-friends.'

'I don't need steroids . . . ' Neil released the banner, which
blew against the woman, wrapping the red-lettered strip around
her like a bandage. 'Good luck, Mrs Rafferty.'

'Dr Rafferty. You can call me Dr Barbara. Now, stand there
and shout with me. Save the . . . *albatross!*'

Neil left her shouting at the bored tourists as they rolled away
in their limousines towards the Waikiki nightclubs. Ecological
movements had always failed to stir him, though he sympathized
with activists who were trying to save the whale or protect the
beaches where rare species of turtle laid their eggs after immense
oceanic journeys. The whales and turtles were swimmers like
himself. But the obsessive do-goodery of so many animal rights
groups had a pious and intolerant strain. It was necessary to test
drugs, like the antibiotic that cured the rare strain of pneumonia
he contracted after swimming the Severn. His mother and Louise
would go on using lipstick and mascara; to spare them from
cancer of the lip or eye a few rabbits might usefully die in the
laboratory rather than the cooking pot.

But something about the lonely campaign of this English
doctor had touched him. The departure of his mother and the
arrival of Dr Rafferty in some way seemed connected. Neil knew
that he was drawn to older women, like the manager of the
rooming house and a middle-aged lecturer in film studies, both
of whom had noticed Neil and begun to flirt with him. As he
waved goodbye to his mother and Colonel Stamford at the
airport, he found himself thinking of Dr Rafferty.

A week later, in downtown Honolulu, he saw the blood-red banner tied to the railings of the Federal Post Office building. A small crowd had gathered, waiting as two policemen cut through the cords. Dr Rafferty stood nearby, chanting her slogans like a scarecrow wired for sound. She was hoping to be arrested, and was more concerned to provoke the bored policemen than convert the passers-by to her cause. An elderly man in a black suit and tie, like a kindly usher at a funeral parlour, tried to speak to her, but she waved him away, watching the traffic for any sign of a news reporter with a camera. The policemen confiscated the banner, and one of them struck her shoulder with his open hand, almost knocking her to the ground. Without complaint she turned and walked past Neil, losing herself among the lunchtime pedestrians.

Despite this set-back, she kept up her one-woman campaign. Neil saw her haranguing the surfers on Waikiki beach, handing out leaflets to the tourists in the Union Street Mall, buttonholing a group of clergymen attending a conference at the Iolani Palace. Often she was tired and dispirited, carrying her banner and leaflets in a faded satchel, the bag lady of the animal rights movement.

Neil was concerned for her, in exactly the same way he had worried over his mother in the months after his father's death. She too had neglected herself, endlessly fretting about Neil and the unnamed threats to his well-being until he felt like an endangered species. Remembering those fraught days, he sympathized with the albatross, wings weighed down by all the slogans and moral blackmail.

To his surprise, he found that there was an element of truth in her campaign. A paragraph in a Honolulu newspaper reported that the French authorities on Tahiti had withdrawn their approval for the re-occupation of Saint-Esprit by the original inhabitants. Army engineers were extending the runway, and it was rumoured that the government in Paris might end its moratorium on nuclear testing.

Neil secretly admired the French for their determination to maintain a nuclear arsenal, just as he admired the great physicists who had worked on the wartime Manhattan Project. As a young air force radiologist in the 1960s, Neil's father had attended the British nuclear trials held at the Maralinga test site in Australia, and his widow now claimed that her husband's cancer could be traced back to these poorly monitored atomic explosions. She often stared at Neil as if wondering whether his father's irradiated genes had helped to produce this self-contained and wayward youth. Once, Neil rode out on a borrowed motorcycle to the cruise missile base at Greenham Common, moved by the memory of the nuclear weapons in their silos and by the few women protesters still camping against the wire. Without success, he tried to ingratiate himself with the women, explaining that he too might be a nuclear victim.

The power of the atomic test explosions, portents of a now forgotten apocalypse, had played an important part in drawing him to the Pacific. As he screened cold-war newsreels for the modern-history classes in the film school theatre he stared in awe at the vast detonations over the Eniwetok and Bikini lagoons, sacred sites of the twentieth-century imagination. But he could never admit this to anyone, and even felt vaguely guilty, as if his fascination with nuclear weapons and electro-magnetic death had retrospectively caused his father's cancer.

What would Dr Rafferty say to all this? One afternoon in Waikiki he was buying an underwater watch in a specialist store when he saw her unpacking her banner and leaflets. Neil followed her as she wandered past the bars and restaurants, shaking her head in a dispirited way. She stopped at an open-air cafeteria and stared at the menu, running a cracked finger-nail down the price list. Suppressing his embarrassment, Neil approached her.

'Dr Barbara? Can I get you a sandwich? You must be tired.'

'I am tired.' She seemed to remember Neil and his artless manner, and allowed him to take the satchel. 'Look at this place – buy, buy, buy and no-one gives a hoot that the real world is disappearing under their feet. I've seen you somewhere. I know, steroids – you're the body-builder. Well, you can help rebuild my body. Let's see if they serve anything that isn't packed with hormones.'

They sat at a table by the entrance, Dr Barbara handing her leaflets to the passing customers. She ordered a tomato and lettuce sandwich, after an argument with the waitress over the origins of the mayonnaise.

'Avoid meat products,' she told Neil, still unsure what she was doing in the company of this British youth. 'They're crammed with hormones and antibiotics. Already you can see that men in the west are becoming feminized – large breasts, fatter hips, smaller scrotums . . .'

Neil was glad to let her talk, and watched the sandwich disappear between her strong teeth. For reasons he had yet to understand, he enjoyed seeing her eat. Her clear gums and vivid tongue, the muscles in her throat, all fascinated him. At close quarters Dr Barbara was far less dejected than the woman he saw arguing with the police and tourists. Her strong will overrode the shabby cotton dress and untended hair.

She sat back and polished her teeth with a vigorous forefinger. 'I needed that – you've done your bit today for the albatross.' She noticed Neil glancing proudly at his rubber-mounted underwater watch. 'What is it? One of those sadistic computer games?'

'It's a deep-water chronometer. I'm planning to swim the Kaiwi Channel to Molokai.'

'Swim? It's rather a long way. Why not take the plane?'

'That isn't a challenge. Long-distance swimming is . . . what I do.' Trying to amuse her, he added: 'Think of it as my albatross.'

'Really? What are you trying to save?'

'Nothing. It's hard to describe, like swimming a river at night.' Exaggerating for effect, he said: 'I swam the Thames from Tower Bridge to Teddington.'

'Is that allowed?'

'No. The river police had their spotlights on. I could see the beams through the water . . .'

'Long-distance swimming – all those endorphins flowing for hours. Though you don't look under stress.' Dr Barbara pushed aside her leaflets, intrigued by this amiable but obstinate youth who had come to her aid. 'Perhaps you're a true fanatic. Physically very strong, but mentally . . . ? When did all this start?'

'Two years ago, after my father died. He was a doctor, too. I needed to stop thinking for a while.'

'Good advice. I wish more people would take it. What about your mother?'

'She's fine, most days. She married an American colonel. He's kind to her. They've just gone back to Atlanta.'

'So you're alone here in Honolulu, planning to swim the Kaiwi Channel. Do they know about it?'

'Of course. They don't think I'm serious. It's too far, even with a pace-boat. But that's not the point.'

'What is?' Dr Barbara leaned forward, trying to see through the hair over Neil's eyes. 'Or don't you know?'

Neil covered the dial of his chronometer, as if keeping a secret sea-time to himself. 'People think you're alone on long-distance swims. But after five miles you're not alone any more. The sea runs right into your mind and starts dreaming inside your head. You won't understand.'

'Perhaps I do.' Dr Barbara's manner was less brisk. She held Neil's hand between her own, as if welcoming him across a threshold. 'Now you know why I want to save the albatross.'

Neil felt the pressure of her fingers on his palm, broken nails searching for his heart and life lines. He could smell her breath, keen and freshly scented. Already he had warmed to this older woman; perhaps she would protect him as well as the albatross?

'When I swim to Molokai you could come along. It's best if there's a doctor in the pace-boat. Are you qualified?'

'I certainly am. I was a Hammersmith GP for six years. Still, I don't think you'll ever need a gynaecologist – unless you use too many steroids.'

'My father was a radiologist at Guy's. Once he took an X-ray photo of my skull.'

'I wonder what he found.' Dr Barbara brushed the hair from Neil's broad forehead. 'Now, do you want to help me pass out these leaflets? I'm going to the airline office across the street.'

'Well . . . it's not my –'

'Come on. Being embarrassed will do you good.'

She waited as Neil paid the cashier, smiling at no-one in her self-absorbed way, as if she was digesting more than a sandwich. Neil followed her through the tourist crowds. Like all older women, she had easily taken the initiative from him. Too shy to help with the leaflets, he stood behind Dr Barbara, pretending that he had nothing to do with this eccentric Englishwoman.

However eccentric, Dr Barbara surprised Neil by recruiting her first disciple. When he next saw her, on the steps of the University Library, she was accompanied by a tall and deep-chested native Hawaiian in his late thirties, who gazed at the world with a slight convergent squint that gave him a look of permanent irritation. He thrust the leaflets into the hands of the passing students like a debt-collector reminding them of their dues. Neil at first resented him, naively believing that he alone had discovered Dr Barbara.

The scowling Hawaiian was Kimo, a former sergeant in the Honolulu police, a long-standing anti-nuclear and animal rights protester who had been forced to resign from the police after taking part in a campaign for an independent native Hawaiian kingdom. In 1985 he volunteered to sail aboard the Greenpeace *Rainbow Warrior*, which resettled the islanders of Rongelap Atoll, 100 miles to the east of Bikini. Many of the Rongelapese had been contaminated by the radioactive ash that fell on them after the Bravo hydrogen bomb test in 1954, and over the decades suffered from high rates of leukaemia, still births and miscarriages. The *Rainbow Warrior* moved the islanders to Kwajalein Atoll, and later sailed for New Zealand, where she was sunk by French agents hoping to put an end to anti-nuclear protests in the South Pacific.

Dr Barbara had known Kimo for the past two years, and it was the former policeman who told her of the threat to the wandering albatross on Saint-Esprit. Inspired by the image of the great sea-bird, Dr Barbara launched her one-woman campaign, which Kimo had now decided to join, hoping that public concern for the albatross would revive the flagging anti-nuclear cause. Offering his savings, he paid for the printing of a new leaflet, which reproduced a photograph of dead birds lying beside a vast runway filled with implacable nuclear bombers.

Kimo's arrival restored Dr Barbara's waning energies, and brought Neil into the group as its cadet member and dogsbody. He tagged behind them as they strode through hotel lobbies and department stores, guarding the leaflets while Dr Barbara hectored everyone in her piercing English voice. To Kimo, forever flexing his shoulders at the nervous security guards, Neil was little more than Dr Barbara's chauffeur. A foot taller than Neil, he stared straight over his head whenever he conveyed Dr Barbara's latest command.

Still uneasy in Kimo's presence, Neil drove the jeep, collected the leaflets from the printer and helped to paint the banners. He remained unsure of Dr Barbara, and was sceptical that she was a doctor at all, until the evening when Kimo was injured in a fracas outside a pool hall.

Neil drove him to Dr Barbara's single-room apartment at the rear of the children's refuge. As she treated the Hawaiian's bruised hands, working confidently with the instruments in her ancient leather valise, Neil gazed around her dingy room, at the leaflets piled on the dressing-table and the unironed clothing heaped at the foot of the narrow bed. The modest apartment, looking out onto fire escapes packed with broken furniture and beer crates, defined the meagre existence of this woman doctor.

Why did she not practise her medical career and join one of the established animal rights groups, instead of serving as a glorified children's minder at the underfunded refuge? Neil had noticed that the Greenpeace and environmental activists kept their distance from Dr Barbara, as if they suspected that her passionate defence of the albatross concealed more devious aims.

Nevertheless, Neil found himself increasingly committed to the great white bird. Chanting 'Save the albatross' gave an unexpected focus to his life. When, two months after their first meeting, Dr Barbara told him that she and Kimo had decided to sail to Saint-Esprit, Neil took for granted that he would be a member of the crew.

As the last of the helium balloons floated towards the sea, the sounds of the protest rally drummed at the windows of the hospital room. Neil forced his head into the pillow, trying to ignore the pains that played their hourly medley across the strings of his leg. He watched the silent television screen and the closing moments of Dr Barbara's speech. Jaw-bones straining from her cheeks, blonde hair forgotten in the wind, she raised her elbows to reveal the damp armpits of her safari suit. She seemed happier and more determined than Neil had ever seen her. Was she genuine or a fraud? In some way she transcended the question of her own authenticity, and was able to believe sincerely in the threatened bird while manipulating the emotions of her audience.

All along, Neil assumed, she had hoped that the French soldiers on Saint-Esprit would seize them, while Kimo escaped with the video-camera and its precious footage. The Hawaiian had hidden for a few last moments among the waist-deep ferns, and had filmed Neil being shot down by the sergeant, a scene endlessly replayed on television across the world. The existence of the camera, a present from Colonel Stamford, had probably prompted their mission to the island. The French government insisted that it had no plans to resume nuclear testing on Saint-Esprit, but Dr Barbara and the albatross were launched and airborne. A defence committee was formed while Neil and Dr Barbara were held at Papeete, and protesters demanding their release marched through London and Paris. Donations flowed in, and environmentalists argued her case from a hundred pulpits and lecture platforms.

By the time of her return to Honolulu, two weeks later, Dr Barbara was the new heroine of the ecological movement. Yet her real motives, like his own, remained a mystery to Neil.

3

The *Dugong*

DEFENDER OF THE ALBATROSS, champion of islands, and all-purpose media star, Dr Barbara Rafferty had far stranger sides to her character, as Neil discovered on the day before he left the hospital.

Among the last of his mail was an anonymous get-well card attached to the latest issue of *Paris-Match*, which devoted its leading feature to the saga of Saint-Esprit. Bored by photographs of himself – his mother had tactlessly released a family snapshot of Neil, aged 4, in a paddling pool – he was about to slide the magazine into the waste basket when he recognized an unexpected face. Among the images of dead birds and camera-towers beside the nuclear lagoon was a grainy close-up taken in 1982 of a younger Dr Barbara.

Dressed in a dark suit, eyes lowered to the pavement, she was leaving the London headquarters of the General Medical Council after being struck from its register of licensed physicians. A sharp-eyed journalist at *Paris-Match*, his memory nudged, perhaps, by the French security services, had raided the picture library and re-opened the celebrated case.

Ten years earlier Dr Barbara Rafferty had been tried for murder in the British courts. Two of her women patients, elderly cancer sufferers in a Hammersmith hospice, had been eased from their last ordeal by a massive sleeping draught. This lethal cocktail of potassium chloride, chloroform and morphine was openly administered by Dr Barbara with the agreement, she claimed, of the patients and their relatives. But not all the relatives had been consulted. Contesting the will, a sister of one

39

of the women visited the police and brought a complaint against Dr Barbara.

The police seized the hospice's clinical records and discovered that Dr Barbara had practised euthanasia on at least six terminal patients over the previous year. She freely admitted the charge, claiming that she had secured her patients' consent after an extended period of bedside counselling. At their request, she had put an end to their pain, defended their dignity and their right to self-respect.

Convicted on eight counts of manslaughter, Dr Barbara was given a two-year suspended sentence. An action group of sympathetic doctors and relatives rallied support, but she lost her appeal. Interviewed outside the High Court, she stated that her further behaviour towards her dying patients would be guided by her conscience, a scarcely veiled threat that led the General Medical Council to strike her from the register. A public debate ensued, during which she appeared prominently on television, arguing her case with a passion and stridency that to some observers verged on the self-righteous. Alienated by her chilling manner, even her closest colleagues turned away from her. From then on she was unable to practise as a doctor and became a director of a fringe company designing a female condom, but after six months she resigned and went abroad. Years of exile followed, in Malawi, South Africa and New Zealand, where clandestine medical work was inevitably followed by the exposure of her past, until she came to rest in Honolulu.

Now Dr Barbara had discovered the animal rights movement, and devoted herself to life rather than death. Neil stared at her photograph propped against his pillow, almost dazed by the revelations. The slim, over-intense face of the guilty physician, shadowed by the dark tones of her suit, might have belonged to a war criminal or psychopath. Nonetheless, he felt a curious concern for this outlawed doctor. He realized that she had once been young, and wondered what the young Dr Barbara would have thought of him, or of her scatty older self and her dreams of facing down the French navy.

When she arrived that afternoon, making her last visit to the ward, Neil left the magazine open on the bedside table. Brushing past Nurse Crawford, she swept into the room with her palms raised to the ceiling, and strode to the window as if only the sky was large enough to contain her excitement.

'Neil – astonishing news!'

'Dr Barbara?'

'You won't believe it. All I can say is that dreams come true. First, though, how are you?' She picked Neil's case notes from the foot of the bed and ran a brisk eye over them. 'Good, they haven't done too much damage. Over-prescribing, as usual, and all these tests – they must think you're pregnant. How do you feel?'

'Fine.' Neil found himself smiling at her. 'Bored.'

'That means you're ready to leave. I warn you, there's a lot to do and not much time.'

Neil let her hand brush his cheek. She sat on the bed, gazing at him with undisguised pleasure. When she was alone with Neil she usually turned down the volume control of her public persona, as if this teenaged boy touched some lingering need for the intimacy of private life. But today she was unable to restrain herself.

'Listen, Neil – it's what we've prayed for. I've found a ship!'

Neil pulled her hands from the air and pressed them together, trying to calm her. 'That's great, doctor. But I'm out of training – I won't be ready for the swim until October or even later.'

'The swim? I'm not talking about that. We're sailing back to Saint-Esprit! We have a real ship – the *Dugong*. It's moored in Honolulu harbour.'

'Sailing back . . . ?' Neil felt the veins throb in his injured foot. 'You're going back to the island? You'll get killed, doctor.'

'Of course I won't.' Dr Barbara smoothed his sheets and pillow, as if taming the white waves. 'It's everything I've worked for. This time we'll have the whole world behind us. The French will have to listen.'

Unable to sit still, she sprang to the window and gripped the sill, already on the bridge of her vessel. Neil listened as she told him of the billionaire benefactor who had joined the albatross campaign. This was Irving Boyd, a reclusive thirty-five-year-old computer entrepreneur now living in Hawaii. He had recently

41

retired after selling his software company in Palo Alto to a Japanese conglomerate, and now devoted himself to wild-life causes.

Neil had seen him in a rare television interview, a bespectacled and almost schoolboyish figure with a row of pens clipped to his breast pocket, an earnest reader of science fiction who in some ways had never needed to grow up. Rare species of aquatic mammals such as the manatee were his speciality, and his marine sanctuary on Oahu contained the only breeding pair in captivity. Impressed by Dr Barbara's poverty and dedication, he had begun to support her with cash donations, and supplied her with an office and free telephone at his Honolulu television station. His most important gift was the *Dugong*, a 300-ton Alaskan shrimp-trawler which he planned to equip as a floating marine laboratory.

'But first it will take us to Saint-Esprit.' Dr Barbara blew the blonde hair from her eyes. 'We leave in three weeks – that's not much time, but I want to keep everything on the boil. There should be ten of us, including you and Kimo, and Irving's television crew. We'll set up our sanctuary, whatever the French do.'

'They'll torpedo you,' Neil told her matter-of-factly. 'They'll sink the ship. Look what they did to the *Rainbow Warrior* in Auckland harbour.'

'This time they won't dare!' Already in full interview mode, Dr Barbara inflated her lungs, nearly bursting the buttons of her safari suit. 'Neil, the world will be watching. There'll be a satellite dish on board to link the film crew to the TV station here. Try to imagine it – everyone will see us reclaim that dead nuclear island and give it back to the living world. The twentieth century criminally misspent itself. When the year 2000 arrives we'll hand to the next millennium a small part of this terrible century that we've redeemed and brought to life again. It's a wonderful dream, Neil, and thanks to Irving Boyd it's within our grasp.'

Dr Barbara gazed at the distant sea, breast heaving as she caught her breath. Her eyes swept across the bouquets and greeting cards, and came to rest on the open copy of *Paris-Match*. Scarcely surprised, she stared at the photograph of her younger self.

'Irving told me he'd seen this. It says everything about him that he wasn't in the least worried. It had to come out – better now than later . . . '

She sat with the magazine in her hands, and then dropped it into the waste-bin, as if discarding an out-of-date calendar. Waiting for her to speak, Neil realized that she had wholly detached herself from the disbarred doctor photographed outside the High Court ten years earlier.

Seeing that Neil was still unsure of her, the sheet drawn up to his chin, she spoke calmly as if to a child.

'I was terribly naive then, far too idealistic. I thought I could do good, but people resent that, judges and juries above all. Doing good unsettles them. Believe me, Neil, nothing provokes people more than acting from the highest motives.'

'The dead patients . . . ' Neil searched for a tactful way around the question. 'Did you really kill them?'

'Of course not!' Dr Barbara seemed genuinely puzzled by Neil. 'Their minds were already dead, they'd given up long before. Only their bodies were alive, covered with sores and ulcers. All I did was put their bodies to rest.'

'Then you did . . . '

'Neil . . . ' Dr Barbara smiled at him indulgently. 'Doctors have to do a lot of things that people would rather not know about. Some of these patients were only minutes away from their deaths, but cruelly the clock had stopped. I merely started it again for them. Old women deserve special care, they're not looked after as gently as old men. Think of them – exhausted, incontinent, riddled with cancers, only able to breathe sitting up, crying out with pain if you even touched them. What I did, I did openly, because I knew it was right. Even the judge didn't dare send me to prison . . . '

As if tired of having to justify herself to this moralistic teenager, Dr Barbara turned to the bouquets lying on the table by the television set. Beyond the chrysanthemums and gladioli was a visionary kingdom of her own, filtered through the scented petals, where she could walk untainted by any moral opprobrium and where the albatross would forever fly above her

43

head. A film of moisture, as pale as hope, ran from her high forehead to the tip of her strong nose.

'I've made you famous, Neil.' She pointed to the childishly scrawled messages. 'They all love you.'

Neil flexed his numbed foot, counting his toes under the sheet. 'They'd love me even more if I died – that would really save the albatross, doctor.'

'Neil . . . ' Dr Barbara shook her head at this mischievous sally. 'Think how proud your father would have been. You do remember him?'

'All the time. It's my mother who's trying to forget him – that's why she's . . . '

'Drawing away from you a little? You can understand that. In bereavement there's a time to remember and a time to forget. Sometimes they're the same thing. When does she expect you in Atlanta?'

'Next month. But I might stay on here for a while.'

'Well, we leave in three weeks, Neil. You'll have to decide. Kimo and I want you to come with us. We need someone your age who'll encourage other young people to join the sanctuary. In time they'll take over from us. It's not a crusade but a great relay race. Will you come?'

'Well . . . there might be a nuclear test. I'll have to think about it.'

'Good. I've always depended on you, Neil. When you're older we'll be very close . . . '

This unveiled threat, uttered in a quietly confident tone, floated through Neil's mind during his days of convalescence at the swimming-pool. When he left the hospital, blushing through the crowd of teasing nurses, Dr Barbara drove him in the jeep to his rooming house, but she set off immediately for the docks. There were stores to be loaded aboard the *Dugong*, cabins and the galley to be equipped, satellite communications gear to be installed.

Neil promised vaguely that he would help, but he had secretly decided not to join the expedition. Television and press re-porters were already visiting the shrimp-trawler in Honolulu harbour, describing in provocative detail the preparations for the ecological sea-raid on a military outpost of the French colonial empire. The Defence Ministry in Paris neither confirmed nor denied that nuclear tests were to re-start on Saint-Esprit, but warned that any unauthorized vessel entering the exclusion zone would be boarded and seized.

Neil returned to a quixotic mission of his own, the marathon swim across the Kaiwi Channel. The months in hospital had softened the muscles of his legs and shoulders, and his first twenty lengths in the university pool left him too exhausted to climb from the shallow end. Weeks of intense body-building and pool practice would be needed to return him to fitness. Rising at six, determined to work himself back to a hundred lengths a day, he tried not to think of Dr Barbara, Saint-Esprit or the albatross.

But memories of the disbarred physician and her passionate breath tugged like the waking nerves in his injured foot, distracting him as he mapped the currents of the Kaiwi Channel on the U.S. Navy charts. Curious to see her before she sailed, and aware that he might never meet her again, he decided to drive to the harbour to say his goodbyes. The revelation that she had killed her elderly patients lay in the back of his mind like an old newspaper in an attic, fading in a moral climate that took a more tolerant view of euthanasia and, tacitly, even approved of the process. Few of her new-found admirers had lost faith in her or stepped back for a moment to ponder her multiple murders. *Paris-Match* now lauded the transformation of 'Dr Death' into 'Dr Life'. All lives were precious, but the albatross and manatee now outranked the lowly human being.

Moreover, Neil knew, he missed Dr Barbara, her strong will and her disconcerting coarseness and affection. He remembered how she bullied him during the voyage to Saint-Esprit, while her fingers forever ran across his chest, reading the braille of some invisible desire in his urgent skin. He thought of the thuggish French marines with their rubber truncheons, and wondered how to dissuade her from sailing to the atoll.

On the first Sunday after leaving the hospital he parked the jeep near the harbour and hid himself among the strolling tourists. The *Dugong* was moored beyond the inter-island ferry station, high bows already pointing towards the open sea. On a steel platform below the bridge a satellite dish cupped the sky. A military staff car stood on the quay, and men in camouflage fatigues climbed the gangway.

Neil limped forward, pushing between the tourists. He hoped that the American government, under pressure from the French, had decided to impound the vessel before it could set sail. But when he reached the staff car he found a driver with a bandit moustache and shaven head lounging behind the wheel. Transfers of a dugong, manatee and great white shark were stuck to his neck, and a rondel on the door was emblazoned with 'Wild-Water Kingdom Inc. Live and Love – an Irving Boyd Planetary Project'.

Neil approached the gangway, stepping past a dozen crates packed with tents and camping equipment, cartons of macrobiotic and vegetarian food, a portable ocean of bottled mineral water, camera lights and silver umbrellas. Gazing calmly upon all this from the bridge was Captain Wu, the Hong Kong Chinese skipper, a small, trim figure in white shorts, knee-length socks and peaked cap. Beside him was the philanthropist and software genius, pale eyes taking in every detail through his over-large spectacles. He noticed Neil standing uncertainly at the foot of the gangway and gave a gentle wave, like an absent-minded pope extending his benediction.

'Neil, don't fall in!' Dr Barbara stepped from the cabin below the bridge. She waited by the gangway and caught his arm when his numbed foot missed a worn rubber cleat. She pulled him onto the deck, surprised but glad to see him, weighing the stronger muscles of his arms like a farmer's wife pleased with the growth of a prize bullock.

'Neil, we've all missed you. Are you coming with us?'

'Dr Barbara, I wanted to –'

'Good. I knew you would.' Dr Barbara stood back and then embraced him fiercely, strong hands searching his rib-cage and shoulder blades, reassuring herself that the bones of old still lay within the newly confident muscle. 'We couldn't have gone without you.'

'Dr Barbara . . .' Neil wiped her gaudy lipstick from his forehead. 'What about the French navy? They're waiting for you . . .'

'Don't worry! There's a new wind blowing.' She consulted her roster. 'We'll find a cabin for you later, but first I want you to meet Monique Didier, our very special new friend.'

She put an arm proudly around Neil as a vigorous, dark-haired woman in white overalls stepped onto the deck below the bridge and emptied a waste-bucket of soapy water into the sea.

'Monique is a chief steward with Air France,' Dr Barbara told him. 'But she's given everything up to join us. Monique, this moody chap is Neil Dempsey, champion swimmer and my right-hand man.'

'So . . . of course, I saw you on TV. You're practically a film star.' The Frenchwoman bowed steeply, holding Neil's hand as if touching an icon. 'I know all about your trip to Saint-Esprit. You're really my hero.'

Despite her ironic tone, Neil found himself reddening again. During her hospital visits Dr Barbara had often described this high-principled air hostess. Now in her late thirties, Monique Didier was the daughter of one of France's first animal rights activists, the writer and biologist René Didier. She and her father had set up a wild-life sanctuary in the Pyrenees for an endangered colony of bears. For years they endured the abuse and hostility of local farmers angered by the bears' sheep-killing and their sentimentalized image in the metropolitan press. All this had made Monique prickly and defensive, but she was dedicated to her campaign, brow-beating her first-class passengers on the Paris-New York and Paris-Tokyo runs. After repeated warnings, Air France had lost patience and sacked her.

Neil was already wary of her sharp tongue, but Monique seemed genuinely reassured by his arrival. He was tired after walking along the crowded quay, and wanted to sit on the platform of the satellite dish, but she hovered around him as if eager to fasten his seat-belt and slip a plastic tray onto his lap.

'It's excellent that you're coming,' she told Neil, still sizing him up. 'We have to get ashore very quickly, and you know the secret pathways to the airstrip.'

'They're not really secret . . . ' Neil realized that Dr Barbara had been busy mythologizing the island. 'What about Kimo?'

'He'll be with us, of course. But we must take care not to expose him.' Monique rattled her bucket with a show of distaste. 'Those French officers are so racist. One chance and they'll shoot him down like a pig.'

'They shot me.'

'But not again!' Monique's eyebrows bristled. 'You're an emblem, Neil. The TV screen is your shield, no bullet can pierce you. Is that right, Barbara?'

'Of course, Monique, though I wouldn't put it quite like that.' Dr Barbara tried to pacify her. 'Let's hope no-one gets shot.'

The endless bedside interviews and television appearances had done their work, Neil reflected. He was now a talisman of the animal rights movement, to be carried shoulder-high like the stuffed head of a slaughtered bison. When Dr Barbara took him onto the bridge she introduced him with a flourish to Captain Wu and Irving Boyd, as if his appearance guaranteed her own credentials.

The computer entrepreneur greeted him with a grave bow, eyes slowly blinking behind the thick lenses like an ever-wary alarm detector.

'We prayed for you, Neil,' he said in a soft Texan voice, to which he listened as if the words contained a concealed code. 'When you were shot the planet held its breath. I think even the manatees and the dugongs prayed.'

'I prayed for the albatross, Mr Boyd.'

'Everyone prayed for the albatross. Meanwhile, I hope you take part in the sanctuary island project.'

'No-one's asked me – is that a TV series?'

'Irving means Saint-Esprit,' Dr Barbara pointed out. 'I think we can look forward to some awfully high ratings.'

'We want you there, Neil.' Boyd's eyes were fixed on Neil with all the humility of a film producer discovering a face of Christ-like pathos among a crowd of extras. 'There's a starring role for you.'

'Well, maybe . . . I don't know much about acting. I'm still coping with reality.'

'Reality? That's a public service channel, Neil. I'm planning to put up the first privately operated ecological satellite. We'll beam you and Dr Barbara into every home on the planet . . . '

As Boyd outlined his prospectus it was clear to Neil that the entrepreneur saw the expedition to Saint-Esprit as little more than the reconnaissance for a television programme. But Dr Barbara bundled him down the stairway before he could reply.

'For God's sake, Neil! He's lent us the ship.'

Neil was pleased to see her annoyed with him. A few minutes in Dr Barbara's presence was more of a tonic than all the hundreds of lengths in the university pool.

'The *Dugong*'s a stage-set, Dr Barbara. Like the replica of the *Bounty*. For him everything turns into television.'

'Maybe, but he still controls the off-switch. Now meet Professor and Mrs Saito. And no jokes about atom bombs.'

A young Japanese couple broke off their work in the galley to bow to Neil. Both professional botanists, they had flown in from Tokyo the previous day after abandoning their careers at the University of Kyoto and placing themselves at the service of Dr Barbara's vision. They had brought with them two small suitcases, a plastic tent and a set of folding chairs, like overgrown children about to play on a holiday beach. They treated Neil to a pair of synchronized smiles that had scarcely faded when he left the *Dugong* an hour later, promising Dr Barbara to return and help with their preparations for departure.

Trying to make sense of this naive but muddled crew, Neil drummed his forehead so fiercely against the jeep's steering wheel that he bruised the skin. Already he knew that some way had to be found of preventing Dr Barbara and her ship of fools from ever leaving Honolulu. During the next days, as he swam his lengths, he listened to the pool-side radio. Media interest in the *Dugong* remained high, prompted by the immense white wings which Kimo had painted along the trawler's hull. Already a novelty designer in Waikiki had turned the striking image of wave and wing into a natty series of badges and lapel buttons.

Every afternoon Neil drove to the harbour, hoping to find that French agents had scuttled the ship. Dr Barbara was usually absent, lobbying the French consulate with a party of sympathizers and addressing the last fund-raising rallies. Captain Wu and his seven Filipino crew continued to load the stores, fuel and fresh water, watched by the solitary figure of Irving Boyd, brooding between the white wings of the ship like Poseidon lost in a dream of his oceans.

A group of New Age hippies carrying an anti-vivisectionist banner had taken up residence on the quay. Shaking their tambourines, they danced among the stall-holders selling balloons and environmentalist geegaws to the tourists. Even Irving Boyd stirred from his meditations and tapped the air to the cheerful rhythm. He invited the troupe onto the bridge, where they danced around a bemused Captain Wu and then conducted a gentle mock-religious rite beside the satellite dish.

Watching this antic ship and its antic crew, Neil was sure that they would never leave port. But a week after his meeting with Dr Barbara he met the latest volunteers to join the expedition and realized that the *Dugong* would not only set out from Honolulu but had every chance of sailing straight into the French guns.

A film crew of three – Janet Bracewell, the Australian director, and the camera-man, her American husband Mark, together with the Indian sound-recordist, Vikram Pratap – were to be Irving Boyd's ambassadors to Saint-Esprit. Detached from the Wild-Water sanctuary, they would record the progress of the expedition and transmit live pictures of any hostile French action to Boyd's TV station in Honolulu and from there to the world's watching networks. Already they were filming the reporters and animal rights activists who roamed the *Dugong*, interrupting the work of the Filipino crewmen and earnestly questioning them about their attitudes to nuclear testing and the environment.

Incited by the camera's presence, the visitors turned the shrimp-trawler into the venue of a continuous party. Passers-by pilfered the unloaded stores and helped themselves to the bottles of donated wine. By the time Dr Barbara and Monique returned in the evening they found tourists dancing on the quay to the New Age tambourines, eco-banners floating on the cool harbour air and an amiable wraith of pot-smoke lifting through the Chinese lanterns. Delighted by this festive atmosphere, Dr

Barbara danced with Monique while Captain Wu paced his darkened bridge and a disapproving Kimo sat with his paint store in the high bows of the *Dugong*.

But Kimo was not alone in being puzzled by Dr Barbara's failure to control her sympathizers. As he watched from the pier of the inter-island terminal Neil had noticed a tall, white-haired American in his early forties standing beside his rented car on the quay. Driven by his wife, he usually arrived in mid-afternoon, stepped from his seat and spent an uncomfortable hour gazing at the ship. The sight of the unguarded stores and the three inflatables on their trailer seemed to unsettle him. While his wife sat stoically at the wheel he would pace around the rubber craft, wiping the wine-stains with his handkerchief, and only relaxing when the Filipinos finished their interviews and returned to work. Sometimes he would shout at the milling tourists, and then break off to practise his tennis backhand, sweeping his long arm in a compulsive way, as if trying to land a difficult shot in his opponent's court. ·

Neil assumed that he was forcing himself to decide whether or not he should join Dr Barbara. On his fourth visit to the quay, the American saw her arrive after her last day's work at the children's home. He avoided her eyes when she strode past, leaned his elbows on the window sill of the car and stared at his patient wife. Before she could speak he turned with a nervous tic of his shoulders and followed Dr Barbara to the *Dugong*, counting her steps aloud to himself. Holding his arms above the heads of the Japanese tourists, he climbed the gangway, his eyes clear and all his doubts apparently resolved.

Neil soon learned that this was David Carline, the last volunteer to join the expedition. The president of a small pharmaceutical company in Boston, he had been on holiday in Honolulu when he learned of Dr Barbara and her mission to save the albatross. The family firm had for decades supplied its pharmaceuticals to the third world, and Carline had frequently taken leaves of absence to join American missionary groups in Brazil and the Congo, teaching in mission schools and delivering lay sermons at the open-air church services. Intelligent, rich and eager for hard work, he was the first sane presence on board the *Dugong*.

Neil disliked him on sight. From the moment that Carline came on deck, swinging his expensive, travel-worn suitcase up the gangway, Neil was certain that he would restore order to the ship, concentrate Dr Barbara's wayward mind and see that the trawler set sail as planned. Sure enough, within little more than a day Carline had assumed the deputy leadership of the expedition. Both Monique and Dr Barbara were glad to defer to someone with the management skills needed to restore order to the crates heaped chaotically in the forward hold. Captain Wu welcomed him to the bridge, recognizing a fellow spirit, and Irving Boyd happily ceded his place to Carline and returned to his television station in Honolulu.

Carline soon set about trimming the ship. First he persuaded the Bracewells to save their film footage, and affably suggested that they join the other expedition members in the job of winching the silver-skinned inflatables from their trailer on the quay. Once the camera vanished from the scene many of the tourists and New. Agers drifted away, taking the stall-holders with them. The work of loading stores resumed, and Kimo descended from his perch, eager to support Carline's brisk new regime.

Carline greeted Neil with a testing handshake, sensible enough to ignore the English youth's hostility.

'Neil, you're the reason I'm here, all the way from Boston. We're proud of you and everything you did on Saint-Esprit.' He gestured to Mrs Carline, sitting sombrely in the car parked by the gangway. 'Even my wife respects you – a great deal more than she respects me, I can tell you. I'd like you to meet her, she admires your guts in sailing to Saint-Esprit and taking on the French. It might help her to understand why I had to join you.'

'Why did you join?'

'Hard to say, Neil. I guess I need to go to Saint-Esprit to find out. Of course, I want to save the albatross, but there's more to it than that. In a sense I want to save Dr Barbara. The world needs people like her, people with conviction and faith in the rest of us. For so long we've behaved as if we're all about to leave the planet for good, as if the Earth was some kind of dying resort area. We need more Saint-Esprits. I saw you and Dr Barbara on the TV news and, do you know, I left the hotel and drove straight down here. Anyway, enough of me. Are you fit for work? Kimo's keen to get the outboards loaded.'

For the rest of the day, as they settled the heavy motors in the hold, Neil kept a careful watch on the American, a nightmare-come-true of integrity and good humour. He reminded Neil of the chaplain at his boarding school in England – always eager and understanding, always ready to make the first rugby tackle on the practice pitch. The chaplain had resigned after an affair with the sports master's wife, and already Neil saw Carline as his chief rival for the attention of Dr Barbara.

'Kimo tells me you want to swim across the Kaiwi Channel,' Carline commented as they rested in the hold, surrounded by the engines and inflatables. 'It's a long way. Do you think you can do it?'

'Maybe not. But it's worth trying.'

'Good for you. Now that's no day-dreamer's philosophy. How do you feel about going back to Saint-Esprit?'

'It's dangerous . . . ' Neil said nothing of his decision to re-main in Honolulu even if the *Dugong* sailed. 'The French have patrol boats and a corvette.'

'You're wary, and it's sensible of you. Remember, though, you weren't frightened to face that French bullet.'

'I was running away.'

Carline laughed at this. 'Well, at least you weren't frightened to do that either.'

As he helped Carline to rope down the engines, it occurred to Neil that it would be surprisingly easy to sabotage the *Dugong*. Captain Wu had talked to Boyd and Dr Barbara about their contingency plans if the trawler was hit by gun-fire: they would either run her aground in the lagoon or scuttle her astride the reef. The cargo-hold and engine-room seacocks were never guarded, and at night only the Saitos and the Filipino crew slept aboard the ship. Carline returned with his wife to their Waikiki hotel, and Dr Barbara and Monique to their apartments in Honolulu. The quay was patrolled by a group of French students who had flown in from Tahiti, opposed to their government's decision to end the moratorium on nuclear testing and suspicious of the treacheries of the Deuxième Bureau. They sat around a kerosene lamp by the gangway, handing out leaflets to any midnight visitors who wandered down the quay, while a look-out monitored the waters around the *Dugong* in a small dinghy.

The cabin that Neil would share with Carline and the Indian sound-recordist was a narrow steel box with three hinged bunks, barely six steps from the door into the forward hold. The Filipinos slept aft in the engine-room and would hear Neil if he approached, but a single open seacock would flood the *Dugong* and sink it to the harbour bed.

Neil watched the news bulletins at his rooming house, waiting for the French intelligence agents in Honolulu to carry out the same act of sabotage that had sunk the *Rainbow Warrior*, and so save him the pain of betraying Dr Barbara. At the end of June, a week before the *Dugong*'s departure for Saint-Esprit, he packed a travel case with enough clothing and personal tackle to convince anyone that he meant to live aboard the ship.

He arrived at the quay by dusk, as the French volunteers sat in their deck-chairs beside the gangway, their anti-nuclear banners swaying in the riding lights of the ship. Neil stowed his bag in the cabin and tested the unlocked door into the forward hold. He joined Professor Saito and his wife in the galley, where he shared their modest macrobiotic meal. Afterwards they invited him to their cabin, where they earnestly discussed the damage to Japan's wild-life by the post-war policy of industrialization at any cost.

A dedicated taxonomist, Professor Saito was a slim, unsmiling man who seemed barely older than Neil. The cabin was crammed with textbooks and research reports on the world's myriad endangered species, which the botanist seemed to be classifying single-handedly. He had begun to catalogue the insect life aboard the *Dugong*, and had even noticed a fall in the expected number of rats in the bilges.

Mrs Saito was a small, brisk woman with strong hands that almost pulled Neil's wrists out of joint when she greeted him. She was devoted to her husband, forever watching him like an experienced manager supervising a novice boxer. Through the flicker of her chopsticks she stared at Neil's skin, once reaching out to touch his arm as if she expected to see his radiation burns.

She told him that they travelled to Saint-Esprit as the delegates of all the nuclear casualties of World War II.

'We can save the albatross, Neil,' she assured him.

'Of course we can, Mrs Saito,' Neil replied, uncertain whether her remark was a question.

'If we save the albatross we can help the spirit of many people in Hiroshima.'

'The dead people?'

'And the other people today. They live on in the albatross.'

Her husband sucked at his sake. 'It's England's sacred bird?' he asked. 'A totemic figure?'

'Yes, it is, in a way . . .'

'It's a beautiful bird. Is Saint-Esprit beautiful?'

'It certainly is,' Neil assured him. 'It has a very strange atmosphere, you know. There are all these amazing towers.'

'Towers?' Professor Saito sat up. 'Like . . . obelisks? Stone columns, with religious inscriptions?'

'No. Camera-towers, made of concrete. Waiting for a nuclear explosion . . .'

Neil tried to calm himself, but the silence that followed his brief outburst lasted until he left the cabin and closed the door on the Saitos. He spent the next two hours on the quay, talking to an earnest American woman, a computer sciences major at the University, who prepared coffee for the French students. At midnight he climbed the gangway and went to his cabin. He sat by the open door, listening to the strange scratching sounds that emerged from the Saitos' cabin, and watched the distant lights of Waikiki through the salt-smeared porthole.

For the first time he wondered if he had the courage to turn the seacock and sink Dr Barbara's dreams to the harbour bottom. Even a few feet of water in the forward hold would postpone their departure long enough for Irving Boyd to have second thoughts about the voyage.

The students were drowsing in their deck-chairs, and the scent of cannabis drifted over the silent ship. Neil stepped from the cabin and eased open the door into the hold. As he turned the wheel of the seacock he vowed to work hard for Dr Barbara and somehow reinstate her as a practising physician.

Headlights flared across the hatchway above his head, illuminating the foremast which reared into the night like a crippled gallows. As the Saitos stirred in their cabin, Neil climbed the oily ladder to the deck and crouched behind the satellite dish. The students were shouting to each other and there was a panic of running feet on the gangway. A taxi approached at speed along the quay, its beams dipping and flaring as the driver braked beside the moored craft, searching for the *Dugong*. Dr Barbara leaned over his shoulder, pointing to the white wings that veered from the dark water.

Seeing her, Neil felt a surge of relief. He knew that he could sink the ship, but not while Dr Barbara walked its bridge. He met her on the gangway, taking her hands when she stumbled towards the deck. Her hair was uncombed, and she gasped through her smeared lipstick, as if she had just been embraced by a violent lover.

'Neil, thank God you're here. I knew I could rely on you.'

'Dr Barbara? What is it – did someone attack you?'

'They've attacked all of us!' Dr Barbara stared wildly at the ship, as if unable to focus her eyes. 'The French have informed the United Nations. Nuclear tests resume at Saint-Esprit on July 15. Neil!'

'July 15 . . .?' Neil tried to restrain her whirling hands, moving across the night air like deranged birds. 'Dr Barbara, that means there's no point in going. We'll never get there.'

'We will, Neil. If we leave tomorrow.' She clasped him in her fierce arms, forcing his cheek against her hot breast. 'Think of it, Neil – they're setting off a nuclear bomb. You'll have to come with me now . . .'

4

The Shore Raid

AN ELABORATE AIR-AND-SEA ballet was taking place, an over-rehearsed performance that rarely deviated from its agreed scenario. The sombre stage-set of Saint-Esprit rose in the background, a thundercloud sitting like a disgruntled genie on its peak, underskirts lit by the ceaseless flurry of the surf against the beaches of black ash. The sea shifted, its surface criss-crossed by a maze of wakes, a frantic choreography marking the thrusts and counter-thrusts of the daily confrontation.

Legs braced against the rolling bows, Neil stood on the foredeck of the *Dugong*, shielded from the cold spray by the white bowl of the satellite dish, at that moment transmitting the afternoon's first performance to the watching world. The only element missing, he often reflected, was a floating orchestra and chorus on a ceremonial barge above the reef. Driven by Kimo and David Carline, the two inflatables swerved across the bows of the *Champlain* as the French supply vessel manoeuvred on the sliding sea outside the entrance to the reef. Powered by their violent outboards, the inflatables leapt almost vertically through the spray, albatross flashes baiting the weary captain as he once again signalled astern to his engine-room.

For an hour the *Champlain* had been trying to enter the lagoon, and Neil assumed that the captain was under orders not to run down the two inflatables doing their best to provoke him. He released smoke, which the two-seater helicopter overhead fanned into a sooty haze, trying to lure the soft-hulled craft onto the reef. Kimo and Carline turned on their propellers with a flourish, charioteers leaping through a curtain of stage-smoke. They sped past the *Dugong* for an admiring cheer, led by Dr Barbara from the bridge, and raced back to the supply vessel.

But by now the French captain had lost his chance to enter the reef. Reversing his engines, he moved across the swell, ignoring the inflatables while the helicopter came over to buzz the *Dugong*. Neil gripped the cradle spars of the satellite dish, the machete in his right hand raised for the benefit of the Bracewells' camera, ready to cut away the dangling line with which the pilot had been trying to lasso the steel bowl.

The downdraught beat against Neil's face, pummelling his skin and almost stripping the albatross-emblazoned windcheater from his shoulders. Standing on the bridge behind Captain Wu, Mark Bracewell fixed his lens on the circling aircraft, arms steadied by his wife as the sound-man, Pratap, fished the sky with his boom microphone for the ugliest engine snarls. Beside them, Monique swore and railed at the blond-haired pilot, her direst threats against the young man lost in the din. She set off a coloured flare, which soared into the helicopter's wake as it made a weary sweep of the disturbed sea and set off for the landing-strip on Saint-Esprit.

Soon there would be an hour's intermission, giving the world-wide television audience time to refocus its indignation. When Janet Bracewell called to Neil he turned to face the camera, aware that his chief role was to provide a poignant end-credit to the transmissions. He hoped that Louise, watching the evening news in England after a day at her music school, would see him and at least appreciate the finer points of the afternoon's display, and that his mother, sitting on the edge of her chair in Atlanta, would not be too alarmed by the vicious blade in his hand.

Captain Wu waited beside the Filipino helmsman, disapproving of these unseamanlike proceedings, while a breathless Dr Barbara surveyed the churned sea like an impresario viewing the location of a lavish film production. This, of course, was literally true, but Dr Barbara, Neil and everyone aboard the *Dugong* knew that at any moment the good-humoured duel might come to a brutal end. They all assumed that the planned nuclear tests would soon take place. Since their arrival at Saint-Esprit four days earlier Neil had scanned the ancient camera-towers and blockhouses of the atoll, half-hoping to see a mind-searing eruption of vapour rise from the centre of the lagoon.

Meanwhile, a single volley of shots from the *Champlain* would sink the inflatables and put them out of action for good. Yet so far, for whatever political and diplomatic reasons, the French had been sticking to the script. They allowed the *Dugong* to approach the island, and waited patiently as the inflatables performed their water-borne pas de deux. In the late afternoon the corvette *Sagittaire* would arrive and escort the trawler to the perimeter of the thirty-mile exclusion zone, its signal lamp signing off with a choice obscenity that sent Monique enraged to her cabin.

The arrangement suited everyone, and provided the maximum of national dignity and TV coverage at the minimum of risk. But now there would be a radical change to the script, and the French had not been consulted. As the deck rolled against his injured foot, testing the still tender nerves, Neil remembered the bullet that had struck him three months beforehand. If Dr Barbara seriously provoked them, the French would shoot again.

'Neil, are you coming?' Monique shouted to him from the bridge, as she fastened her life-jacket. 'We're leaving now.'

'I'll stay here, Monique.'

'We want you on the island, Neil. It's good for the film.'

'You get shot for me.'

'As you wish . . . ' Monique bared her large teeth, concerned that Neil had mislaid his courage with his boarding pass. 'You should rest more, Neil. These nuclear dreams . . . '

By the starboard gangway, hidden from the *Champlain*'s binoculars, rode one of Irving Boyd's most powerful speedboats, engine rumbling at the sea like an impatient bloodhound. Its seats were loaded with flares, detonators and three Molotov cocktails, which Carline and Professor Saito had assembled, using a brew of ether, palm oil and gasoline. Mrs Saito was already squatting among the glass cylinders, her hands fondling the tapers of cotton waste, excited by the destructive power at her finger-tips. Monique clambered into the craft, and silently mouthed some eco-catechism as she stared at the waiting beaches. The nuclear island incarnated everything these women feared and detested, as Neil knew from their long harangues. Often they trapped him in the galley and threatened him with all the deformations that afflicted the placid turtles of Eniwetok Atoll, the holiest ground of Neil's imagination.

A Filipino crewman calmed the speedboat's engine as its spitting exhaust raked the white hull-plates of the *Dugong*. Professor Saito, his slim face hidden inside the hood of his waterproof, crouched beside the Bracewells and Pratap. The Japanese botanist seemed pinched and nervous, never comfortable when he was more than a few feet from the journals and year-books in his cabin. Between his hands he clasped a terracotta jar of human ashes, a small sample entrusted to him by the keepers of a Hiroshima ossuary, which he hoped to bury beside the dead albatross on the quiet sands of the Saint-Esprit lagoon.

Relieved that he had refused to join Dr Barbara on this shore-raid, Neil waited for her to emerge from the bridge-house. She stepped onto the deck, trussed like a weekend commando into her life-jacket and waterproof, and gave a brave wave to Neil. He helped her down the gangway towards the pitching speed-boat, trying to steady her shaking feet, but she stumbled on the greasy steps, almost losing the albatross bandeau around her forehead.

'Dr Barbara, why don't we . . . ?'

'Neil, what is it?' Regaining her balance, she turned her warmest smile on him, one arm raised to fend the swaying hull of the *Dugong* from his head. 'Don't be frightened by all this.'

'We could wait another day – or even a week. The French might leave.'

'We can't wait any longer, Neil. We must set foot on the island. If we don't, the world will lose interest in us. Now, I want you to stay on board. You've done enough to save the albatross. Promise me you won't try to swim ashore.'

'Dr Barbara . . . ' Neil pointed to the Molotov cocktail clasped between Mrs Saito's thighs. 'Just one bullet – that's all it needs to blow up the boat. The Saitos haven't seen the French.'

Dr Barbara tapped his chin with her fist. 'We've got to get ashore. In ten days we have to go back to Honolulu, and we need something to show Irving we're serious.'

'But Irving isn't serious!' Neil found himself shouting through the *Champlain*'s sirens. 'All this is just a TV programme for him . . .'

'I know, Neil. But this is our last chance. Trust me . . .'

Its wake boiling the sea, the speedboat moved away from the *Dugong*, the raiding party crouched behind the helmsman. The two inflatables still worked like terriers around the supply ship, their outboards moaning. The *Champlain* had drifted through the confused sea, and now lay five hundred yards from the reef entrance. The captain defended his bows, and his crewmen aimed their hoses at Carline and Kimo when they swerved and turned, drenching the two men. No-one noticed the speedboat heading along the outer edge of the reef, where Kimo had found a second breach in the coral wall.

Should he swim ashore? Neil gripped the handrail and gazed at the eager waves, rolling playfully onto their backs as they waited for him. He guessed that Dr Barbara had dropped the idea like a small pebble into his mind, keen to have Neil with the raiding party but unwilling to be responsible for him. This time, she knew, the French would aim higher than Neil's feet. As their tempers rose they had resorted to tougher tactics. Escorting them out of the exclusion zone, the *Sagittaire* had almost rammed the trawler. The officer in charge of the boarding party physically threatened Captain Wu, and his NCOs had manhandled Kimo, silencing Dr Barbara and Monique with their loudhailers when they tried to make an impassioned speech to the Bracewells' camera.

All this they were fully prepared for, and during the voyage from Honolulu they felt surprisingly lightheaded, their spirits kept buoyant by Dr Barbara's steadfast conviction that their mission to the nuclear island would succeed. Engine failure becalmed them for three days, a purgatory of airless boredom broken only by squalls of burning rain. Dr Barbara spent hours in the *Dugong*'s bows, counting the sea-birds, while Monique played bridge with Carline and the Bracewells. Kimo, strengthening his huge body for the confrontations ahead, ran endless circuits of the deck and exercised to a heavy rock beat on his portable sound system.

The Saitos, meanwhile, rested in their cabin and honed their moral convictions. Dropping in for a chat, which he knew annoyed them, Neil was soon informed of their belief that the other members of the expedition lacked a proper understanding of their journey to a spiritual ground-zero of the twentieth century. Professor Saito tried to quiz Neil about the special symbolism of the albatross, viewing the bird as an emblem of the nuclear guilt that ailed Dr Barbara and, by extension, the war-time Americans. Neil, in turn, showed rather too much curiosity about the Hiroshima A-bomb, and Mrs Saito felt obliged to reprimand him.

'Neil! You have a disco mentality. Hiroshima was not a light show.'

'Of course not, Mrs Saito. My father was at Maralinga during the British tests.'

'So. How many people died there?'

'Well . . . I think he did.'

'You think? Yukio, he thinks. The boy . . . thinks.'

Otherwise, Neil mooned around the ship or played chess with Carline, delighted to find that he could easily beat the pale-eyed American. Generous in victory, he ignored the lectures on the true chess mentality.

'Your play lacks any sense of strategy, Neil. You only win by waiting for me to make a mistake.'

'But, David, you never make mistakes.'

'As it happens, I've made nothing but mistakes in my life, or so my wife and daughters like to tell me. That's one of the reasons I'm here.'

'You don't think this expedition's a mistake?'

'Do you, Neil? You probably do. You're a strange paladin for Barbara to have picked. I guess she has something special in mind for you.' Carline stared wistfully at the chess pieces as he set out another game. 'It may seem naive to you, but our cause is just, and it's within our grasp.'

Carline's hopeful but plaintive smile reminded Neil of the insecure grin he had been unable to erase from his face as the *Dugong* pulled away from the quayside at Honolulu. Embarrassed by the sight of his despondent wife, Carline began to practise his backhand to himself. His forced good cheer depressed Neil, as did his self-appointed role as second-in-command to Dr Barbara. Carline was forever striding around the ship, helping Captain Wu with the navigation, supervising the stores, eager to land on Saint-Esprit and find relief for the petty bunion of the heart that had sent him to Africa and South America on his missionary jaunts. During one of his inspection rounds he casually displayed to Dr Barbara the chromium-plated pistol in his suitcase. Seeing that he had horrified her, he promised to hurl it into the sea, but the next day Neil noticed that it still lay in its black German holster.

For all his high-minded sentiments, Carline was not above certain small deceits. Shortly before they sailed, his Waikiki hotel delivered a crate of expensive canned goods to the *Dugong*. This picnic hamper sat under his bunk, guarded by a conspicuous bronze padlock. Although he collected his full daily ration of food from the galley – alternating stew and corned-beef hash prepared by the Filipino chef, who had worked for the American navy at the Subik Bay base – Carline smiled without embarrass-ment when Dr Barbara caught him having a private snack of pâté and quails' breasts. Her eyebrows almost touched her hairline as she pondered this display of a rich man's easy arrogance, but like the Christian missionaries in their up-country stations she valued his energy and determination, and decided to tolerate this quirk of character.

Unsure of Carline despite beating him at chess, Neil tried to make himself useful to Monique, and helped her to prepare the daily commentary on the voyage which she recorded for a radio station in Toulon. However, her irritation with herself over the smallest slip of the tongue and her relentless attacks on her country's ecological policies soon wearied Neil. Reluctant to join Kimo in his earnest pounding of the deck, he found himself in the chart-room with the Bracewells and Pratap, reduced to watching the endless video footage that the film crew had collected. Neil soon noticed that the camera went out of its way to stress his youth and gaucheness as he stared heavy-browed at the sky, a simpleton puzzled by his first sea-bird. Dr Barbara and

Monique seemed just as gawky and amateurish as they swung up and down the bridge like a pair of tipsy spinsters.

'Mark, are you going to show this film?' he asked, wondering how Louise and his mother would respond to the footage. 'It's really weird – we all look drunk, or brain-dead.'

'Neil, come on . . . ' Bracewell joined in the laughter but glanced at his wife in a telling way. He and Janet were a pleasant but secretive couple, always cheerfully on the move around the ship and rather more interested in the expedition members than in the plight of the albatross. 'We can't dress you up in shining armour.'

'Why not? Dr Barbara's completely serious.'

'We know that. Look, I admire her, but why pretend she's Albert Schweitzer? Neil, the whole point of the trip is that you and the others are a cross-section of everyday life – seven people with practically nothing in common who meet up on a street corner and decide to stop a bully beating his dog to death.'

'Exactly, Neil,' Janet agreed, offering him an extra helping of pawpaw as a pacifier. 'The real story is right here on this ship. It's you and Monique and the Saitos . . . Irving knows that.'

'So you're really making a documentary about us – not about the albatross?'

'You seven, *and* the albatross,' Bracewell explained. 'Let's face it, you've got some pretty strange reasons for being here.'

'Does that matter? The important thing is saving the birds.' Neil was surprised to hear himself defending the albatross. 'You make it sound like a sitcom – "The Dugong and the Albatross." Janet, it isn't a joke. The French – '

'Of course it isn't a joke.' Janet touched his nose with a creamy finger-tip. 'You know that better than anyone else, Neil.'

They were fond of Neil, and happy to argue with him all day. But Neil realized that Irving Boyd and the Bracewells saw the voyage to Saint-Esprit as a safari to save an endangered species, perhaps the most threatened of all – Dr Barbara Rafferty and her party of high-minded but innocent enthusiasts.

★   ★   ★

Smoke rose from the island, lifting from the runway beyond the screen of palms. It drifted past the camera-towers and lay against the steam-drenched hill-slopes, stirring the shaggy leaves of the cycads and tamarinds. A series of rapid explosions broke the silence like a string of fire-crackers, and a vivid copper light shone through the palms, isolating the hundreds of tree-trunks. A glowing wind moved across the atoll, and thrashed the dusty vegetation into a tempest of burning dust. A fuel tank had exploded, sending a cloud of oily smoke into the air, and the shock wave rolled over the swells and drummed against the *Dugong*, vibrating the rail between Neil's hands. Carline and Kimo had broken off their harassment of the *Champlain* and sped towards the trawler.

'Captain Wu! The *Sagittaire* is back!'

Neil clambered onto the platform of the satellite dish and pointed to the north-west horizon. The French corvette was barely a mile away, its graceful, threatening profile turning upon the *Dugong*. On the bridge Captain Wu spoke to the engine-room, hands resting palm-upwards on the rail as if he accepted that the sabotage of the fuel tank marked a senseless escalation of the campaign, and would promptly lead to the seizure of the *Dugong* and his own arrest. Kimo had sneaked ashore several times, reporting later that the military base was no more than an airstrip depot where some thirty French soldiers lived in tents pitched under the palms, safely away from the stench of the beaches. The killing of the fish and albatross continued, but to no clear purpose.

The *Champlain* slipped through the reef and set course for its anchorage in the lagoon, leaving the corvette to deal with the *Dugong*. Neil sprinted along the deck to the stern hoist, and waited with the Filipino crewmen for the speedboat to reappear. The fuel fire had subsided, and Saint-Esprit had drawn a curtain of tattered smoke around itself. Neil listened to the laboured churning of the trawler's elderly diesels, and prayed that the *Dugong*'s hull-plates would be strong enough to resist the sharp prow of the *Sagittaire*.

The speedboat swerved sharply from the reef, escorted by the two inflatables. Dr Barbara's chalky face shone like a lantern against the darkening shore, eyes alight as she helped the seasick Monique to vomit over the side. Within moments the three craft jostled alongside, everyone shouting at once, their cheeks flushed with excitement, like a party of students returning from a rag-week jape.

'Neil! I wish you'd been with us!' Dr Barbara clambered up the gangway and seized his shoulders. 'Monique blew up a fuel tank, the whole island's on fire! Are you proud of us?'

'I am proud of you, Dr Barbara.'

'Good – I want you to be. Remember, you and I were here first.'

Still holding Neil around the waist, she stared in a happy daze at the smoke that hung over Saint-Esprit, a plague spectre searching the palms. The Filipino crewmen swung the speedboat onto the deck, while Carline and Kimo waited their turn in the inflatables, fists clenched over their heads.

But already eyes were turning towards the corvette, now only eight hundred yards away, its bows cutting brusquely through the waves. Annoyed with herself, Monique was still retching over her life-jacket, its yellow panels stained with the red wine she had drunk to bolster her courage. Professor Saito and his pale wife stood by the speedboat, clinging to its side as if aware that for the first time in their lives they had lost control of their emotions.

The *Sagittaire* altered course towards them, her captain clearly set on ramming the *Dugong*. Diesel exhaust pumped from the trawler's funnel as Captain Wu rang 'ahead' and 'more ahead' to the engine-room. Driven by the following sea, the vessel moved out of the corvette's path, but the French commander again trimmed his bearing, bows fixed on the *Dugong*.

Sirens blared from the corvette's bridge and a signal lamp flashed in their faces as the warship ran alongside, its heavy hull shouldering the trawler out of its way. It sheared past in a scream of iron, stripping away a section of the starboard rail and crushing the wooden gangway to matchwood. Its wake overturned Kimo's inflatable, and the Hawaiian was swimming in the seething water, trying to grasp Carline's outstretched hand.

Dislodged by the impact, a carapace of lead paint fell from the trawler's funnel and shattered on the deck. Neil, Monique and Dr Barbara sat stunned among the lumpy shards, deafened by the roar of the diesels and the harsh braying of the corvette's sirens as it turned to make a second pass at the *Dugong*.

The Bracewells were first to recover, their camera recording the damage to the ship and the protesters sprawled across the decking. Neil steadied himself against the satellite dish, wondering how long it would take them to swim ashore. At high water they would clear the reef, but how many of them could swim more than fifty yards?

Dr Barbara climbed onto a life-raft in the bows, screaming abuse at the corvette as it overtook them.

'*Assassins! Salauds!* Shoot me, Captain!'

She brushed the spray-drenched hair from her mouth, exposing an ugly bruise above her lip, and helped Monique onto the raft beside her. Vocal chords numbed by her anger, the former air hostess stared at the vomit-stained life-jacket whose harness she had demonstrated so many times in the aisles of her aircraft. She tore at the nylon straps and flung the jacket onto the deck. Raising her cotton shirt, she exposed her right breast to the bored sailors who looked down from the corvette's bridge. The *Sagittaire* swept past, its commander signalling to Captain Wu to cut his engines, and Monique turned to the helicopter that clattered above its wake, screaming like a berserk mother at the young pilot.

Ignoring the corvette, Captain Wu was heading for the open sea, dragging the inflatables across the steepening waves. When the empty dinghy passed Kimo he seized the dented float, righted the craft with his huge arms and wrestled himself aboard. He and Carline straddled their outboards as they leapt through the clouds of spray. Neil waited for the exhausted American to lose his balance, but the years of competitive power-boating at Kennebunkport had hardened his thighs and reflexes.

Determined to make a third attack on the trawler, the *Sagittaire*'s captain bore down on them, and the corvette swept towards the *Dugong* on a fast sea. Mark Bracewell steadied himself against the waist-high rail of the stern docking-bridge, camera held over his shoulder, while an anxious Pratap plucked klaxon blasts from the sky.

'Neil! Get back! Leave the film!'

Dr Barbara was shouting as the two ships sheared past each other in a clamour of sirens and signal lights. The corvette's stern rose on the trawler's bow-wave, and the outer edge of the helicopter platform scythed along the starboard deck of the *Dugong* and struck the docking-bridge from its steel mounting. A wall of surging water threw Bracewell between the colliding hulls and hurled him into the broken wake of the trawler. Through the roar of sirens and the erratic flashing of the signal lamps Neil saw the shattered camera strike the stern of the corvette and plunge into the sea.

Captain Wu stopped his engines and let the *Dugong* drift towards the reef. Everyone stood on the rolling deck among the sections of twisted railing, staring into the torn water a hundred yards behind the trawler, where Bracewell's deflated life-jacket lay slackly on the dark sea. Professor Saito and Pratap seized the distraught Janet when she tried to clamber over the stern. The helicopter withdrew, as if the pilot no longer wished to involve himself in the confrontation, but on a signal from the corvette he returned to the scene and hovered over the floating jacket.

While Monique comforted the weeping woman, pressing Janet's head to her exposed breast, Kimo and Carline started their outboards and set off for the circle of water dented by the downdraught of the helicopter. Through the seething air, stained by smoke and engine exhaust, Neil could smell the stench of dead albatross from the beaches of Saint-Esprit and see the camera-towers of the nuclear lagoon, giant pieces ready to play their roles in an even more deadly game.

He searched for Dr Barbara, worried that she too had been lost overboard. But she was standing alone by the satellite dish below the bridge, her back to the helicopter and the speeding inflatables. Bandeau raised above her pale forehead, she stared at the captain of the *Sagittaire* with the same expression that she had turned upon the French sergeant as Neil lay wounded at her feet.

5

Island People

THE TWIN-ENGINED PIPER was preparing to land, circling the lagoon as the pilot inspected the coral-surfaced runway and the ruptured fuel tank still leaking a sooty smoke among the trees. A platoon of French soldiers waited at the runway's edge, gazing at the dead fish and albatross which a work party from the *Sagittaire* were burying in the sand. They stepped back as the Piper swept in, clouds of dust blanching the parasols of the palm trees with an arctic whiteness that might have been spray-painted for this funereal occasion.

Standing outside the prayer-shack between Kimo and Dr Barbara, an albatross banner draped over his arm, Neil listened to Monique as she sobbed and swore, pushing away the Saitos and Carline when they tried to comfort her. He watched the Piper come to rest at the far end of the runway, aware like everyone else that its arrival at Saint-Esprit marked their own departure.

A few feet from Neil, the American camera-man lay in his open grave, coffin draped in the Stars and Stripes and intricately decorated with albatross wing-feathers. Neil had helped Mrs Saito to fold the pleats, and was glad that Bracewell was being laid to rest among the wild yams and sweet potatoes, on this quiet headland overlooking the dunes where the albatross had once reared their young. He remembered his father's funeral and the eerie non-denominational service in the north London crematorium, with its sliding coffin and remote-controlled curtains, and his mother gasping as the teak doors briefly re-opened before closing for the last time.

Here at least Bracewell lay close to the birds that Dr Barbara had tried to protect, and in full view of a larger world. Four light aircraft were parked under the trees beside the Piper, chartered by French and American journalists. They waited with their cameras, drinking the beer which two stewards from the *Sagittaire* served from a makeshift bar.

Numbed by Bracewell's death, no-one aboard the *Dugong* had been prepared for the world-wide outcry. By chance, the moment of collision between the trawler and the corvette had been relayed live to Honolulu, and the desperate film, ending in a last explosion of spray and steel, showed all too clearly the murderous intent of the *Sagittaire*'s captain. The film's abrupt finale, as the camera was snatched from Bracewell's hands, had seared the consciences of millions of viewers. With remarkable presence of mind, his tearful widow had ordered Pratap to bring a reserve camera from the chart-room, and coldly insisted on recording the search for his body. Standing beside her crushed husband as he lay on the deck, she filmed the *Dugong* when it ran aground on the reef. Captain Wu had loyally followed the orders radioed from his billionaire owner in Honolulu, and the closing transmission showed the camera jolted from the widow's trembling arms.

Wary though they were of the albatross expedition, animal rights groups in the United States and Western Europe greeted the tragic television pictures with angry demonstrations that filled the streets of Washington, Paris and London. Embarrassed by the over-zealous commander of the corvette, and reminded of the threat to tourist revenues, the French Defence Ministry ordered the captain to allow the expedition members to remain on Saint-Esprit until the American had been buried on the island, as his widow insisted. In a last concession his parents – a Honolulu dentist and his wife – were flown from Tahiti in a government aircraft to attend the service.

The bereaved couple stepped onto the runway, helped by a junior officer from the *Sagittaire*. They stared at the shabby palms beside the lagoon, already noticing the stench of dead birds. As

Dr Barbara stepped forward, clearing her throat of the corrosive coral dust and oil fumes, Neil tried to hold her arm, worried that she might exploit the occasion for the benefit of the watching journalists.

But the death had calmed her. In the minutes after the fatal collision, when it was still not certain that Bracewell had drowned, she had done her best to reassure everyone on board the *Dugong*. Later, when a French boarding party arrested Captain Wu on the bridge of the grounded trawler, she restrained the angry Kimo from mounting a single-handed assault on the corvette. Carline had promptly volunteered to join him, offering the Hawaiian his chrome-plated pistol, but Dr Barbara seized the weapon from his hands.

'That isn't the way, David. I know how you feel, but we'll lose everything we've gained.'

'Barbara . . . !' For once, Carline seemed baffled by her show of weakness. 'We must do something – the French killed that poor fellow. God almighty, I gave up everything to come here.'

'And you'll have to give more! Far more than you imagine. We have world opinion on our side, so why throw it away?'

'World opinion?' Carline bared his expensive teeth, so unlike Dr Barbara's snaggled incisors. 'And another handy martyr. Sometimes I think . . .'

'David?' She handed him the pistol, the bruise flaring on her upper lip, but Carline had calmed himself. As if withdrawing into his money, he retreated to the chart-room, where he had moved his picnic hamper, bedding and suitcase from the water-filled cabin.

As the *Dugong* settled on the reef, splitting its keel-plates, the sea soon flooded the engine-room, and the Filipino crew joined Captain Wu aboard the *Sagittaire*. Monique and Dr Barbara stowed their kit in the bridge-house, while the Saitos camped in the galley with their precious taxonomic library, journals crammed among the skillets and saucepans. Kimo dozed in the cockpit of the speedboat, Captain Wu's golf-clubs within reach, ready to deal with any midnight French boarder.

Sedated by Dr Barbara, an almost sleepwalking Janet Bracewell accepted the invitation of the corvette's captain to rest aboard his ship. She took Pratap with her, leaving their equipment in the chart-room, and on the miniature, battery-powered monitor Neil watched a recording of the film that her husband had taken of the raid on the island.

This showed the earnest saboteurs, led by Monique and Dr Barbara, racing across the runway like adventure-holiday commandos. They laid their incendiary flares outside the storerooms, ignited the wooden armature of the fuel tank with the Molotov cocktails, and released two reluctant basset hounds – regimental mascots that Monique termed 'experimental animals' – from their quiet kennels. Unable to cope with the noise and explosions, and frightened by the cannibal gulls devouring the dead albatross on the beach, they returned to their shady dens at the first opportunity.

Surprisingly, no-one was guarding the base. The French engineers were working on the eastern edge of the atoll, laying down a system of landing lights, and the few remaining soldiers had climbed the peak in order to observe the duel between the corvette and the *Dugong*.

As Neil switched off the monitor he noticed Carline standing behind him, watching the fire-ball of the fuel-tank flare against the startled faces of the saboteurs.

'Disappointed, Neil? It's not exactly what you hoped for . . . '

'David?'

'Too bad . . . I guess there won't be a nuclear test at Saint-Esprit. But maybe Dr Barbara can arrange a different kind of explosion . . . just for you.'

The burial party stood by the open grave. Faces hidden by the shadow of the prayer-shack, the captain of the *Sagittaire* and two of his officers waited while the camera-men from the American news agencies recorded the sombre scene. The lenses panned across the runway, taking in the restive Frenchmen, the strong-chinned Dr Barbara and her party of protesters, and then lingered over the rotting albatross on the beach below the ancient blockhouses and towers of the nuclear test-site. Bracewell's coffin had already attracted the attention of a small bush-rat, and the French naval chaplain rapidly concluded his service. Soil flew

72

through the air as the corvette's captain spoke briefly to the dead man's widow and parents.

With a last stricken gesture at the closing grave, the three relatives turned and set off along the runway towards the waiting Piper. The burial party dispersed. Staring lightheadedly at the whitened trees, Professor Saito wandered towards the beach, followed by his scowling wife. With his bamboo cane he struck at the voracious gulls tugging at the carcasses of the albatross. Monique ran after the *Sagittaire*'s captain, her caustic tones lost in the downdraught of the helicopter coming in to land. Within moments the captain had returned to the corvette, while a junior officer supervised the departure of the Piper.

It took off ten minutes later, leaving Dr Barbara still standing beside the grave, as if this trapdoor into eternity was now the expedition's only refuge. The corvette's launch was moored by the pier, its engine running, and the French soldiers were waiting for them to board the *Sagittaire* for the return journey to Papeete and whatever charges the Ministry of Defence in Paris chose to bring against them.

'Dr Barbara . . . ' Neil tried to wake her, aware that all the blood had drained from her face. 'What happens now? The French have won.'

Dr Barbara held his head to her shoulder, and wiped her wet sleeve against his cheek, tears perfumed with Monique's borrowed mascara. 'They can't win, Neil. They can never win. Remember that.'

'We have to leave – Professor Saito and the French captain agreed. What will you do, Dr Barbara?'

'I don't know, I haven't been able to think . . . '

Neil could feel the air sighing from her chest. The bones that once carried her strong neck had been numbed by Bracewell's death. Like Neil, she was aware that all her hopes of saving the albatross had been buried with the camera-man in this island grave.

'We could work for Irving at the Wild-Water sanctuary,' Neil suggested. 'I can leave my big swim until next year.'

'I'm sure your mother will want you in Atlanta, Neil. Are you going to miss me? Who will I have to boss around?'

'You'll find someone, Dr Barbara.'

Despite himself, Neil felt responsible for her. The French soldiers were eager to escort them to the launch, and the fatigue party had given up the pretence of burying the dead albatross and were throwing broken eggs at each other. The last of the press planes took off, sending a cloud of coral dust through the trees. It levelled out and circled the stranded *Dugong*, and then set course for Tahiti, soon losing itself in the steam from the corvette's funnel.

'Dr Rafferty . . . ' Carline called out. He was decorating the marker cross with frangipani he had plucked from a shrub beside the prayer-shack. 'Ask everyone to come back.'

'What is it, David? We're going now.'

'I'd like to say a few words. I didn't know Mark too well, but I want the team to hear what I think – it might help them.'

'All right – Professor Saito, Monique . . . David has something to tell us.'

They stood around the grave while Carline gazed at the frangipani, waiting as Monique fondled the wound-red flowers. Long arms crossed over his chest, hands shielding his testicles, he seemed to be back among his native congregations in Africa or South America, his voice barely audible in the wind.

'Before we go, let's think of Mark, first, and then think of ourselves. Contrary to the general belief, no-one's death diminishes us. Nature in its wisdom created death to give each of us our unique sense of life. We're not part of the main. Each of us *is* an island, every bit as real as Saint-Esprit, and death is the price we pay to keep ourselves from drowning in the larger sea. Like Kimo here, we're all island people – Barbara and Monique, Professor Saito and Miko, and especially young Neil, dreaming about another kind of island. Mark Bracewell lived for twenty-seven years, and his island still floats in the sea of time and space . . . '

Embarrassed, Neil waited for Carline's homily to end. Flurries of emotion plucked at the American's voice, and he wondered if Carline had joined the missionary fathers in order to indulge a curious graveside hobby. Perhaps those who died from sleeping sickness, kwashiorkor, yellow fever and malaria made this

74

insecure Boston aristocrat feel momentarily confident, fully aware of himself for the first time. In his way he was colonizing, not the living of the third world, but the dead within their graves.

As a French petty officer strode up to them he felt Dr Barbara nudge his arm.

'Right, Neil, we'll go now. I think David's finished. But we'll be back.'

She spoke bravely, shaking her head over the dead albatross and the camera-towers as they walked towards the waiting launch. Neil visualized the muted reception that would greet them in Honolulu, and could already see her trying to rally her failed crusade, abandoned by supporters who would soon move to other causes. Kimo would commit himself to the quest for a native Hawaiian kingdom, and Monique would campaign for her doomed bears. He imagined Dr Barbara in her threadbare dress, haunting the Waikiki hotels with her satchel of faded leaflets.

He took her hand, touching the calluses on her worn fingers. He inhaled the tired scent of her skin and thought again of the notion that had been forming in his mind. Perhaps he could marry Dr Barbara, if only to keep her out of harm's way.

'Dr Barbara . . .'

'Yes, Neil?'

'There's something I wanted to say . . . about us.'

'Go on. I know you'll surprise me.'

Neil searched the horizon for inspiration, avoiding the grey threat of the *Sagittaire*'s bows, its paintwork scarred by its collision with the *Dugong*. Beyond the trawler he noticed a white triangle leaning on the rollers as they swept towards the reef. Behind it were three more masts, jib-sails pointing towards Saint-Esprit.

'Come on, Neil. Time to leave the island.'

'Perhaps not, Dr Barbara . . .' Neil pointed to the approaching craft. Already a signal lamp flashed from the bridge of the corvette. The helicopter rose from its landing platform and turned towards the sea.

Everyone searched the wind. Kimo stood in the launch, fending off the French sailors who tried to seat him, and threw his baseball cap into the lagoon. Monique broke off her embittered harangue of the soldiers on the pier, and Professor Saito steered his wife's

75

arm towards the reef. A flotilla of small craft had materialized from the sun-lit mist and was advancing upon Saint-Esprit.

'Neil, wake up!' Carline ran past them, gesturing like a deranged magician at the sea. 'Barbara, open your eyes, for God's sake.'

'What is it, David?'

'You're not alone now. Look – the world's come to save the albatross.'

6

The View from a Camera-Tower

'NEIL, STAND CLEAR! She's going now!'

Far below, David Carline was shouting through the roar of the bulldozer's engine as Neil ran down the path which the French engineers had cut in the hillside. He was breathless after climbing the radio mast with the tow-rope around his waist, and stumbled over a rotting palmetto. He pressed his rust-stained hands against his knees and gasped at the air, waiting for his lungs to catch up with him. Carline was reversing the bulldozer across the airstrip, and the rope stiffened above the forest canopy, frayed threads snapping and spinning. After working all morning with a hacksaw, Kimo had severed three of the steel struts supporting the tower, but the first attempt to topple the mast – the visible symbol of French dominion over Saint-Esprit – had ended in fiasco when he failed to secure the rope, fearing that his huge body would buckle the weakened structure.

Keen to impress Carline, who had commandeered the bulldozer and christened it his 'dune buggy', Neil promptly volunteered to take Kimo's place. Ignoring his bloody shins, he climbed to within a few feet of the aircraft warning light and fastened the rope to the metal shroud.

'Kimo, where's the boy? Neil, she's coming down . . . !'

Already the mast was straining against the sky, its lattice emitting a medley of plaintive cries. Neil reached the foot of the path and sprinted through the ferns towards the runway, flakes of rust from his hands speckling the lilies and morning glory that flowered around the perimeter of the camp. Led by Dr Barbara, a crowd had gathered on the beach. They cheered and clapped as the mast leaned from its plinth, and urged on the bulldozer when its tracks slewed in the milled coral. Carline stood at the controls, working the brake levers with his frantic hands like a fairground organist grappling with a berserk calliope. His cotton fatigues were covered with oil and sweat, but the same high gleam shone from his eyes that Neil had seen when Carline first mastered the bulldozer's controls and crushed the French storage huts.

Neil reached the camera-tower by the runway as the mast began its free fall across the sky. Hurling the trees aside, it swept down the wooded slope in a storm of dust and insects, struck a lava outcrop and broke into two sections. Baseball caps and panamas rose into the air as Carline dragged the upper segment across the runway like the carcass of a vanquished giant.

Everyone ran towards the mast, taking turns to stamp on the aircraft warning light and shatter its quartz lens, determined to put out this cyclopean eye that had gazed down on them during the three-week occupation of Saint-Esprit. Toppling the radio mast, Neil well knew, was more than a moral victory. They had now blocked the runway, preventing any fixed-wing aircraft from landing a surprise commando force.

Unsettled by the mast's demolition, a dozen wandering albatross circled the peak, keeping a safe distance from the crowd whistling to them. Neil was glad to see that the great birds had begun to return to Saint-Esprit. He lay back on the warm concrete roof of the camera-tower, smiling at the albatross as they soared effortlessly on the thermals. When they swooped over the reef, where the *Dugong* lay impaled, he searched the empty sky for any high-level aircraft, and then turned to watch the hectic activity on the beach.

Taking their cue from Dr Barbara, the volunteers were moving back to the tasks she had assigned them. There was no shortage of helpers – more than twenty yachts and ocean cruisers were now moored in the lagoon, their crews eager to defend the island against the imminent naval landing.

No-one was sure when the French military would return, but almost certainly they would put on a show of force intended to deter any future environmentalists from coming to Saint-Esprit. Most of the sympathizers who had sailed from Tahiti and the

Marquesas were themselves French, which made them even more attractive targets for the soldiers' truncheons and tear gas.

Heads would be cracked, and some of Dr Barbara's older supporters might be seriously injured. Twenty feet from Neil, wearing their identical straw hats, were Major Anderson and his wife, a gentle Australian couple in their late sixties, quietly laying the cement bricks of the miniature aqueduct that would carry water from the stream to the reservoir beside the runway. They worked silently in the heat and mosquitoes, never complaining though always glad to talk to Neil. They had sailed their small sloop from Papeete, loaded with food and medical supplies for the albatross expedition. Neil feared for them, wondering how they would survive the violence which the French activists from the schooner *Croix du Sud* would do their best to provoke.

Six well-muscled men and three voluble young women, they were working beside the pier, filling the steel cargo-lighter with rocks and cement blocks that they moved in a makeshift cart from the beach. They intended to sink the craft in the largest of the reef entrances, so excluding the *Champlain* if it tried to return to Saint-Esprit.

It still puzzled Neil that the French naval force had left at all. In the first uneasy week after Bracewell's burial a grudging truce had prevailed, tempers on both sides calmed by the huge oil slick that spilled from the hull of the *Dugong*. After two days of heavy seas its fuel tanks had ruptured, but by then the old shrimp-trawler had done its job. The three yachts that arrived as Dr Barbara was about to be ferried to captivity aboard the *Sagittaire* were followed that afternoon by a further half-dozen protest craft. A sit-down demonstration took place on the beach, each of the crews protecting a member of Dr Barbara's team from the confused soldiers, arms locked together against the raised batons, while other yachtsmen relayed to the world's air-waves a moving eye-witness report of the incident. The crackling short-wave message, reminiscent of the last transmissions from the besieged Dien Bien Phu, depicted Dr Barbara and her beleaguered group clinging to the oil-soaked beaches among the bodies of the poisoned albatross, threatened by the impatient guns of the corvette.

Surprisingly, the exhausted captain of the *Sagittaire* made no attempt to seize the protesters, and the soldiers returned to their bivouac beside the runway. Later they learned that the French prime minister and several members of his cabinet had been jeered and jostled at an election rally in Paris, and that the American State Department had recalled its ambassador to discuss Bracewell's death.

Meanwhile Dr Barbara and her companions sat it out on the beach, gagging on the stench of diesel oil and dead fish, in a shanty town of chart-room furniture, galley stores, dismantled bunks and TV equipment which Kimo and Carline ferried from the *Dugong*. Monique restlessly stalked the runway, berating the soldiers who read their girlie magazines and refused to be provoked. Professor Saito catalogued the dozens of plant and animal species which the oil slick threatened with extinction, while his wife and Dr Barbara bathed the injured sea-birds in buckets filled with detergent.

Neil held the dying birds for them, lumps of greasy mucilage and feathers, aware that the exposure sores on Dr Barbara's lips had reappeared. After three cold nights on the beach, he crossed the runway to the lagoon and swam out to the nearest of the yachts, a ketch owned by a New Zealand engineer and his wife. Concerned that the expedition had lost most of its supplies in the stricken trawler, they rowed Neil back to the beach with a large carton of fresh fruit, vitamin supplements and mosquito repellent.

But Dr Barbara was too distracted to thank them. She lay silently on the black sand and picked at the calluses on her hands, as if aware that her dream had ended, accepting that the French would soon tire of their presence on Saint-Esprit and were merely waiting for the media hubbub to die down.

Even David Carline had lost heart, sitting on the ashy beach beside his hamper, the dead birds at his feet. Avoiding Monique's eyes, he unlocked the hamper and handed the last of his cans to Neil, who passed them around the expedition members. Silently they consumed the pâtés, truffles and *foie gras*, the rare cheeses and pickled eggs. Later, Carline set off for the pier, ostensibly to send a message to his wife by short-wave radio, but in fact to see if he could arrange his passage to Papeete.

The next morning they woke into the cold mist that clung to the dripping parasols of the forest, and found that the French had gone.

Three yachts had arrived during the night, anchoring within the reef, and their crews stood on deck, searching for any signs of the corvette. Both the *Champlain* and the *Sagittaire* had raised steam and slipped away under cover of darkness. The engineers and soldiers guarding the runway had also vanished, taking their basset hounds, weapons and galley equipment with them. Overnight Saint-Esprit had become a stage-set whose cast had disappeared in mid-drama, carrying away every copy of the prompt-script.

Dazed by the sight of the deserted camp, Dr Barbara led everyone to the airstrip. Joined by the yacht-crews who were coming ashore, they wandered past the abandoned latrines, across the scuffed ground where the tents had once been pitched, now littered with old newspapers and cigarette packets. They tested the open doors of the empty storage sheds, and Kimo found a coil of telephone wire which he slung protectively across his chest, guarding the secret calls concealed within these devious spirals. Like children in an empty school, they glanced uneasily at the eye of the radio mast high above them.

Neil broke the spell, aiming a stone through a window of a storage shed. Monique and Mrs Saito joined him, and within a few excited moments every pane had been shattered. The women shouted each other on, and for an hour led a delirious rampage around the camp, destroying anything that might be of use to the returning military. Only when Carline started the engine of the bulldozer and began to flatten the storage sheds had Dr Barbara called a halt.

Flushed and happy, she pointed to the radio mast. A huge white bird with black wing-tips had approached the island from the sea and now soared in a wide circle around the peak.

The first of the wandering albatross had returned to Saint-Esprit.

★   ★   ★

Remembering this signal moment, the fruit of all Dr Barbara's dreams, Neil dozed on the concrete roof and watched the great birds sailing above the forest, their solemn eyes searching for the vanished radio mast. Their reappearance across the empty skies of the south Pacific had given a new confidence to both Dr Barbara and the volunteers flocking to Saint-Esprit. A silver-hulled ketch was entering the lagoon, a banner draped from its foretop.

'*Bravo Albatross! Bravo Dr Rafferty! Bravo Neil Dempsey!*'

Neil listened to the rattle of the anchor chain. Aware that he was the only person on the island not working to save the sanctuary, he climbed from the roof of the camera-tower. Like everyone else, he found himself repeatedly peering at the sky, waiting for a tell-tale vapour trail that might mark a high-altitude reconnaissance plane. The French government had given no reason for their abandonment of Saint-Esprit, but even if they returned in force the albatross sanctuary would soon be so well established that a vast international outcry would greet any attempt to expel them.

'Neil, stop dreaming . . . ' David Carline sat at the controls of the bulldozer, a jaunty smile on his thin mouth, dust rising around him like incense around a buddha. 'It's safe to wake up now.'

'I'm dreaming of the albatross, David.'

'You don't need to – they've come back to Saint-Esprit.'

'That's my dream . . . we're all inside it.'

'Even Monique and Dr Barbara? You're a shaman, Neil – you'll live in the forest with Professor Saito and count the winds.'

'Even Monique and Dr Barbara. But maybe not you, David.'

Carline ignored this, still trying to win Neil's friendship. He had offered to teach him how to drive the bulldozer, but Neil was wary of the American. Since leaving Honolulu, Carline had shed every trace of plumpness from his face, which was now as hard and angular as the camera-towers. So far he showed little interest in the albatross, and spent his time scouring the old bunkers for barbed wire, as if he planned to take over from the French the task of constructing a military base. Four canvas tents donated by the crew of the *Croix du Sud* were pitched at the northern end of the runway, aligned by Carline's exacting eye. He had drawn up plans for a mess-hall, clinic and plant laboratory that left Dr Barbara nodding at him like a mechanical toy.

Monique and the Saitos were standing on the pier, checking the latest gifts of food and medical supplies. Neil would have offered to help, but they already treated him as their messenger-boy, ordering him about on endless errands, and he crossed the runway to the aqueduct of cement and plastic tubing which the elderly Australian couple were building.

Despite their work on the aqueduct, Major Anderson and his wife drank only the bottled mineral water stored in their sloop, as if the stream running down the hillside was reserved for Dr Barbara and her team. Neil liked to sit with them, helping to stir the fast-setting ciment fondue which the French engineers had used to construct the underwater foundations of the pier. He was impressed by their dedication to the sanctuary, though they rarely mixed with the other yacht-crews. As the Bracewells had soon noticed, the would-be saviours of the albatross had little in common apart from their vague yearnings for the mythical bird.

'Are you hungry, Neil?' Mrs Anderson put down her trowel and rooted in her wicker bag. 'We brought some canned fish for you.'

'Thanks, Mrs Anderson. I'll eat it later.'

'Eat it now – no-one will see you, they're all so busy. You must be hungry after climbing the mast.'

'I'm always hungry.' Neil read the label on the can. 'Dr Barbara says we shouldn't hunt the fish in the lagoon. She claims it's their sanctuary too.'

'That's high-minded of her, and I dare say she's right.' Major Anderson pressed the can-opener into Neil's hand. 'I imagine you can eat this fish – it was probably making a nuisance of itself somewhere.'

Neil tucked into the greasy mackerel with a plastic fork. His spirits rose as he remembered the savoury anchovies from Carline's hamper that he had devoured on the beach. The waters of the lagoon teemed with snapper and coral trout, blue-fish and sea perch that many of the yacht-crews, not yet indoctrinated by Dr Barbara, grilled on open fires in the evening.

'The way Mr Carline brought down the mast . . .' Mrs Anderson waved away the flies. 'That was a sight. I thought the whole island was falling into the sea. Either that or the French had landed again.'

Neil tossed the empty can into the undergrowth. 'Do you think they will land again?'

'We have to assume so, Neil.' Major Anderson pushed back his straw hat and surveyed the endlessly circling albatross. 'Serious fellows, aren't they? But they have a lot to be serious about. I've never known the French give up anything without a fight. Verdun, Indo-China, Algiers – history penned in their own blood.'

'That's what I tell Dr Barbara,' Neil agreed. 'She thinks they're bored with us. I expect they'll be here within a month.'

'Who knows?' Major Anderson ran a military eye over Neil's broad shoulders. 'Whenever they come, they'll knock heads, so be careful.'

'Yes, be careful, Neil,' his wife agreed. 'We'll be here to look after you, but don't let Kimo and Mr Carline get you fighting with the French soldiers.'

'Dear . . . ' The major calmed her. 'Neil knows that – he's already been shot by them.'

'We don't want him shot again. Have you thought of going back to Atlanta, Neil? Your mother must be worried. And Louise – she sounds as if she needs you.'

'I talked to them on the *Croix du Sud*'s radio-phone. I said I'd go back when I finished helping Dr Barbara.'

'Well, she needs you too. Dr Barbara's the sort who always needs people. You'd best look for her, Neil.'

'She's by the beach with Mrs Saito, cleaning the birds.'

'That's good, Neil.' Mrs Anderson took the plastic fork from his restless hand. 'You go and help her.'

'No – the birds are all dead. It's a waste of time.'

'Neil . . . ' Mrs Anderson stilled his hands. 'It's Dr Barbara's way of mourning for them.'

★　　★　　★

84

Waving to the Andersons, Neil crossed the runway towards the beach. He liked the elderly couple, two more of the surrogate parents he regularly recruited, only to find that their affection suffocated him. There were no youths of his own age on Saint-Esprit. The Frenchmen from the *Croix du Sud* called to him from the beach as they rested after filling the lighter with rocks and sand, but they were ten years older than Neil and only interested in their endless games of volley-ball.

Neil passed the prayer-shack where Bracewell lay in the small cemetery among the wild yams. He added a single lily to the wreaths left by the visiting yacht-crews, and gazed at the wreck of the *Dugong* on the reef. A storm had torn away the funnel and a section of the bridge, and the oil slick was drifting along the beach to the rocky cascade below the cliff.

Neil waded through the shallow water, searching for edible crab and bivalves. Fortunately the lowly creatures lay in a zoological niche beyond the reach of the animal rightists. The cheerful cries of the *Croix du Sud*'s crew sounded above the thump of the volley-ball. Despite their hard work, they managed to enjoy themselves, inviting Monique and any spare women from the fleet of ocean craft to join their camp-fire parties on the beach. Saint-Esprit and the albatross were a game to be played like the water-sports at a holiday resort.

Buoyed by the clear skies and the returning birds, everyone's confidence was high. The forty or so volunteers worked together without any supervision, clearing the forest beside the runway, digging latrines and setting up the camp. The water supply, the kitchen tent and donated stores would keep the original members of the albatross expedition going for at least a month. More sea-birds had been killed by the *Dugong*'s leaking oil than by the French soldiers in their months of occupation, but at least the albatross now soared above the peak.

Despite this success, Neil felt distanced from the rest of the expedition. He missed Louise, and had been unsettled by her self-immersed chatter on the radio-phone. More than a planet separated them. He wanted to leave for Hawaii and a flight back to London, and knew that he was staying on Saint-Esprit, not to save the albatross, but in the hope that the French would resume their nuclear tests. At times, when Dr Barbara or Mrs Saito caught him gazing wistfully at the blockhouses, he guessed that they were fully aware of his real motives for joining the expedition.

A slick of engine oil lay in a small cove, a greasy quilt of blackened plumage, dead fish and beach debris nudged by the waves rolling in from the reef. Neil climbed the sandy slope and walked towards another of the camera-towers hidden among the trees, its cracked cement streaked with rust from the armature bars. There were a dozen towers around the perimeter of the lagoon, built in the 1960s to house the remote-controlled cameras. During his first week on Saint-Esprit he had explored them all, swimming between the sand-bars that made up the rim of the atoll, but none showed any sign that they were being prepared for a fresh round of tests. The towers on the high island had been swallowed by the advancing forest, ancient megaliths left behind by a race of warrior scientists obsessed with geometry and death.

A faded vanilla shrub filled the doorway of the tower, its leaves dissolving into dust as he pressed past it to the steps. Neil rested his elbows on the window ledge of the observation chamber and gazed at the open expanse of the lagoon, visualizing the immense flash that might one day light its surface. Memories of his dead father and the atomic proving grounds at Maralinga seemed to haunt its calm waters, a myth more potent than the albatross.

Voices sounded outside the tower, the laughter of a man and woman flirtatiously sharing a joke. Neil reached through the camera slit and pushed aside the palm fronds below the sill. The couple had left the forest path that ran from the beach to the airstrip and strolled like idling lovers between the shadowy trees. Neil recognized Pierre Bouquet, the skipper of the *Croix du Sud*, a mathematics teacher at a Papeete *lycée*. Bouquet had helped to clean the birds trapped by the oil slick, and his arms were still marked by the dark smudges. He smiled attentively at the woman, listening to her strong voice as she laughed at something he had said, admiring her with a dozen covert glances.

The woman was Dr Barbara. She had taken off her shirt and walked naked to the waist, stains of oil on her left shoulder. But all thoughts of the drowned birds were far from her mind. She was revealing an off-duty version of herself that Neil had never known, like his after-hours glimpse in the Honolulu hospital of an intimidating senior sister relaxing with a tumbler of whisky in the chief anaesthetist's office.

As always, she was doing all the talking, but Bouquet was content to listen. He was openly admiring her bare breasts, chafed by a succession of safety pins, his hand lightly taking her waist. While the shadows dappled their backs they strolled deeper into the forest, voices lost in the chitter of insects.

Neil leaned against the camera slit, his forehead pressed to the cool concrete, trying to adjust himself to the notion that Dr Barbara had a life beyond the albatross. He had gladly thought of her as a substitute mother, though Dr Barbara could not have been more different from the anxious and unconfident woman who depended on Colonel Stamford to tell her the time of day. He was angry with Dr Barbara, not for taking one of the young Frenchmen as a lover, but because her passion for the albatross was less single-minded than he imagined, and coexisted with other needs and appetites. Saint-Esprit was tainted by more than the death of the birds and the waiting ghosts of its nuclear future.

In a sudden insight into himself, he thought: I have to protect the island from Dr Barbara.

One of the yachts was raising anchor, its jib-sail tapping at the wind. Earlier that morning everyone on Saint-Esprit had said their goodbyes to the crew, a retired American naval commander from Honolulu named Rice, his elderly wife and their middle-aged daughter, the widow of a Canadian airline pilot. Having given most of their supplies to the expedition, they were about to return to Hawaii.

Their place would soon be taken by one of the new arrivals who anchored in the lagoon every day, but Neil was sorry to see them go. They had attended Dr Barbara's rallies in Waikiki, and had visited him in hospital, bringing a small library of environmentalist texts. During the second week at Saint-Esprit he had slept aboard their sloop, glad of the mosquito net and a soft bunk. All three sensibly accepted that the French navy would return, and were concerned, like the Andersons, for Neil's safety.

The sloop's engine rumbled faintly, the propeller sending a faint wake across the water as Rice wound up the anchor. Seeing Neil on the beach, Mrs Rice cheerily saluted him from the cockpit where her daughter held the tiller.

Neil waved in return, and stepped into the shallow surf. He felt the cool tug of the undertow drawing him into the deeper water, reminding him of his dream, now shelved, of swimming the Kaiwi Channel. The Rices' sloop was three hundred yards away, but well within his range. He knew that they would be happy to take him with them to Hawaii – they had seen Neil's mother on television being comforted by Colonel Stamford after Bracewell's death.

Neil waded into the deeper water, the cold sea clasping his thighs. The black sand raced around his heels, urging him down the slope. The duffle bag containing his clothes, the diver's watch and other personal kit lay in the pup tent he shared with Kimo, but there was no time to collect them, and he would never be able to explain to Dr Barbara, Monique or Professor Saito why he had decided to leave.

A wave struck his chest and rolled past to the shore, breaking among the dead fish and birds. The sloop's engine was still idling, as Rice trimmed the jib. Already Neil was swimming towards the yacht, pausing as the next wave hit his face, then settling into his powerful crawl.

He was fifty yards from the sloop when Mrs Rice noticed him crossing its wake.

'Charles . . . it's Neil. I think he wants to – '

She pushed past her daughter and reached over the stern, but her husband was staring out to sea, binoculars to his eyes. Above the low beat of the sloop's engine, drumming at Neil's ears as he rolled his head in the water, came the hard clatter of an approaching helicopter. The crews of the anchored yachts emerged from their cabins, pointing to a white-hulled ship that advanced towards the reef. As Neil took Mrs Rice's outstretched hand he saw the concern for him in her eyes, and heard her husband shout:

'They're back . . . ! The French are back . . . !'

7

The Rainbow Pirates

A PAIR OF FRENCH combat boots entrenched themselves in the sand beside Neil's head, their cleated soles cutting through the ashy slope. As he rested after the long swim to shore, he raised his eyes from the boots to the camouflage fatigues, designer sunglasses and close-cropped white hair.

'David? You look like a French commando . . . '

'I'm flattered, Neil. That's kind of you. I'm trying to raise a defence squad.' Carline took off his sunglasses and watched the helicopter circle the atoll. 'I'm sorry to say there's no heart left for a fight.'

'Where's your pistol? And the German holster?'

'Safely hidden away. Where else? We have a real battle on our hands.' Carline whistled cheerfully, unconvinced by the combat uniform he had assembled from the abandoned lockers in the storage sheds. 'I'm glad to see you, Neil – for a moment we thought you were leaving us.'

'I wanted to say goodbye to the Rices.' Neil sat up and let the last water drip from his shirt. 'They're sending a message to my mother.'

'Good. She must be worried about you. But the French won't harm you, Neil – you're the albatross boy.'

Neil frowned at this and searched the horizon for the *Sagittaire*. He assumed that the corvette would wait out of sight until the aerial reconnaissance of Saint-Esprit was complete. Meanwhile the tank-landing craft – more than a hundred metres in length, with a high stern bridge and helicopter deck – lay at anchor beyond the reef, sitting on the sea like a huge white ammunition box. Behind its fierce ramp an amphibious armoured car or even a light tank might be ready to launch itself at the nesting albatross. Or were nuclear weapons and their support equipment moved around in these armoured arks?

Either way, a military landing was imminent. A tender lowered from the stern had set off for the beach, but no-one had tried to intercept the craft. Despite the excitements of the past days a sudden mood of resignation had swept the island at almost telepathic speed. Having given everything and endured so much to gain their foothold on Saint-Esprit, they could no longer rally themselves to defend its oil-sodden shores.

Besides, the intimidating presence of the landing craft touched too many memories of the D-Day landings. Dr Barbara stood under the trees by the prayer-shack, quietly picking at the ulcers on her lips. Kimo squatted across a fallen palm trunk, throwing shells into the waves. Monique and the Saitos left the kitchen tent and wandered towards the beach, and only Major Anderson and his wife continued to work at their aqueduct. The yacht-crews waited under their awnings, and even Bouquet and his usually combative companions aboard the *Croix du Sud* watched the tender's approach without comment. The time of protests and slogans had passed. Like children, Neil reflected, they hoped that if they held their breaths the French would go away.

The helicopter was first to land. Satisfied that Saint-Esprit was undefended, the pilot came in across the lagoon and settled his floats into the calm water beside the pier.

A small, perspiring man in a rumpled safari suit, binoculars around his neck, released the safety harness and slid his cautious feet into the shallow waves. Head down, he waded to the beach, where Monique waited to greet him, arms folded across her breasts. Neil expected her to launch into one of her legendary tempers and scream abuse at the visitor. But after listening to him through the soft cuffing of the helicopter's fans, hand raised in disbelief to one ear, she waved to Dr Barbara.

'Barbara! Come down, please!'

'What is it?' Dr Barbara stood behind Kimo, steadying herself against his shoulder. 'Be careful, Monique . . . '

'You'll enjoy this, Barbara.' Monique was laughing for the

first time since Neil had met her aboard the *Dugong*. 'Let me introduce Monsieur Kouchner – he's very interested in Saint-Esprit.'

'I won't deal with him.' Dr Barbara's hands cut the air as she stared down at the portly figure trying to squeeze the water from his trousers. 'Who does he represent? The Ministry of Defence?'

'Worse than that. Much more sinister . . . ' Monique shook her head sombrely. 'Still, there's good news from the Elysée Palace this morning – the government has made Saint-Esprit a wild-life special zone. The moratorium on nuclear tests will continue – Monsieur Kouchner is quite definite.'

'But who is he?' Jaw set, Dr Barbara advanced across the sand, followed by the Saitos. 'Foreign Service? The Colonial Office?'

'No, Barbara – Club Méditerranée.' Monique spoke straight-faced. 'Monsieur Kouchner is a field scout. Club Med may open a beach resort on Saint-Esprit . . . '

They stood still, staring lightheadedly at each other. Dr Barbara sank to her knees and clasped a handful of black sand, which she threw playfully at Monique. The two women embraced, laughing with relief. The first yacht-crews were coming ashore in their dinghies, waiting for the tender to clear the reef.

'You're safe here, believe me,' Kouchner happily assured Carline and the Saitos as they questioned him. 'Saint-Esprit belongs to the world. The publicity and demonstrations, they're all too much. The President decided on a magnanimous gesture, especially as Peugeot and Renault are boycotted in the United States. Green issues are a big factor in the parliamentary elections . . . '

'They've just pulled out?' Still sceptical, Carline pointed to the landing craft. 'Then what about the LCT? What's hiding behind that ramp – a brigade of marines?'

'Far more dangerous – TV crews, journalists, publishers' agents. Unlimited destructive power at every finger-tip.' The cheerful travel agent raised his short arms to embrace the island. 'Everyone is coming to Saint-Esprit.'

'And the LCT?'

'The *Palangrin* – an old car ferry which the American networks chartered in Papeete.' The Frenchman cast a hopeful eye at the oil-stained beaches with their dead birds and fish, already visualizing the native huts clustered around the bar-restaurant, aerobics gym and holistic massage room. 'The navy may be back, just for inspection, but not for some time – the death of the American was a big turning point. Saint-Esprit is yours for many months. Relax, you can all go on vacation!'

The tender carrying visitors from the *Palangrin* had entered the lagoon and docked alongside the pier. The journalists and news photographers stepped ashore, followed by the TV crews, already staking out the most promising panoramas of the modest island. An assertive woman interviewer from a French fashion magazine soon spotted Monique and Dr Barbara and began to question them, thrusting her tape-recorder into their faces. The first camera strobes flared against Dr Barbara's high forehead, illuminating the exposure sores on her scalp, which a thoughtful make-up girl concealed with her powder puff.

For the rest of the day Saint-Esprit became a series of movable press conferences, which sprang spontaneously from the air around the expedition members like dust-devils. Bouquet and the crew of the *Croix du Sud* set up a bar on the airstrip beside the bulldozer, and this served as the combined nerve-centre and casualty station of the island. Dr Barbara and Monique led the journalists on a tour of the albatross nesting among the dunes, provoking only two of the pairs to abandon their eggs.

Professor Saito and his wife were interviewed by a team from a Japanese TV channel, who set up a small studio against the tranquil backdrop of the camera-towers and the nuclear lagoon. Waiting his turn, Neil wondered whether to startle the Hiroshima and Nagasaki viewers by extolling the merits of atomic weapons, but felt Carline's cautionary hand on his shoulder.

'Leave out the nuclear weapons, Neil. Just congratulate the French President on his good sense.' He was amiably tipsy on the wine brought ashore from the *Croix du Sud*. 'Remember, you're the only one they managed to shoot. Don't let the Saitos take the credit.'

'David, it might all be a trick . . . How far can you trust the French?'

'About as far as I trust the British. Maybe a little further. They'll stay away for a while, long enough for us to save a few more of the birds. Tell me – what *do* you see from these camera-towers?'

'Nothing, David.'

'Really? That's a pity – an interesting experiment is about to start soon, and not the kind you record with a geiger counter.'

Barefoot, at the Japanese director's request, Neil submitted to his interview, sending greetings to his mother and Colonel Stamford, to the nursing staff at the Honolulu hospital and, lastly and most awkwardly, to Louise, who already seemed a memory of his early adolescence. Blushing with embarrassment, he raised his right foot to show the bullet scar, standing one-legged while the camera lingered obsessively over the wound.

He left the interview to find Dr Barbara beaming at him with all the pride of a stage mother. Neil was glad to see her so buoyed by the French government's decision, the chatelaine of Saint-Esprit assured of her tenancy. She had borrowed Monique's lipstick and rouge, and her face was more animated than Neil ever remembered. She was flattered by the attentive cameras that followed her up and down the runway, and touched by the congratulations of the yacht-crews who cheered her on as she swept about her island on a wave of adrenaline.

At last, speaking to the assembled cameras beside Bracewell's grave, she made a passionate plea to the world's television audiences.

'First, I want to thank the French President and the French people. They've saved a great deal more than the albatross. They've saved Saint-Esprit and its wild-life, and above all they've saved hope – hope throughout the planet for a better world, where all species can live together without fear. The twentieth century is nearly over, but it still carries with it the terrible possibility of nuclear and chemical death. I want Saint-Esprit to be a beach-head, the doorway through which we step into the next century. Save the albatross, save Saint-Esprit, and save the twenty-first century . . . '

'Dr Rafferty, you'll continue your work when you leave?' asked a Swedish woman journalist wearing a collection of pro-abortion badges. 'You'll take your message to the whole world?'

'Leave . . . ?' Dr Barbara seemed puzzled by the notion. She frowned at the camera lenses and clutched the safety pin that secured her ragged shirt. 'I'm never going to leave Saint-Esprit. My work and life are here, on this island. Saint-Esprit is a refuge for all living creatures, not just for the albatross. I want every threatened plant and animal to know that it can find asylum here. Go back to your countries and tell them – Saint-Esprit is a sanctuary for the entire planet and everything that lives on it. My arms are wide enough to welcome the world!'

More than fifty people had gathered around the cameras as Dr Barbara extemporized her new credo. The yacht-crews switched off their portable radios and listened intently. After a moment's respectful silence a loud cheer drummed against the roof of the prayer-shack. Carline took off his camouflage forage cap and saluted Dr Barbara as she smiled and blushed, accepting the embraces of Monique and Mrs Saito.

'Did you see that, Neil?' he asked almost dreamily, glad to be seduced by Dr Barbara's words. 'The purest draught of evangel-ism – complete sincerity hand-in-hand with the widest eye to the main chance.'

'Is this how new religions begin? David, it could be happening.'

'Neil, Neil . . . there's nothing new here. It's the oldest religion there ever was – sheer magnetic egoism. But she's absolutely right, it's just what I expected from her. Still, back to work – every fly with a sore foot and every trampled blade of grass is already on its way to Saint-Esprit.'

*   *   *

94

Events moved faster than Neil imagined possible. A rush of dreams, plans and hopes swept aside the barrier which the French military threat had built across their minds. Though thrilled at first by her own daring, Dr Barbara soon calmed herself. The decision to remain indefinitely on the island, in this shabby realm of rotting fish and oil-stained beaches, had provided a new image of herself to live up to, as if she had set out to test the further possibilities of her own fame.

Accompanied by Professor Saito, she strode around the island, inspecting the fern-covered hillsides and drawing up her plans for the sanctuary. While the journalists and camera-crews stumbled behind her, Kimo brought up the rear with machete and marker pen, and soon lines of stakes set out the animal enclosures and plant terraces of her new Eden. There would be shaded enclaves for rare species of fungi, and irrigated beds for obscure water-plants whose habitats were threatened with extinction by pollution and deforestation. Large mammals, reluctantly, would be excluded, but the smaller natives of woodland and desert would be bred and nurtured in their caged environments, and eventually turned free to roam the island. No creature, however violent or self-destructive, would be rejected, since a true asylum welcomed the vicious and deranged. One day, even the most virulent bacteria might be succoured.

Throughout all this Professor Saito was in a taxonomist's heaven, keeping track of Dr Barbara's ambitions and adding an eager commentary of his own, which he dictated into the tape-recorders that Mrs Saito borrowed from the journalists and pressed into his hands. Diagrammatic forests of genera and species reared through his mind, branching into the remotest limbs of the biological kingdom, along which he mentally scrambled to rescue a rare parasite or endangered predator.

'And how long will this take, Professor Saito?' asked a sceptical British tabloid reporter. 'Three months? A year?'

'Many years, possibly decades.' Professor Saito modestly raised his small hands to the dense foliage, smiling as his wife stared stonily at the moss-covered trees and the tangle of vines and ferns. 'But in nature everything fits together, nothing can escape. A blueprint within us is already mapping out the sanctuary. There's an ancient garden inside our heads, waiting to greet us.'

'I'm glad you mentioned that, Professor.' The reporter gestured at the sweating journalists, tormented by the flies and mosquitoes. 'You've left one endangered species out of your sanctuary. Is he banned, and how long for?'

Professor Saito waited genially as his wife tittered at this. 'I'm sure we'll find room for *Homo sapiens*. At first he'll be on the staff side, and work his way back into the good favours of mother nature. But we'll happily protect you, if only from yourself . . . '

Mrs Saito chuckled over the sally all the way down to the airstrip.

Despite these grandiose pronouncements, and the complete lack of progress on any practical level, the establishment of the sanctuary prompted considerable interest well beyond the shores of Saint-Esprit, as Neil noticed when he and Kimo took the tender to the *Palangrin* and watched the satellite TV transmissions in the communications room. Eating breakfast cooked by the admiring chefs in the galley, he watched himself stuttering shyly through his interviews. But at least Louise, his mother and step-father would see that he was well. Neil's familiar image – broad shoulders, determined chin and, most affectingly of all, his small but pronounced limp – again bounced between the satellite dishes of the world, an electronic ambassador for Saint-Esprit. Green and animal rights groups in Europe, America and Japan had already responded to Dr Barbara's open-armed invitation, and the first threatened plants and birds were being prepared for their long journey across the Pacific.

Even Club Med yielded to the inevitable, accepting that the new islanders would have no time for either leisure or pleasure. Exhausted by all this environmentalist zeal, M. Kouchner retreated to the landing platform behind the funnel of the car ferry. Sitting under the drooping blades of the company helicopter, he gazed wistfully at his maps of the Marquesas and the Friendly Islands, aware that a romantic vision of the Pacific first dreamed by Gauguin and Robert Louis Stevenson was giving way to a far more puritanical one.

Joining Kimo on the bridge of the *Palangrin*, Neil found him scanning the skies to the north-west, as if expecting an early asylum-seeker, some endangered cockatiel or condor released from its cargo crate at Papeete airport.

'It's a bit soon, Kimo. Are you waiting for one of the rare birds?'

'You bet – Irving's supply Dakota. Let's hope he remembers us.'

'Dr Barbara talked to him on the radio – he said they were loading the plane.'

'Sure. He's so busy with his TV station he forgets this isn't a game show.'

'We could row around the yachts – people give us anything we ask for.'

'I know . . . ' Kimo turned away from Neil, as if his frankness unsettled him. 'But I don't like doing it. Anyway, they're running short. In a few days you're going to wake up and find everybody's gone. You'll be sitting alone on that beach again.'

'Won't that be good, Kimo? It's what you always wanted.'

'Right on – I can't wait. Too many people coming to Saint-Esprit. Nobody's thinking about the albatross any more. Let's get that Dakota down and then we can go from there.'

After returning to the island, Neil paced along the waiting runway, now cleared of all obstacles. The reserves of food, fuel and medicines which they had salvaged from the *Dugong* had been exhausted, and their modest meals of rice, fruit and canned fish depended entirely on donations from the depleted larders of the visiting yacht-crews. Monique and Mrs Saito were strict in their rationing, but Dr Barbara made sure that Neil received extra portions of protein. If only for the cameras, it was essential that he remain lean but not haggard, or his parents and a dozen child-protection agencies would agitate to rescue him from the sanctuary.

Yet he tried to share his rations with Dr Barbara, leaving his unfinished plate in her tent. For all her elation and the endless interviews, she had begun to neglect herself. The exposure sores and the ugly rash on the backs of her hands were spreading.

'Not enough vitamins, Neil. Let's hope the Dakota comes soon.'

'I'll go fishing, Dr Barbara – the lagoon's full of perch and snapper.'

'No, Neil . . . ' Dr Barbara calmed him with a distracted smile. 'Saint-Esprit offers asylum to every living thing. The lagoon is their sanctuary.'

'But they're not threatened. The French have stopped poisoning them. Professor Saito says they're fit to eat.'

'You're threatening them, Neil.' Dr Barbara lifted the flap of her tent and pointed to the runway, where Kimo and Carline, Monique and the Saitos sat under the palms beside the bulldozer, watching the clouds. The surface of ground coral had been swept by Kimo to befit the arrival of a queen. 'Waiting for the sky – we're turning into a cargo cult.'

Fortunately for the fish, the relief plane from Honolulu arrived before Neil could win his wrestling match with Dr Barbara's conscience. Two days after the *Palangrin*'s departure, in a tumult of cheerful sirens and discarded video-tape, the elderly Dakota circled Saint-Esprit, flew in over the broken-backed shrimp-trawler and touched down on the runway.

Irving Boyd had done everything he promised. As the hatchway opened, Neil recognized the bald-headed driver with the manatee transfers pasted to his neck, whom he had last seen on the quayside at Honolulu. Scratching his tattooed scalp, he gazed in awe at the coral-dusted figures approaching him along the runway, like an over-worked UN aid official greeting a party of spectres.

The stores soon revived them. Donated by support groups throughout the Hawaiian Islands, there were crates of canned meat and fish, cartons filled with oranges, pomelo and pineapples, supplies of organically reared eggs, flour and pasta. There were enough waterproof tents to house fifty volunteers, camp beds and sections of duckboarding, paraffin stoves and water-purifiers, mosquito netting and portable latrines. A thousand tomato seedlings in plastic trays were soon wilting in the sun, nibbled by two suspicious goats that Kimo lifted from the Dakota in his arms. A dozen hens, Rhode Island Reds, blinked at the light from their bamboo cages, where they had spent the flight from Papeete pecking at the sacks of plant fertilizer stowed behind them. Sighing and whistling through her teeth, Mrs Saito climbed into the Dakota and carefully decanted the scattered phosphate into a bucket.

Neil searched through the bales of donated clothing, choosing a shirt in a vivid nightclub blue and a baseball cap with an eco-theme badge lovingly stitched into its peak by a member of a women's group in Sydney. There were oilskin jackets and scuba gear, and a friendly banner painted by children at a Honolulu infant school depicting an idealized Saint-Esprit like an island in a fairy tale, occupied by amiable tigers and dignified crocodiles.

As he dragged away the sack of letters sent by well-wishers all over the world, Neil estimated that the monthly relief flights would supply their needs for the indefinite future. He helped Carline and Kimo to erect the largest of the tents, which would serve as their storage depot, surprised to see that a set of heavy padlocks formed part of the assembly pack.

Only five yachts in the original fleet that defended Saint-Esprit now remained in the lagoon, and their crews, as Kimo warned him, had almost exhausted their supplies. Bouquet and his shipmates on the *Croix du Sud* sailed reluctantly back to their jobs in Papeete, after a night of dancing around a beach fire and a last walk with Dr Barbara among the moonlit waves. Major Anderson and his wife were now *ex officio* members of the sanctuary, thanks to their work on the aqueduct. They were provided with a tent, mattresses and camp beds, and shared the meals prepared by Monique and Mrs Saito.

But when Neil suggested that the remaining yacht-crews

should be given enough supplies to return them safely to Tahiti, he found himself contradicted by Carline.

'I think not, Neil. We need everything for the sanctuary.' Carline fondled the padlock of the storage tent. 'Who knows when the next plane will arrive?'

'They've helped us so much – they gave us everything we had. David, it's a long way back to Tahiti.'

'They'll make it, if they leave now. We mustn't encourage them to hang around.' Smiling sympathetically over their plight, Carline took the cans of beef from Neil and returned them to the over-crowded shelves. 'Don't you agree, Barbara?'

Still wearing her faded shirt, Dr Barbara stared at the bales of gaudy clothing and the cartons of canned food. She took Neil by the arm and steered him into the sun.

'David has a point, Neil. The sanctuary isn't a chandlery for any passing yacht. We must think of ourselves and all the work we have to do.'

Neil freed his arm and turned to face her, as Kimo and Carline watched them from the shadows inside the tent. 'So we give nothing to any crew that calls here? Dr Barbara – even if they're desperate?'

'Of course not. Obviously we help anyone in real need. Look at me, Neil, I've taken nothing.' Dr Barbara clasped the rusty safety pin between her breasts, a talismanic brooch. 'But we do have to draw the line. In fact, a lot of lines are going to be drawn in the next few weeks. And you'll help draw them, Neil . . . '

As if to prove her point, three days after the last of the yachts had set sail for Tahiti an unexpected arrival lowered anchor within the reef. This storm-battered sloop was the *Parsifal*, and its hull and patched sails were painted with psychedelic colours, slashes of mauve and acid green that flared from the waves like the fins of a deranged kraken. The craft had sailed straight out of the nineteen-sixties, manned by a crew of nautical hippies, long hair in pony-tails, studded leather bands on their wrists, rainbow pirates drawn to Saint-Esprit by some pot-induced vision of their own.

The two young men were drop-outs from a Stuttgart architect's office, and their passengers were a pair of German women and a small child whom they had picked up in Vancouver. Neil was surprised that they made no attempt to approach the camp and greet the expedition members. They kept to themselves, lighting driftwood fires on the beach, playing with the child and swimming naked around the reef as they hunted for coral, which they later cut into necklaces.

Their presence irritated Monique, who found the feckless young men a distraction from the serious business of establishing the camp. Kimo laughed at them, while to the Saitos they were scarcely visible at all. But to Carline they were a constant aggravation. Guarding the storage tent as Kimo swept the runway, he warned Dr Barbara that the hippies' food supplies would soon run out.

'I can see them rustling a chicken, Barbara, and spit-roasting it on the beach. We may have the beginnings of a security problem.'

'They'll leave eventually.' Dr Barbara rested in her tent, accepting a mug of tea from Neil, and refused to be worried by the Germans. 'We can't fence the island, and I can hardly expel them.'

'I could draw up a guard roster,' Carline suggested. 'And maybe build a look-out post on the beach.'

'You sound like the French.'

'The sanctuary has to be defended, Barbara. A lot of rare species are going to be landing here soon.'

'There's one already. Listen to him, Neil . . . ' When Carline strode away to test his padlocks she sipped the tea and stared at the sky. 'He'll go one day, then Kimo and the Saitos. Sooner or later I'll be alone here. I wonder if you'll leave me, Neil . . . ?'

For once Neil decided not to reassure her. Sustained by little more than the cups of sweetened tea, Dr Barbara lived among the clouds with the great albatross. More than a hundred had returned to Saint-Esprit, after crossing an ocean as wide as Dr Barbara's dreams. Her spirits soared on their wings. She refused to take part in the earnest debate about rationing their food stocks, as if deliberately forgetting that they depended on the charity of the Dakota. Neil noticed that she had not read a single one of the letters in the mail-bag beside her bed.

'Neil, I'm off to work,' she told him. 'Make sure David doesn't play the fool with that pistol.'

She devoted her time to helping Professor Saito set out the plant and animal terraces on the hillside. Taking a stout spade with her, she climbed among the cycads and ferns, stabbing at the dusty undergrowth as she began the laborious task of clearing the first of the terraces.

Two hours later, when Neil took the spade from her exhausted hands, she sat beside him on the lower section of the radio mast and watched the white birds wheeling in the sky. She smiled at them like a wistful parent, as if already accepting that one day they would leave the island. Massaging her shoulders, Neil realized for the first time that she would only be happy when she was alone on Saint-Esprit, when Kimo, Monique and the Saitos had gone and even the albatross had abandoned her.

8

The Gift Mountain

THE WORLD, HOWEVER, had no intention of leaving Dr Barbara alone. Three days after the psychedelic sails of the *Parsifal* brought their lurid spectrum to Saint-Esprit, a white seaplane appeared in the sky over the island. Neil, glad to rest from the back-breaking task of forest clearance, threw down his machete and set off for the runway, ignoring Monique's irritated calls.

'Neil, you're so lazy,' she shouted after him. 'No-one ever taught you to work.'

'I'm just someone to nag, Monique . . . '

Carline was sitting in the radio-cabin, head-phones over his pale hair, enjoying his new role as air-traffic controller. He cleared the two-engined seaplane, owned by a charter firm in Papeete, and watched it circle the lagoon. It touched down, cutting the calm water in a bravura display of racing foam.

'I always wanted to manage a small airport,' he reflected as he removed his head-phones. 'You get to be a kind of harbour-master. There are tides in the sky, Neil.'

'Where are they running, David?'

'Deep inside our heads, but you'll never see them. You're swimming in your own little sea. Now, check out our visitor – Captain Garfield, Inter-Island Air Charter. A fresh pomelo would kick-start the day . . . '

The seaplane taxied towards the pier and moored beside the landing-stage. The Australian pilot, a sixty-year-old Queens-lander with a beard as white as his aircraft, hailed Neil through the cockpit hatch.

'Sanctuary Island? The Barbara Rafferty show? Laddie, you look like you're saving the albatross.'

Neil stepped under the starboard propeller, an icy spear that trembled above his head. 'If you want to join us you'll have to see Dr Barbara. Who are you, anyway?'

'Father Christmas, by the feel of it. I've got everything here except sleigh bells and a sprig of mistletoe.' Garfield shouted to his two native crewmen waiting by the open cargo-hold. 'Right, start unloading the gift-shop . . . '

The dark cavern of the cargo hold resembled a cut-price Aladdin's cave, crammed with wooden crates and cardboard cartons. Neil was suspicious of the old pilot's facetious tone, sensing that some elaborate practical joke was about to unfold.

'Gifts – from where, exactly?'

'Lad, never ask. I've more than half a mind to start saving an albatross myself. As it happens, donations from the good peoples of Papeete, Sydney and Honolulu.'

When Garfield took off two hours later, after respectfully shaking hands with Dr Barbara and Mrs Saito, a cornucopia of equipment sat on the pier, the first instalment of a gift mountain being assembled from all over the world in the gymnasium of a Papeete *lycée*. A consortium of local businessmen had chartered the seaplane, and a twice-weekly shuttle would continue as long as the gifts arrived.

For the rest of the day all work on the sanctuary ceased. The crates had been lovingly packed by the school-children, decorated with coloured ribbons and goodwill messages. There were portable radios and cassette-players, cartons of wine, soft drinks and mineral water, battery-powered video-games, barbecue grills with a year's supply of briquettes, flippers and wet suits, deck-chairs and sun-umbrellas.

'They must think we're on holiday . . . ' Dr Barbara handed Monique a spangled swimsuit still in its sales-wrapper. 'They've ransacked every department store and patio on the Pacific rim. I only wish we'd had their support in the early days.'

Monique picked her way among the knick-knacks with the

disdain of a French housewife inspecting an inferior street-market. 'It's unfair of me, Barbara, but I resent all this . . . it's such a weird idea of what we need.'

Kimo settled his huge body into a sun-lounger, polishing the bright chromium with his thumb. 'Nothing says we have to be uncomfortable, doctor.'

'These video-games make me uncomfortable.' Dr Barbara pressed a button and frowned at the bizarre electronic images, the treasured realm of some concerned teenager in a Sydney suburb. 'Monique, I'll be working on the terraces with Professor Saito. Neil, we're still waiting for you and Kimo to clear the ferns above the aqueduct. There's far too much to do . . . '

Nevertheless, Dr Barbara's plans for the sanctuary were soon interrupted. As promised, the seaplane returned within three days. Nursing an uneven port engine, Captain Garfield left it running as the crew unloaded the sections of a prefabricated plant laboratory, donated by a manufacturer of scientific equipment in Florida. A maze of pumps, condensers and cooling circuits would maintain the right temperature and humidity for any rare plants sent to Saint-Esprit from their endangered habitats.

The Saitos were enthralled by this palace of glass and aluminium, and even Dr Barbara was mollified, treating the sceptical Garfield to a rare smile. After moving the heavy sections away from the airstrip and its flying grit, Neil and Kimo spent the rest of the day assemblng the laboratory on the level ground beyond the mess-tent. Ready now to catalogue creation, Professor Saito took up his tenancy of this new domain, and watched proudly as Mrs Saito carried his camp bed from their tent and set it up among the sinks and specimen trays.

They were barely rested the next morning when the supply Dakota appeared through the clouds. It touched down in the mist of coral dust that now hung permanently over the airstrip. The largest part of its cargo was a desalination plant donated by an American chemical company in Ohio. The gleaming complex of reaction vessels and separation chambers filled with ion-exchange resins sat under the trees like a machine deity, its bowels emitting curious noises and a few drops of rusty water.

The air-traffic in and out of Saint-Esprit was now so intense that Carline moved his sleeping bag to the radio-cabin, where Neil brought him his meals. The unsettled albatross strutted among the dunes, beaks testing the wind for the scent of some less popular island. Taking pity on them, Carline turned away a tourist turbo-prop with a party of American sightseers, but allowed in an executive jet carrying two field representatives of a Japanese travel company. The Saitos declined to speak to them, so they climbed the dusty hillside to the forest clearing among the taro and breadfruit trees, where they tried to negotiate with a distracted Dr Barbara, describing the working holidays they were eager to arrange for ecologically minded Japanese volunteers. A coolie army of accountants, dentists and computer operators was waiting to serve the sanctuary.

Too busy to consider this, Dr Barbara hacked away at the undergrowth, and at last Monique took pity on them and told them to consult the desalination plant, which she described as the island's oracle. For ten minutes they stood patiently beside the machine, listening to its throaty grunts, and then were guided by a silent Mrs Saito to their jet.

But the first serious test of Dr Barbara's temper occurred when a large hydrofoil anchored within the reef a few hours after the Lear's wheels left the runway. Chartered by an Italian media conglomerate, it carried a film unit ready to make a documentary record of the sanctuary island. Dr Barbara and Monique refused ·to cooperate, and shouted abuse at the Italian director when he approached them, holding his light meter to their faces. Carline did his best to calm Dr Barbara, brushing the dust from her forehead-and trying to ease the machete from her fretful grip.

'Barbara, maybe just one interview . . . or a shot of you digging? We're short of diesel fuel for the bulldozer. If they agreed to transfer a thousand gallons from their reserve tanks . . . '

Dr Barbara slashed at the undergrowth near the Italian's feet. 'Are we short of fuel? You unloaded a dozen jerry cans from the Dakota.'

'Gasoline, Barbara – for the two water-scooters Club Med donated. Now if you gave an interview . . . ?'

But Dr Barbara was adamant. She had addressed the cameras

for the last time. Blonde hair speckled with forest debris, sweat drenching her shirt and mud streaking her forehead, she raised her machete and waited until Carline and the Italian had backed down the hillside and taken refuge in the radio-cabin.

Finally Professor Saito agreed to be interviewed about the first endangered species to be air-freighted to Saint-Esprit, now occupying temporary quarters in the plant laboratory – a pair of slow loris from Indonesia and a dwarf lemur from Madagascar displaced by a logging project. But this scarcely satisfied the director. As Neil rested in a sun-lounger on the pier, admiring the angular lines of the hydrofoil, he overheard the Italian talking earnestly to Kimo and offering to become his literary agent.

'It's a fascinating story,' he insisted, 'maybe the greatest of our time. There should be a book about it, written by someone on the inside. The struggles, the passion, the romance . . . '

'That's not for me.' Kimo sucked his blistered hands. 'If anyone writes a book it should be Dr Barbara.'

'She'll never write anything. She only wants to dig her forest – Mother Teresa has more fun. You're an American, the story of Saint-Esprit could lead to a co-production deal with a big Manhattan publisher, you'd have money for other projects. You could buy an island of your own . . . '

Pondering all this, and the funds that might be generated for his swim across the Kaiwi Channel, Neil joined Dr Barbara in her tent. Impatient with herself, she sat on the camp bed, face in her hands, the sweat from her thighs staining her sleeping bag.

'Did you hear Professor Saito's interview, Neil? I hope he was sensible.'

'He was fine, Dr Barbara. His English is better when Mrs Saito isn't around. He'll make people understand.'

'Good. But I don't think they'll ever understand. I remember all I hoped for . . . we had it in our grasp but now Saint-Esprit's becoming a media toy.' She took Neil's hand and weighed it in her palm, as if testing its resolve. 'Sometimes I think we ought to leave Saint-Esprit altogether.'

'Leave the island? Dr Barbara?'

'Yes, we need to tackle the world head on – demonstrate outside Downing Street and the White House. It isn't just the rare plants and animals we need to look after. We have to think of ourselves.'

'You're right, doctor,' Neil agreed, taking his cue. 'Tell me, do you think I need an agent?'

'An agent?' Dr Barbara sat up and stared at Neil. 'What sort of agent, good God? A press agent?'

'A literary agent. Being serious, Dr Barbara . . . '

'Serious? If you're thinking of getting a literary agent it's a great deal more serious than I thought.'

To Dr Barbara's mounting despair, the world continued to force its attentions upon Saint-Esprit. The seaplane piloted by Captain Garfield made its bi-weekly landings on the lagoon, disgorging a medley of stores, gifts and equipment. A Tokyo manufacturer of solar panels promised to provide enough units of electricity to light a native village, but made the mistake of insisting on regular maintenance reports. An airfield construction company in Seattle offered a free second runway in return for becoming an official sponsor of the expedition.

Two anthropologists from the University of Southern California arrived with their own camping gear, ready to observe the social and behavioural patterns of the sanctuary community. They set up a hunter's blind on the camera-tower beside the airstrip, where they sat behind a screen of camouflage netting with their stop-watches and binoculars. After four days of this, Kimo lit a fire of palm fronds on the staircase of the tower and, an hour later, escorted the smoke-blackened pair to Garfield's seaplane.

Despite these interruptions, the work on the sanctuary continued, and a week later, when Garfield returned with a group of Greenpeace observers, they were impressed to find a secure settlement in the open clearing between the plant terraces and the lagoon. There were half a dozen tents linked by duckboards, the animal pens and plant laboratory, a kitchen and mess-tent, and a two-roomed prefabricated cabin that served as Dr Barbara's clinic and medical store.

Monique's father, the aged René Didier, had joined the flight from Papeete after a long journey from France, determined to visit his daughter, though much against Dr Barbara's wishes. Sharp-eyed and resolute, despite his advanced years, the old animal rights campaigner clasped Monique's shoulders and raised his cane in astonishment.

'My God, Monique, it looks like Bora Bora – you have everything here except a Hilton . . . '

'We've worked hard, Papa, all of us. Even Neil here,' she added as Neil carried the old man's suitcase. 'He's lazy and I have to trick him, but he's done his best.'

'The young angel of Saint-Esprit.' Didier stopped to inspect Neil, evidently approving of his mosquito bites and skinned knuckles. 'It's thanks to him that you're here at all. And to the good doctor. You know, I'd like to be buried here – just my ashes, I wouldn't want to pollute your animal haven.'

'Papa – nothing dies that comes to Saint-Esprit . . . '

Before resting in his daughter's tent, Didier insisted on seeing the albatross. After the long walk down the runway, he stood smiling among the dunes, counting the great white birds still flying in from the sea, all the vastness of the Pacific in their solemn eyes.

But for Neil the most problematic of the visitors drawn to Saint-Esprit were members of his own age-group. A second piratical craft had joined the psychedelic *Parsifal*, a dishevelled ketch with scarecrow sails and a rotting shark's head lashed under the bowsprit. A squatters' camp of a dozen hippies – British, German and Australian – occupied the beach where Dr Barbara, Kimo and Neil had first landed. They wandered up from the shore and helped themselves to the supplies and equipment sitting in the open air beside the runway, and carried away a dome-shaped greenhouse intended to house a colony of bonsai trees.

This glass structure became their tribal wigwam, around which they gathered in the evenings to smoke their pot. Once their food supplies were exhausted they returned to the runway and searched the stocks of canned goods and wine. Mrs Saito and Monique, now in charge of the catering, protested to their leader, a pock-marked Scot with an oily pony-tail springing from the back of his bald head. He waved them away, claiming that he and his companions had an equal right to the supplies. At night a wild music drummed through the trees, and an acrid smoke rose from the palm logs drenched in gasoline from the tanks of the water-scooters. Their shallow latrines fouled the forest floor, and the beaches were soon littered with empty cans and broken wine bottles.

Their sallow-cheeked women – a feral tribe of high-school runaways and college drop-outs – drifted around the camp, irritating Dr Barbara and Professor Saito with their requests for drugs. One of them, a San Diego psychiatrist's daughter with spiky pink hair and needle-punctured arms, asked Dr Barbara to perform an abortion, offering to pay with her father's stolen credit card.

Intrigued by the young women, Neil began to join the hippies on the beach in the evenings. As the gasoline flames lit the dark surf at his feet, he lay beside the fire of palm logs, watching the erratic video picture on a battery-powered TV set embedded in the sand. The two German women from the *Parsifal* took turns to breast-feed their baby, an amiable infant with rolling eyes under a swollen Down's forehead. Wondering which of the women was the child's mother, and assuming that the other had left her own baby in Vancouver, Neil enjoyed the pot and mulled wine which the bearded captain of the *Parsifal* offered him.

The hippies' erratic but undemanding presence made a pleasant change from Dr Barbara and her puritanical regime. The albatross were returning to Saint-Esprit, however deep he dug the camp latrines, and Neil felt less concerned with the fate of the slow loris or a threatened species of dwarf bamboo from the uplands of Nepal. He inhaled the sweet smoke, thinking sometimes of Louise, now as remote from him as the nuclear tests that would never come to the sanctuary island.

An hour before dawn he woke in his tent, aware that Dr Barbara was leaning over his bed. Her face was touched by the light reflected from the surf, and he could smell the strong scent of her body as she worked herself into one of her passions. He listened to the sea breaking on the reef, and the mournful, fluted music of the waves rushing through the hull of the *Dugong*. His nostrils quickened as Dr Barbara searched the mosquito net. He guessed that she had climbed the peak through the darkness, eager to be close to her beloved albatross, an ascent she made whenever she weighed an important decision. Pacing among the birds, she would have seen Neil and the hippies on the beach.

She raised the mosquito net and sat beside him, a hand pressed to his abdomen.

'Neil – time to wake up.'

'Dr Barbara?'

'Not so much noise. Listen to me – can you drive the bulldozer?'

'Of course.'

'You understand the controls?'

Neil sat up, rubbing the cannabis resin from his lips. 'Do you want to build another runway, doctor?'

'Another runway? We have one too many as it is. Get up and put on some clothes.' ·

She waited while he dressed, her eyes never leaving his naked body. After straightening his mosquito net, she raised the door-flap and beckoned him into the darkness. They moved through the silent camp, past the tent where Monique slept beside her aged father. The riding lights of the Andersons' sloop seemed to drown in the blackness of the lagoon. Water rilled from the zinc cascade of the aqueduct, inaudible against the breaking waves.

Dr Barbara strode through the night air, the sweat cooling on her forehead. Still fuddled by the cannabis, Neil stumbled into a rut left by the Dakota's wheels. Dr Barbara steadied him and pointed to the bulldozer, parked beside the long line of packing cases and donated stores.

'Neil, I want you to start the bulldozer.'

Neil listened to the *Dugong* sighing on the reef. The flames still lifted from the hippies' log fire, but they were asleep in their shanties and lean-to huts.

'Start the engine? Where are you going, doctor?'

'Nowhere. I'll stay here with you. Now, listen to me – I want you to push everything into the sea. The whole lot, as deep as you can.'

'The shacks, doctor? There's a baby there. One of the girls has malaria.'

'Not the shacks! I'll deal with them later.' She gestured at the wooden crates in their cargo netting. 'Get rid of them! Drive them into the sea!'

Neil tried to calm Dr Barbara as the coral dust rose from her nervous feet. 'We need the supplies, doctor – they're here to help us.'

'They're not!' She seized his arm and propelled him towards the bulldozer. 'We don't need them, and they're not helping us. They're turning Saint-Esprit into a playground. We have to begin again and do it on our own. Now, get into the seat and start the engine!'

'But what about the food . . . ?' Neil pressed his hands against the steel track. 'We only have enough supplies at the camp for three weeks?'

'Throw the food away!' Enraged with herself, Dr Barbara drummed her fists together. 'We'll make do with what we can grow ourselves. Try to understand, Neil – I want the world to leave Saint-Esprit and forget us. Then we can find who we really are!'

Thirty minutes later Neil switched off the engine. He leaned against the metal seat, his lungs filled with the foul breath of the diesel exhaust, skin drenched in lubrication oil sprayed from a leaking gasket. A small fire which two of the hippies had lit with splinters from the packing cases burned on the open ground above the beach, its flames reflected in the greasy control levers.

Everyone was standing among the trees, watching as the waves swept in from the reef and seized greedily at the crates and canvas bales. The surf raced through the gulleys which the bulldozer's tracks had cut into the sand. Already the sea was breaking up the wooden cases, the undertow dragging the barbecue kits and sun-loungers into the deep water. Sections of duckboarding floated on the waves, and the surf swilled among the mosquito nets that drifted out to sea like discarded shrouds.

Hundreds of food cans rolled back and forth on the sighing gravel, taking part in a series of frantic races.

Dr Barbara paced the shore-line, her shirt soaked by the waves, smiling with the pride of a destructive child at the one-time gift mountain disintegrating on the black sand. One of the hippies waded into the surf and retrieved a can, wrapping its label around his wrist. Another pulled a recreation bicycle from the deeper water, wheeled it through the waves and threw it onto the sand at Dr Barbara's feet.

Neil rested against the control levers, too tired to step down from the bulldozer. No-one at the camp had woken until the last of the stores had slid beneath the waves. The hippies were the first to appear, emerging from their shanties to watch the storehouse that had so generously supplied them with food and drink vanish into the sea. Major Anderson and his wife sat in the cockpit of their sloop, sharing a blanket, observing the action through their binoculars. The Saitos had hurriedly dressed in their yellow weatherproofs and stood solemnly under the palms, while a bare-chested David Carline, pistol tucked into the waist-band of his pyjamas, shook his head over the destruction, hands raised to the night air as if trying to weigh the deviant sky. Only Kimo smiled with open admiration, still eager to be impressed by Dr Barbara and her wayward temper.

'Barbara! I'm with you . . . !'

Monique ran down to the water's edge. Fastening her dressing-gown, she embraced Dr Barbara and kissed her cheeks. Arms around each other, the two women stood in the seething surf, as the last of the packing cases tumbled into the waves.

PART II

9

The Ecology of Paradise

BARELY A WEEK had passed since the destruction of the supply store, and Neil was still shocked by what he had done. The sanctuary had turned in upon itself, and the members were now preoccupied by their own survival. Their original reason for coming to Saint-Esprit, to save the albatross from the threatened nuclear tests, had faded into the dusty forest as soon as the support flights and media attention had ceased. In the evenings, after a meagre meal, they sat on the beach and watched the hippies trawl the waves for cans of food, aware of the suddenly vaster sky over their heads.

On the first morning, before any of them had recovered from the violent night, Dr Barbara called a meeting in the mess-tent and set out her survival plan for the immediate future. As she waited for them to assemble under the canvas awning she seemed more confident than ever, mistress of her island domain and certain that the expedition was back on its proper course. Lungs flushed with air, blonde hair flying from her forehead like a battle pennant, she resembled a warrior queen who had mounted a successful coup against her own followers.

Clearly intimidated by her, Professor Saito sat like a nervous schoolboy in the front row, pencil and notebook on his lap. Mrs Saito was calmer than her husband, eyes fixed coolly on Dr Barbara as if admiring the way she had seized control of the expedition. Monique helped her ailing father to a seat, concerned by his unsteady gait and fretting hands. But the old Frenchman's resolve and pugnacity had been recharged by the night's destruction. After complimenting Neil on his heroic act he assured

Kimo that the French naval forces were less likely to return to Saint-Esprit once the spotlight of world interest moved from the island. The Hawaiian treated this to a sceptical shrug, but he surveyed the peak above the forest slopes as if already seeing the flag of his independent kingdom flying from the plinth of the radio mast.

Carline was the last to enter the tent. Carrying one of the food cans he had found on the beach, he lingered by the radio-cabin, still undecided whether to charter a private jet, or so he had confided to Neil. Only when Dr Barbara began to speak did he stroll across the runway and take his seat behind the others.

'Right everybody, I'm glad you're here.' She stood by a large blackboard, a gift from the Papeete *lycée* that Neil guessed would now come into its own. 'Neil, sit up and stop staring at the camera-towers. There's a lot to do. First of all, I want you to block the runway.'

'Doctor – ?' Major Anderson, sitting with his anxious wife beside the Saitos, tried to protest. 'It's our main link to the outside world. We need that runway.'

'We don't need it.' Dr Barbara turned brusquely from her blackboard, breaking the chalk in her hands. 'In fact, it's been a large part of our problem here. People will still visit Saint-Esprit, but they'll have to come by sea, and that may cool their ardour. We must be left alone, so we can get on with the sanctuary. David, do I see you straining to say something?'

Carline stood up, the can in his hand, as if about to lob a grenade at Dr Barbara. Yet he watched her with the respect he had always shown to this maverick physician, disagreeing with her but curious to see where her imperious imagination might lead them.

'I take your point about the runway, Barbara. That was a grandstand display last night. But before I eat today's breakfast I'd like to think there's another coming tomorrow.'

'Of course there is,' Dr Barbara replied briskly. 'If you work for it.'

'Work? Well, that's a word everyone understands.' Carline gestured at the canvas roof. 'A heck of a lot of people worked to put that over our heads. All those stores young Neil bulldozed into the sea were their investment in us, their commitment to a dream. People all over the world are trying to help.'

'But are they?' Dr Barbara bared her chipped teeth and pointed to the beer-cans and wine bottles lying under the trees beside the runway. 'I'm grateful to people for the gifts they've sent, but look at what they've achieved – Saint-Esprit isn't a sanctuary, it's a rubbish tip picked over by TV crews. You may not realize it, David, listening to your head-phones, but you've been running a cargo cult.'

'And what about the dream, Barbara? We shared that once.'

'We still do. I want Saint-Esprit to be a sanctuary, not a holiday camp for ecological tourists. The hippies on the beach aren't interested in saving the albatross or anything else. If we wait much longer Saint-Esprit will be a haven for druggies and drop-outs. Everyone has to work, and we can't work when we're sleeping off last night's hangover. We came here to get away from the world, but it's caught up with us again. You don't need to go to Brazil or Burma to find deforestation and pollution – just pay a visit to Neil's psychedelic friends.'

'They'll quit soon.' Kimo tried to pacify her. 'That still leaves us, doctor. If we're going to make the sanctuary work we need all the basics – tools, equipment, food. Especially food.'

'We have enough to keep us going,' Dr Barbara replied. 'For a good two months if we ration ourselves. We have the goats and chickens, there are wild yams and breadfruit, taro and sweet potato. Professor Saito tells me there are dozens of edible plants in the lagoon. We'll soon see how many of us the island can support, and then we'll shut the door on the world. I hope you'll join me, especially you, David – we're all grateful for the medical supplies you asked your company to send us. I'll stay on even if I'm alone here. If any of you decide to leave you can take the last seaplane tomorrow. Then we'll tell Captain Garfield we want nothing more. All we ask is to be left alone . . . '

There was an uneasy murmur, and a sharp quarrel over nothing between Mrs Saito and Monique's father, but before anyone could disagree Dr Barbara began to chalk the work-tasks and rosters on the blackboard. Neil would care for the animals in the farm enclosure, while Dr Barbara, Carline and Kimo cleared the plant terraces. Monique and Mrs Saito would be in charge of the kitchen. To the Andersons she assigned the lighter work of extending the vegetable garden of donated seedlings and root crops.

Everyone would devote two hours a day to crop-hunting, gathering breadfruit and taro, manioc, coconuts, yams and sweet potatoes. Professor Saito was already compiling a biological inventory of the island, searching for edible plants and fungi. From this they could calculate the resource base available for the endangered species they would admit to Saint-Esprit once the sanctuary was established.

'We're going to be busy, damned busy,' Dr Barbara told them, slapping the chalk from her hands. 'I'll work beside you until I drop. Things will get a lot tougher, but it's worth the effort. Think of Saint-Esprit as the ultimate environmental project – we're engineering the ecology of paradise!'

Did anyone believe her? Neil waited for the first defectors to fold their tents and set off for the pier, suitcases in hand, but no-one decided to leave. Uncertain of themselves, but buoyed by Dr Barbara's fierce conviction in her cause, they set to work. As she frequently reminded them, *they* were now the endangered species, more vulnerable than the lemur and slow loris. Their survival dominated the next days – moving the storage tent with its stock of food to a more secure position beside the kitchen, digging storm-drains around the camp and, above all, searching the hillsides for the smallest edible root or berry. The world had drawn closer to them, no more than an arm's length away, at the end of a hoe, spade or machete.

Dr Barbara bullied them along. Even the protected animals in their enclosures were nervous of her, retreating into their dens when she approached. She soon devised a repertory of playful routines for each of the expedition members, joshing Kimo out of his meditative pauses whenever the Hawaiian daydreamed over his machete, teasing Professor Saito to provoke his wife into working harder, complimenting Carline on his newly muscled arms.

Carline tolerated all this good-humouredly, but Neil was still surprised that he had decided to remain on Saint-Esprit. At times he suspected that the American had taken the place of the two ill-starred anthropologists whom Kimo had smoked from their blind atop the camera-tower. For reasons Neil had yet to understand, Carline seemed pleased that Dr Barbara had become more authoritarian.

'Shoulders back, Neil,' Carline told him when he paused over the latrine they were digging for the clinic. 'You have to give everything you've got for Dr Barbara.'

Neil raised his hands and licked at the burst blisters. 'There isn't any more I can give.'

'Don't be so sure . . . ' Carline watched Dr Barbara sprint up the clinic steps. 'Our lady commandant has large plans for her gulag.'

'She works the hardest.'

'Of course she does. And the longest hours. Still, she has the most at stake.'

'You're crazy, David. Dr Barbara doesn't have a cent in the world.'

'Believe me, Neil, she has a great deal invested here. If the sanctuary fails she'll be destroyed.'

Neil pondered the American's frank but unmalicious smile. 'Do you want it to fail?'

'Should I? Maybe it's already failed – I don't think any of us can match Dr Barbara's expectations. Not even you, Neil.'

'But you're still staying on here?'

'Of course. What's so impressive is that she's absolutely right. Every decision she's made since we left Honolulu has been borne out by events. It took real guts, but she was right to face the French guns. She was right to dump all that stuff in the sea and close the runway.'

'She's testing us – she needs to see if we can take it.'

'No, Neil.' Carline took the spade from his hands and struck at the sandy soil. 'She's testing herself . . . '

Were they all waiting for rescue, before the sanctuary broke and exhausted them? Whenever an aircraft flew over Saint-Esprit they rested on their tools and watched its vapour trail through the forest canopy, wistfully dreaming of the food parcels and fresh fruit in the seaplane's cargo hold. Aware that Neil was losing weight, Mrs Anderson brought a can of pressed beef from the sloop. As he watched Kimo scraping and pounding the taro roots, then heating them to release the starch, Mrs Anderson slipped the can discreetly into his hand.

'Mrs Anderson . . . ' Neil followed her to the kitchen garden. 'I can't take this – you'll need it when you sail back to Papeete.'

'Go on, Neil.' She watched as he opened the can and forked the fatty meat into his mouth. Her son, a soldier with the UN peace-keeping force in Lebanon, had died in a terrorist ambush in 1987, and Neil often suspected that he resembled the dead youth. When he finished the beef she took the can from him and hid it away. 'Good. I never enjoyed *Robinson Crusoe*, but Dr Barbara seems to be playing it backwards. Every day we have less and less, and feel more and more uncomfortable.'

'Doesn't Dr Barbara want things to get better?'

'I really don't know – perhaps she wants them to get worse.'

'Why, Mrs Anderson?' Neil asked. 'What would be the point?'

'To see what we're made of, I suppose. And if we're strong enough to stay in the sanctuary.'

'But if we're strong, we wouldn't need a sanctuary?'

'It all depends what you mean by one – and what you're hoping to protect there.'

'Aren't we protecting the albatross?'

'Something more, I feel . . . something special that belongs to Dr Barbara.'

Neil remembered this cryptic aside on the day of the Dakota's arrival. All morning he had helped Monique to care for her ailing father. A chronic kidney infection had flared up, resisting the antibiotics that Dr Barbara injected, so Kimo carried the old man to the clinic and laid him on the mattress in the cool sick-room. Monique and Mrs Anderson bathed him, but Didier was barely conscious and clutched at his daughter's hands, pressing them to his inflamed cheeks.

Distracted from her work on the terraces by the Dakota's engines, Dr Barbara strode down the hillside towards the runway, now blocked by the bulldozer and the radio mast.

'Dr Rafferty!' Mrs Anderson called from the clinic. 'Would you come, doctor?'

Dr Barbara hesitated, her attention held by the scattered albatross and the Dakota's silver wings as they turned across the lagoon.

'I've only a moment. What is it?'

'Monique's father – I think he should return to Tahiti. Monique agrees with me, his fever is worrying . . . '

'I'll have a look.' Dr Barbara stepped into the clinic and stood in the modest sick-room, where the old Frenchman lay within the mosquito net, his skin so pale that he was barely visible through the white mesh.

Monique drew back the net, unhappy even to look at her father. 'Barbara, I have to take him to Papeete. We should clear the runway and tell the pilot to land.'

'The flight might do more harm than good.' Dr Barbara smiled winningly at the old man. 'You're getting well, Monsieur Didier. We're feeling better today, aren't we?'

'Dr Rafferty – ' Mrs Anderson was listening to the changing note of the Dakota's engines, aware that the pilot might turn away. 'This may be his last chance. I really do recommend . . . '

'Barbara, I'll be back,' Monique assured her. 'In a month, at the minimum.'

'Monique, I need you here.' Dr Barbara closed the mosquito net. 'Believe me, your father is through the worst. Putting him on the plane will kill him.'

Neil stepped forward and picked up the old man's canvas bag. 'I'll clear the runway, doctor.'

'Neil!' Dr Barbara raised her hand to slap his face, but caught herself as Mrs Anderson stepped between them. 'Go back to your work! If anyone speaks to the pilot, I will . . . '

*　　*　　*

The Dakota circled the atoll, its slipstream scattering the ever-cautious albatross, their confused wings like leaflets dropped from a rescue aircraft. As if aware that any messages of good cheer would never reach the ground, Kimo and Major Anderson scarcely raised their heads while they doggedly hacked at the wild yams in the cemetery. Professor Saito came to the door of the plant laboratory, shielding his weak eyes as the Dakota flew over the broken-backed wreck of the *Dugong*, and then returned dutifully to his endangered fungi before his wife could tap his elbow.

Monique and Mrs Anderson stood on the steps of the clinic, waiting for Neil to drive the bulldozer forward and clear the runway. But no signal had yet been given by Dr Barbara. She leaned from the doorway of the radio-cabin, microphone in hand, waving to the aircraft as she reassured the crew and any journalists aboard that all was well.

Would she allow the Dakota to land, unload its consignment of stores and evacuate Monique's ailing father to Papeete? Neil remembered her speaking to Captain Garfield during the sea-plane's concluding visit, insisting to the sceptical Australian that they had ample stocks of food and equipment and would survive comfortably on their own. While she urged the captain to restart his engines the expedition members had wandered towards the pier, staring at the wooden crates filled with fresh fruit, mineral water and shampoo like the inmates of a prison farm.

Now Monique expected Dr Barbara to tell the pilot to land. But Neil was certain that she would never order him to clear the runway. She had stopped herself from slapping his face, but he could almost feel the stinging blow when he remembered the anger she had turned upon him.

For a moment a vent of hell had opened, and another Dr Barbara had glared out at him. He listened to the rumbling murmur of the diesel engine, and watched the bulldozer's exhaust float across the runway to the radio-cabin. Already Mrs Anderson had turned away, shaking her head in dismay, and took up her vigil in the sick-room.

Neil switched off the engine and stepped onto the white coral.

Avoiding Dr Barbara, he walked to the headland beside the cemetery and watched the Dakota set course for Tahiti.

Dr Barbara had insisted on having her way, but a wary silence hung over Saint-Esprit, deepened by the old Frenchman's illness and the sense that they were cut off from the world beyond the horizon. By shutting everyone else out they had also shut themselves in. The black beaches of the atoll were effectively a wall, and the whole Pacific was Dr Barbara's moat.

Few craft visited the island now that the publicity barrage of the early months had passed. A week after the Dakota's departure a catamaran crewed by three off-duty officers in the Peruvian Navy anchored in the lagoon. Dr Barbara invited them to inspect the sanctuary, and spent an hour in the mess-tent, sharing the bottles of wine which they brought ashore. None of the expedition members joined them, but Neil and Carline rowed out to the catamaran and recorded messages that the Peruvians would later transmit to Neil's mother and to Mrs Carline.

Listening to himself as he reassured his mother that all was well, and then to Carline's proud description of their success in establishing the sanctuary, Neil was aware that their words no longer matched the reality of Saint-Esprit. He spoke truthfully to his mother, saying that the mosquitoes and sand-flies bothered him, that he was working hard, ate well and had not been ill, and that the bullet wound on his foot had healed completely. But he sensed that he and Carline were reading from an old script. A different Saint-Esprit had emerged, with a phantom runway inside Dr Barbara's head, on which strange cargoes were being landed.

When the Peruvians set sail, an hour before dusk, only Dr Barbara waved them goodbye. Afterwards she stripped and swam in the sea, then dressed and climbed the path to the peak, where she stood in the darkness among the albatross.

The next morning Neil was not surprised to find that the radio-cabin had burned down during the night, and that everyone assumed the hippies were responsible.

★ ★ ★

'Barbara, there's a time to do nothing and a time to act!' Pistol in hand, Carline paced around the still smoking embers of the cabin, a heap of charred wooden boards that had collapsed over the gutted radio. 'In football there's an offensive game as well as a defensive. We've been far too passive.'

'Have we?' Dr Barbara seemed unconcerned by this act of vandalism. She waved the smoke into her face, savouring the tang of pine-oil distilled from the burnt timber. 'What do you suggest – a punitive expedition?'

'I suggest drawing a line!' Carline pointed to the distant shanties. 'They have sex on the beach, drink our water from the stream, smoke their pot and beg for food.'

'It sounds like sheer heaven. I may join them.' Dr Barbara rested an arm on Neil's shoulder. 'We must be charitable, David. Nothing is more irksome than the sight of people working all day. Besides, does it matter? Since no planes will be landing here we hardly need a radio link.'

'Barbara . . . ' Exasperated, Carline raised the pistol to his temple. 'What's next – the mess-tent, the clinic, the plant lab? They destroyed my airport! We have to act!'

'All right. We'll send Neil down there. He knows them well – perhaps he can find what happened.'

'A fifth column? Good thinking, Barbara.' Carline holstered his revolver, smiling at Neil. 'Now, Neil, all you have to do is build a wooden horse . . . '

Thoroughly briefed by Carline, Neil set out for the beach. The second of the hippie yachts had left with its British and Australian crew, leaving the two German men on the *Parsifal*, the two women and the retarded child. Sometimes they drifted up to the camp, hanging around the kitchen in the hope of finding powdered milk for the baby. Trudi, a small, dark-haired woman in her twenties with a pallid but attractive face and an atlas of dead veins on her arms, often carried the child to the animal enclosure, begging Neil for a pail of goat's milk and a few eggs.

Liking the child, he usually helped her, and declined the LSD tabs she offered in exchange.

'Go on, they're good,' she always assured him. 'You'll see a new island, filled with birds.'

'They've already come back, Trudi.'

'But inside your dreams.'

Despite Carline's hostility, the Germans greeted Neil affably, ready to share with him the cans of food they had rescued from the sea, stripped of their labels by the rushing surf.

'Every meal is a surprise,' Werner, the *Parsifal*'s skipper, told Neil as they settled around the fire. 'That's what God intended when he made the Earth. Maybe we ate nuts or fruit, or the fish in the sea. Now we know exactly – lasagne, Wiener schnitzel, eggs benedict – it's so boring.'

A stocky Rhinelander with a tattooed cheekbone, he dandled the child on his knees, opening the door of a miniature house he had built from driftwood and shells.

'This is your house, Gubby, we're all going to live here.'

Gubby chuckled noisily, struggling to add more shells to the roof and fending off the playful fingers of Wolfgang, the yacht's navigator, a quiet, emaciated man whom Dr Barbara suspected of harbouring TB. The two men were happy to play with the child and watch the women work. Trudi scavenged the beach for coconut husks and palm fronds, which she stuffed into her sling. Inger, a once robust blonde with dyed yellow hair and a pockmarked face, thighs covered with needle scars, fed the fire and selected one of the cans from their modest cache.

'Say a spell, Inger,' Wolfgang urged as she opened the can. 'For asparagus soup, bratwurst or pickled herring . . . ?'

'Shoe polish – I'll paint Gubby's bottom.' She leaned over and drew two horns on the child's swollen forehead. 'Now he's a little devil . . . '

Trudi picked another can. 'He's a devil already. Gubby, you'll frighten Dr Rafferty's beloved birds.' To Neil, whose broad shoulders she was always appraising, she said: 'So you came to save the albatross?'

'Yes . . . in a way.'

'What way? You mean you don't want to save them? I'll tell Dr Rafferty.'

'He wants to see a nuclear war,' Werner explained. 'One sun is not enough for Neil.'

'Maybe he's crazy,' Inger surmised. 'Island fever, there's no cure. Gubby, he pushed all your food in the sea.'

Neil played with the baby, still trying to decide which of the women was the mother. Lamely, he said: 'I had to – Dr Barbara ordered me to get rid of everything.'

'And you always do what she orders?'

'No. Mostly when she tells me to do things I don't do them. Only the important ones.'

'Those are the ones you shouldn't do.' Inger picked at the enlarged septum of her nose. Milk from her breasts stained her faded denim vest, but she seemed too drained to feed a child. 'When people say something is important, never do it.'

'You're right, Inger.' Neil lay beside the fire and watched the baby laughing at the waves. The treasures of the reef were almost exhausted, but the hippies were unconcerned. They were under-nourished and easily tired, but he found them refreshingly pleasant company after Dr Barbara's rigorous regime. He knew that they were uninterested in the sanctuary, and would never have bothered to burn down the radio-cabin. Their ocean-battered yacht rode at anchor and one day, on the merest whim, they would decamp and sail away.

Meanwhile, however, their lassitude was infectious, and more dangerous to the sanctuary than Wolfgang's T B. The sudden drop in their food ration left the expedition members with little energy to spare. After the day's work they lay in their tents, or wandered along the beach in the hope of finding a few cans surrendered by the waves. Only Carline now seriously believed that the hippies had burned down the radio-cabin but Dr Barbara, concerned by the decline in morale, seized on the notion and did her best to provoke the dormant hostility to the idle and workshy Germans.

After their supper one evening Trudi walked up from the beach, and Dr Barbara made a point of barring her from the mess-tent. Strangely torpid, Gubby lay in Trudi's arms, his laughter gone.

But Dr Barbara was in no mood to compromise, and sent Monique back to the kitchen with the cup of goat's milk she had brought for the child. 'I haven't any medicines to spare,' she told Trudi. 'Besides, the only medicine the baby needs is food. If you're not eating enough your milk will dry up.'

'There isn't any food, doctor – the sea's empty now. Neil can give us some eggs. I have acid left.'

'Trudi, we don't want your drugs, and the eggs are for Monsieur Didier.' All reasonableness, Dr Barbara explained: 'If you haven't any food you'll have to sail away.'

'But we can't leave without supplies – it's six days to Tahiti.'

'Then you'll have to work like the rest of us. The four of you can easily gather enough food from the forest. You could even fish outside the reef.'

'That's too tiring. And we don't like the food in the forest.'

Carrying the inert child in her sling, Trudi turned back to the beach as Dr Barbara stood hands on hips. Neil and Kimo avoided the young woman's dejected gaze, unhappy with the lack of charity shown by the sanctuary.

Aware that Monique's father had been too ill to taste a single egg, Neil asked: 'How is Monsieur Didier, doctor? Monique says he's stopped eating.'

'He's as well as we can hope. But he is very old, Neil. One day soon he'll probably leave us. The sanctuary is a wonderful place to say goodbye to everything.' She watched the goats foraging in the undergrowth beside the animal enclosure, their heads through the wire fence. 'Still, we have to think about the living. We've done so much, but everyone seems rather down.'

'They're tired, Dr Barbara. Maybe they need the television cameras to keep them going.'

'Let's hope not. I've got to find some way of rallying them, especially David and Kimo. The women are starting to do all the work. We can't sit back or the sanctuary will run to seed. Remember that we're not alone on Saint-Esprit.'

'Werner and Wolfgang won't harm us, doctor. They're stoned most of the time.'

'Perhaps. But they may become desperate, Neil. We really must keep our guard up . . . '

*   *   *

129

As he cleaned the chicken hutches the next morning, Neil discovered that one of the birds was missing. He was certain that the Germans had not stooped to stealing the hens, but decided to say nothing until he had searched the surrounding forest. Wading through the dense ferns below the plant terraces, he noticed that Dr Barbara was already at work, preparing the ground for her endangered bamboos and orchids. Already he suspected that she had removed the chicken, just as he was sure that she had set fire to the radio-cabin.

He watched her arms rise and fall as the hoe struck the knotted soil. It was only eight o'clock, but already she was bathed in sweat and dust, while the rest of the expedition team sat on their beds and pondered the day ahead. Dr Barbara was impatient with them all, eager to turn the screw. He knew that she had refused to allow Monique's aged father to leave Saint-Esprit, not because she had closed the runway but in order to provoke everyone with her apparent callousness. Dr Barbara loathed the status quo, and thrived on tension and conflict. Yet he still admired her more than any woman he had ever met, and liked to watch her strong arms striking the hard soil and the way she brushed her fraying blonde hair from her forehead as if dismissing an insolent breeze.

Hearing him, she turned to stare through the trees. Neil stepped into the shadow of a eucalyptus, and decided to make his way down to the beach to satisfy himself that the Germans were innocent of stealing the chicken. Pushing aside the waist-high ferns, he strode into the deep forest, feet sliding on the spongy soil and rotting bark. The stream slid down the hillside, a silver serpent that briefly showed its back to him. He reached the path through the dappled world where Dr Barbara and the skipper of the *Croix du Sud* had walked arm in arm, and approached the camera-tower hidden behind its screen of vines and palmettos.

The fronds swayed in the sea air that cooled the narrow valley, giving Neil a glimpse of a bizarre image within the foliage. A demented artist had recently been at work, using a palette confined to a single primary colour. A bloody scrawl covered the grey concrete, drawn from the diary of an obscene child.

.Neil separated the branches and stared at this crude finger-painting, in which threads of animal tissue and a few feathers were smeared onto the cement. A grotesque goat stood on its rear hooves, immense penis swinging between its legs, ready to mount a woman with pendulous breasts and a strong, pointed nose.

The blood had scarcely dried, daubed onto the wall in a few violent seconds. In the entrance to the tower was a dark pool, speckled with fat and gristle, where a chicken had been slaughtered, its head, feet and gizzard lying on the stone. Neil stepped across this greasy ooze and climbed the staircase, following a blurred trail of bloody heelprints. The camera chamber was empty, and a dusty light filtered through the leaves beyond the aperture, but Neil could see the white rag that lay in the corner. Kneeling down, he held it in his hands, and unfolded the stained tatters of one of Dr Barbara's cotton shirts, saturated like a tampon with the chicken's blood.

He squeezed the drenched fabric, as if pressing the sex from Dr Barbara's pubis, and felt the blood run onto his hands. He tried to guess who had drawn the threatening goat poised to copulate with her. The artist had deliberately left the shirt for him to find, as if inciting Neil and everyone else on Saint-Esprit to enter an even more violent future than that which had once awaited the albatross.

10

The Attack on the Beach

THE ATTACK WAS ABOUT TO BEGIN. Parting the ferns with a cautious hand, Neil crept towards the trees above the beach as the other members of the raiding party took up their positions. Led by Carline, they had crawled down the hillside through the undergrowth, unnoticed by the sunbathing hippies, and were now ready to launch their punitive assault.

Twenty feet away, Professor Saito and his wife waited in a shallow gulley beside the stream, a camouflage of forest debris taped to their foreheads, hands clasping the bamboo spears they had freshly sharpened after breakfast. Neil was still surprised by their new-found taste for action. For a few hours they ceased to be dedicated botanists and reverted to the spirit of the Japanese infantrymen who tenaciously defended the Pacific atolls during the Second World War, waiting above the beaches for the American marines to wade ashore. The Saitos were eager to defend Saint-Esprit against waves of hippies, hotel developers and documentary makers, and their casualty rate might be equally heavy, to judge by their grim expressions.

Bored by the long wait, Neil pulled a parasol of dead palm fronds over his head, converting his shallow lair into a hunter's blind. Lying on his back, he raised his wooden club and aimed it at the largest of the albatross soaring above the wreck of the *Dugong*. He was about to squeeze his trigger finger when the blind collapsed in a flurry of dirt and leaves, and a sweating figure flung herself onto the ground beside him.

'Neil, what are you doing? This isn't a game!'

Monique crawled into the space under the parasol, her face

streaked with mud. As usual on these raiding parties, she had lost herself in the undergrowth and emerged with a spitting temper.

'Where are the Saitos? Neil! Have you been playing with yourself? Dr Barbara told me to watch you.'

She stared short-sightedly at the surrounding ferns, like a harassed hostess who had mislaid her passengers. Even on Saint-Esprit her world seemed to be populated by rowdy tourists refusing to wear their seat-belts, unruly teenagers such as Neil, or misfits who were potential hijackers. They hovered in the aisles of her mind, ignoring her demonstrations of the oxygen mask and life-jacket.

'The Saitos – are they here yet?'

'Monique, they've been here for half an hour.' Neil pointed to the Japanese couple in the gulley. 'We can all have a rest now.'

'There's no time to rest.' Monique crawled forward, her strong shoulders and buttocks pressed against him. Neil looked at the dark freckles on her neck and the scar on the lobe of her left ear – a love-bite, perhaps, left by some handsome co-pilot in a stop-over hotel? More likely, he decided, she had been nuzzled by one of her over-eager bears. Yet her fierce, unplucked brows guarded surprisingly delicate eyelashes. The heady scent of her body, the dark curves of her neglected breasts, had transformed the blind into an arbour of adolescent lust.

She thumped his head with her elbow. 'Neil! We're ready now – David is signalling . . .'

Below them, little more than thirty yards away, was the hippie settlement. Smoke rose hopefully from a cooking fire of driftwood and palm leaves, where Trudi and Inger sat with the baby. But there was little to cook. Despite the bright sunlight, the women were wan and dejected, barely able to brush away the flies that pestered their faces. The four Germans and Gubby suffered from chronic under-nourishment, and were too tired to bail out the *Parsifal*, now sinking slowly at anchor. They tried to beg from the visiting yacht-crews, but their derelict appearance and needle-sharing put off any would-be donors.

At low tide, even the sea seemed discouraged, rolling slackly against the black sand. Werner sat alone on the beach, gazing at the flaking acid paintwork of the yacht. He spent his time brooding in his driftwood shack or tending a plot of marijuana plants among the nearby palms. Meanwhile Wolfgang wandered along the shore-line, searching for the last of the stores that Neil had bulldozed into the sea, his tattooed thighs flinching at the cold waves.

'Neil, we're going! *Vite, vite!*'

Professor Saito and his wife had leapt from the gulley and plunged into the sand. Carline was racing along the water's edge towards the shacks, silver pistol in one hand, spray breaking around his long legs. He snatched the canvas awning that formed the roof of Werner's hut and dragged it into the sea, then scooped up the black sand and hurled it into the face of the patient German.

Pulling Neil by his shirt, Monique burst through the ferns and bellowed at Trudi and Inger in a hoarse voice that sounded like a garbled cabin announcement. Neil followed her to the beach, waving his cudgel in the air. The German women sat beside the fire, watching without any change of expression. Gubby noticed Carline's whooping figure, rolled his eyes and began to chortle. The Saitos stopped beside the fire, trembling with indignation. Professor Saito glared at the passive women as if they were the most shiftless of his students, while his wife scattered the embers with a vicious kick.

Neil waved reassuringly to Trudi, patted the baby's head and ran on, swinging his cudgel at the salt-stained screen of the television set half-buried in the sand. The sharp explosion startled everyone. Gubby began to cry and Trudi rocked him against her breast. Wolfgang gave up his trawl of the sea-bed and waded back to the shore, while Werner shook his head over Neil's clumsy aim.

The commando raid was over. Led by Carline, who had confiscated the last food cans from the hippies' store, they ran along the beach towards the runway. Neil hurled his club into the sea and limped past the grove of marijuana plants, careful not to damage them.

'Yukio, well done! Good work, Monique!'

Carline was waiting for them behind the bulldozer, pale eyes flushed by the excitement. Kimo, although a trained policeman, refused to lead the raids, but Carline took an almost boyish pleasure in harassing the hippies. Like a scout-master supervising an inter-school contest, he exhorted them to make the maximum effort but was careful that no-one was actually hurt. The chrome-plated pistol was his referee's whistle, and Neil sensed that Carline had found his real vocation on Saint-Esprit. For all his inherited wealth, the pharmaceutical company left to him by his father, and the prestige of his missionary trips to Africa, these raids against the hippie settlement on the beach made him feel useful for the first time. Games, for anyone rich from birth, were always the most serious business in life.

'Neil, are you all right? You've cut your foot.' Carline pointed to the blood on the white coral. 'Did one of the women bite you? Watch out for these Germans – they'll stop at nothing.'

'It was the television set. I didn't mean to hit the screen.'

'Must have been a lousy programme. Get Dr Barbara to check it for you. Anyway, you were great, son. They won't try stealing from us again.'

Carline set off along the runway, followed by Monique and the Saitos, each carrying one of the looted cans. They were eager to be congratulated by Dr Barbara before returning to the more mundane task of hunting for yams and sweet potatoes. Neil waited for the war-whoops to subside, picking the glass spurs of the television screen from his feet. When all was quiet he walked back to the hippie camp and helped Inger and Trudi to rebuild their shacks, kindled another fire for them and played with the baby.

The raiding parties were a charade but they served their purpose, binding everyone together and sustaining the illusion that the sanctuary was beset by enemies. In part they were a tribal display, but the raids also introduced a few welcome moments of tension into the boredom and monotony of sanctuary life.

Work now dominated their days on Saint-Esprit, above all the ceaseless search for food. Helped by the reserve stocks in the padlocked storage tent, and a few gifts of fresh fruit smuggled ashore from visiting yachts, they had managed to survive, confirming Dr Barbara in her belief that they should reject the world. The group was now more tightly knitted than ever before, disciplined, self-obsessed and wholly dedicated to hard work.

To Neil's surprise, all this had begun to irritate Dr Barbara. He had expected her to welcome the relentless activity, but she soon became bored with the job-rosters and work-targets that Carline and Professor Saito devised. The flower-beds around the clinic and mess-tent planted by Mrs Saito, the decorative stone pathways laid out by Monique, the ever-deeper storm-drains dug by Kimo, together provoked Dr Barbara into fits of impatience. By making a fetish of self-discipline and the work ethic they were institutionalizing the sanctuary and suppressing the anarchic spirit that had brought them to Saint-Esprit. Monique's dourness had come to the forefront, like Kimo's tendency to isolate himself on his bed with his dreams of an independent Hawaiian kingdom, a realm that Neil guessed was shrinking to the floor-space of his tent. The Saitos rarely strayed from the plant laboratory, while Carline, conversely, had taken to roaming the island on his own, his tall and long-boned figure following the ancient trails of the original natives as if hunting for new opponents.

In the six weeks since the destruction of the radio-cabin the sanctuary had come to resemble the encampment of a religious sect. A fence of telephone wire enclosed the tents and animal enclosures. No longer were the goats and hens free to roam at will, defecating in the kitchen, nor were the laundry lines spattered with the droppings of exotic birds. The creatures were penned within an elaborate steel and glass aviary donated by a farm-equipment manufacturer in Idaho.

At times, as he fed the loris and lemur, the Bolivian peccaries, the kangaroo rats and the Javanese palm civets, each in its labelled hutch, it seemed to Neil that he was running a zoo, the opposite of the free-range sanctuary that the expedition had vowed to establish. How long would it be, he wondered, before they began to cage the albatross?

Of course, the cages were for the creatures' benefit. Unfettered freedom, as Professor Saito pointed out, soon led to chaos. By placing Saint-Esprit on a more military footing they had increased the effectiveness of the sanctuary. The populations of the protected mammals had begun to grow, and the rare plant species flourished on the terraces and in their laboratory seedling trays.

Not everyone, however, thrived on the new regime. The chilling hours of spear-fishing in the lagoon – a temporary expedient, Dr Barbara assured him, to increase their protein intake – left Neil shivering in his sleeping bag. Concerned for him, Dr Barbara began a series of blood and urine tests, and even suggested that he spend a few days at the clinic.

But Neil declined, relying on the warmer weather at the year's end to heat the lagoon. Despite the pleasure he felt as Dr Barbara ran her hands over his diaphragm and liver, searching his bony ribs and shoulder blades, he was always uneasy inside the clinic. The narrow bed, with its open mosquito net, resembled a trap waiting to catch its next patient.

No-one had yet been cured by the clinic, but Monique's father had died there, in circumstances that not only the Andersons found distressing. The ordeal of Didier's first month on the island and the nights of feverish sleep had wasted the old ecologist. When Neil began to fish in the lagoon the nutritious *bouillabaisse* that Monique prepared soon revived him. He sat up, became alert again and offered Neil an informed commentary on the odours emanating from the animal cages.

Tragically, on the very evening that he made his first steps to the latrine, Didier had suffered a massive stroke. Monique found him the next morning when she brought him his breakfast. Drained of all blood, his small face resembled a wizened pomelo, blanched lips splayed against his tobacco-stained teeth. Professor Saito remarked to Dr Barbara upon the bruises to his chin and forehead, but he helped to bury the old man in the cemetery beside the prayer-shack. Carline delivered a brief sermon, and Dr Barbara did her best to comfort Monique, assuring her that everything had been done for her father.

Neil, however, had seen more than the bruises. Dr Barbara had burned the soiled linen in a brazier behind the clinic, and when she sent Neil to stir the ashes he found that the pillow-case had been too drenched to ignite. Smears of blood covered the torn cotton, marking out the image of a face in which cheekbones, chin and brow-ridges were clearly visible. Watching the flames consume the fabric, Neil imagined someone stepping through the darkness, parting the mosquito net and pressing the pillow over the old man's face, and the long teeth splitting his lips as he struggled for breath.

Neil remembered the obscene graffiti on the walls of the camera-tower and the sexual threat against Dr Barbara. Someone had mutilated the chicken and drawn the priapic goat coupling with the strong-nosed woman – Kimo, Carline, perhaps Werner in one of his deranged acid reveries? Had the German crept into the clinic in the hours before dawn, thinking that Dr Barbara was asleep under her mosquito net . . . ?

Neil tried to warn Dr Barbara, but as he spoke she smiled at him and stared at his blood and urine samples lined up on her desk like the pieces on a chess-board.

'No-one would want to harm me, Neil. Not even Werner. I've sacrificed everything for the sanctuary.'

'I know, doctor. But the dead chicken and the painting on the camera-tower . . . ' He was too embarrassed to describe the image. 'It was a kind of warning.'

'Neil . . . ' Dr Barbara moved a vial of blood as if about to mate a king. 'You were probably running a slight fever, or dreaming of nuclear war. Saint-Esprit is at peace with itself. Too much so, I sometimes think . . . '

And so it seemed to the outside world. Major Anderson and his wife had been distressed by Didier's death, standing apart from the other mourners at the funeral, but they would say nothing to Neil when he tried to question them. The few visitors to Saint-Esprit – curious journalists alerted by the closure of the runway, passing Australian and American yacht-crews with gifts of endangered animals, and a party of French environmentalists with a large consignment of threatened plants – found the albatross returning in their thousands to the island, guarded by a taciturn group under the leadership of a strong-willed but restless matriarch. They had rejected the world beyond the reef, like any fundamentalist sect, and politely refused the offered gifts, merely asking the visitors to assure their friends and relatives that all was well. Long before the newsreel cameras recorded the scene they had returned to their simple tasks of hoeing, planting and carrying water. Around this dour tribe the endangered plants and animals thrived and bred like visitors from another planet.

Neil's only respite from the spartan regime was the time he spent with the hippies, slipping Inger and Trudi the few scraps of food he could scavenge from the kitchens. For all the attention to life on Saint-Esprit, he sensed that a darker island lay waiting to emerge, willed into being by Dr Barbara as she played with her vials of blood, and by the artist of the sinister graffiti on the camera-tower. Neil had come to Saint-Esprit dreaming of the nuclear flash, but a different kind of death waited in the wings, ready to take the stage.

After the punitive raid, when he had rebuilt the fire for the women, he came across Werner in the clearing beside the tower. The German spent hours wandering the hillside, searching for rare barks and fungi, from which he had already distilled a modest pharmacopoeia of hallucinogens. As Neil approached the tower, hiding among the cycads, he saw that Werner was kneeling beside a dead albatross. The German was plucking its wings, as if to find a quill with which to embroider the obscene painting of Dr Barbara and the goat.

When he stepped behind Werner, ready to challenge him, Neil realized that he was digging a grave for the bird. Werner muttered a mantra over the creature, plucked a feather from its wing and stitched it through the collar of his sheep-skin jacket. Blades of grass, a withered flower and a chicken's foot already decorated his lapels, as if he intended to become a walking reliquary of everything that had died on Saint-Esprit.

'Neil? Where's your battle-spear?'

'I threw it in the sea.' Neil raised his palms in apology. 'I lit the fire again for Inger and Trudi. I'm sorry about the raid, Werner.'

'We're used to it now. Anyway, there was no battery for the TV set. But it was nice for Gubby to look at.'

'I'll find another set for him. It's just David, he gets carried away. He isn't really serious.'

'I think he *is* serious.' Werner turned to examine Neil, as if measuring him for a grave. 'Everyone is serious here, except you. Be careful, Neil. He's a small man but he has a small island that makes him big again.'

Neil helped him to lay the bird in the grave and scoop the sand over its blurred plumage. Trying to reassure the German, he said: 'Nothing lasts forever, Werner, even on Saint-Esprit. You can't have a funeral for every leaf that dies.'

'You've been talking to Dr Barbara too much. There should be a ceremony for everything. Each breath you take is a celebration, with a special ceremony for the last breath. Not just our last breath but the last breath of every bird and flower.' Werner's nostrils caught the smell of wood smoke from the fire. 'You'll eat with us, Neil?'

'No, it's for you and Gubby. I'll try to bring some rice tomorrow.' Before leaving, he asked: 'Werner, what would you do if a shark was washed ashore – or a whale?'

'I'd wear its eyes, Neil. Like I'll wear yours. Then they'll see a new life far away from Dr Barbara.'

Shortly before dusk, Trudi and Inger shuffled down the airstrip and appeared at the gates of the camp. They sat in the dust, Gubby lolling in a sling around Trudi's neck. The swollen moon of the child's head swayed on its weak neck, and its eyes searched the trees as if unable to find anything to laugh at. Taking pity on them, Kimo brought a rucksack from his tent and handed each of them a candy bar. While they licked the chocolate from their fingers Carline prowled the nearby fence, smiling uneasily to himself, and Mrs Saito emerged to berate them in a torrent of Japanese.

Roused by all this, Dr Barbara at last strode from the steps of the clinic. She glanced with some irritation at Monique, who was still scouring the cooking pans outside the kitchen, and kicked aside one of the ornamental tiles that the Andersons had laid on the pathway.

Hands on hips, she surveyed the two women through the wire, treating their thin arms and pallid faces to a show of sympathy. 'Inger, if you're going to spend the night here you should bring a blanket.'

140

'We have no more food, doctor.' Inger spoke matter-of-factly. 'We can't steal from the ships and the people give us nothing. This afternoon you took our last cans.'

'You stole them from us in the first place. We need them just as much as you do.'

'We found them in the sea. All of them. Neil swam for one of them.'

'Then go back to the sea.' Dr Barbara was staring at the wreck of the *Dugong*, already bored by the hippies' plight. 'Take your yacht and fish beyond the reef.'

'Fish?' Trudi pressed the baby's head to her empty breast. 'We're too tired – you can fish all day and only catch enough for one person.'

'Then go back to Tahiti – why stay and starve?'

'We like the island, doctor. It's our island too.'

Dr Barbara struck the wire gate with an angry fist. 'It's not your island! Saint-Esprit belongs to the albatross and any other creature that needs sanctuary . . . '

'My baby needs sanctuary.' Trudi comforted the restless child. 'Give us a little milk for Gubby. Just for the baby.'

'The dried milk is for emergencies only. Besides, it's not good for the child.'

'Dr Barbara . . . ' Kimo steadied the trembling gate, his huge arms raised as if to calm the air. 'We can give something to the baby. Just for now.'

'Of course – and tomorrow?'

'I'm thinking now, doctor.'

'And I'm thinking about the future.' Dr Barbara stared challengingly at the others, as if reminding herself that they shared the sanctuary with her. 'David, I'm sure you agree with me?'

'Of course, Barbara . . . ' A series of contrary scowls crossed Carline's face as he fidgeted with himself. 'It's a difficult one, but I go along with you.'

'Good. Yukio, what about you?'

'We can adjust the food schedules . . . ' Nervous of his wife, the botanist temporized. 'Maybe the schedules are right.'

'They certainly are. We spent enough time on them.'

141

Watching the scene from the steps of the clinic, Neil sensed that he was witnessing a shrewd but cruel experiment. The rightness of the hippies' claim to food was a secondary matter. Dr Barbara was testing the resolve of the sanctuary members, as she tested everything on Saint-Esprit. The albatross, the endangered plants and animals and all those on the island were taking part in an endless trial to see if they matched Dr Barbara's fierce expectations of them.

Surprisingly, it was the women who were most stalwart in their refusal to aid the two hippies and their ailing child. Mrs Saito and Monique were united against the wavering men, and glowered at the cowed trio beyond the gate. Seizing upon their support, Dr Barbara strutted along the fence and tested the rusty wire.

She was snapping her fingers at the air when Neil appeared beside her, two cans of dried milk in his hands.

'What are those, Neil? Did you find them on the beach?'

Neil showed her the intact labels. 'I took them from the shelf in your office.'

'Did you?' Dr Barbara's gaze was fixed upon Neil with an intentness he had never known before, as if she was curious to see his response to the confrontation she had devised. 'Well, now you're going to take them back.'

'No, doctor. I'm giving them to Trudi for the baby.'

'And what happens when all the cans have gone? When there isn't any food left because we've been too busy being kind to each other?'

'That hasn't happened, Dr Barbara. Not yet. We look after the animals. And the albatross.'

'They're in danger, Neil. That's why we started the sanctuary. But even here we have to be selective. Not everything can be saved.'

'We can still be kind, doctor. You looked after me when the French soldiers wanted me to die.'

'And I'm still looking after you. Things may not always go well here, and then you'll come to me again. Now, take the cans back to my office.'

'No – ' Neil stepped through the gate and stood beside the

squatting women, smiling at the unsettled child when it waved to him. 'If I can't give the milk to Gubby I'll go and live with Trudi and Inger on the beach. I'll fish for them and leave the sanctuary.'

'Neil!' Dr Barbara tried to hold him. 'We came to Saint-Esprit together. You can't leave . . . '

'We'll start our own sanctuary, Dr Barbara.'

Carline strode forward to separate them, beaming tolerantly like a missionary separating two rival natives. 'Barbara, let's take time to think this over. I can air-freight a ton of powdered milk into Saint-Esprit. You'll be able to bathe in the stuff.'

'Neil's our best spear-fisher,' Kimo pointed out. 'We need him here, doctor.'

Neil waited, a milk-can in each hand, aware that Monique and Mrs Saito had sided with Dr Barbara. Both were already treating Neil as if he were an outcast.

'He's a lazy boy,' Mrs Saito insisted. 'He never works, he's just dreaming all the time.'

'Let him go, Barbara,' Monique agreed. 'He's already living on the beach. Better to take the women. We can teach them to work.'

'Yes . . . ' The suggestion cooled Dr Barbara's temper. She nodded to Monique, and turned to assess the two German women. Already she seemed to be thinking far ahead, to another island and another sanctuary free of kindness.

'All right, then. Monique, tell them that they can bring the baby and live in the camp with us. Neil, you're in charge of them. They can stay, but only if you feed them.'

11

The Breeding-Station

DR BARBARA WANTED A CHILD – not her own, she had made clear, but an infant sired by Neil and conceived by either Inger or Trudi, a sanctuary first-born who would celebrate the new kingdom of Saint-Esprit. As Neil broke the surface of the lagoon and swam towards the beach the two women were waiting for him beside the barbecue. Regrettably, they were still far more interested in what Neil might bring to fill their stomachs than in any gift to Dr Barbara that he could place in their wombs.

He waded ashore, weary after the hour of deep-water swimming, and the weight of the wet-suit and oxygen cylinders. Inger cheered when she saw the dying grouper impaled on the steel arrow. Gubby swayed forward, chuckling to himself at the absurdity of its size, while Trudi ran into the surf to steady Neil.

'Neil! It's so big. Jonah never saw such a fish . . . '

Trudi struggled with him in the bullish waves, her arms streaming with the grouper's blood. Inger left the fire and pulled Neil from the water, relieving him of fish and spear-gun.

'Poor Neil! It must have been a battle for you.' Inger rubbed away the pressure bruise around his mouth. 'Trudi, he's been kissing someone again. I think Neil has a lady friend in the sea . . . '

'We'll give you the biggest share,' Trudi assured him as she carried the grouper to the fire. 'You have half, and we take the rest. What a swimmer – you could swim back to Honolulu.'

'Don't give him an idea. We'd be starving without Neil.'

Neil stood swaying in the ashy sand, and flicked drops of water at the delighted Gubby. The women unbuckled the shoulder harness and lowered the oxygen cylinders to his feet. They unzipped the wet-suit, rolled the collar and flayed the black rubber skin from his shoulders. Inger squatted on her heels and pulled his swimming briefs to his ankles, plucked a strand of kelp from his scrotum and sat him down on the sand.   •

Waiting to catch his breath, Neil played with the baby while the women gutted and cleaned the fish, their forearms smeared with the entrails. The butcher's blade flashed between their hands as they severed the head and tail, stripped the heavy skin and impaled the scarcely dead beast on a bamboo stake.

Satisfied by the first sounds of fat hissing on the charcoal, the women draped a towel around Neil and dried him vigorously.

'Neil, you're the new Johnny Weissmuller,' Inger told him. 'Maybe you'll take us to Hollywood. Think, a Tarzan with two Janes . . . '

'No-one can fish like Neil,' Trudi agreed as she licked the blistering flesh. 'Not Wolfgang, and definitely not Werner. One day soon we'll love you, Neil . . . '

An hour later, when they had finished their meal, Neil reflected that it was a perfect day for a seduction, but it was the women who would seduce him, and in their own good time. Sea, sun and sky could not have been arranged more skilfully had Dr Barbara herself been in charge of the *mise en scène*. The sanctuary island was Neil's amatory bower, or so Dr Barbara hoped. After a week of storm-cloud and incessant gales, a benign sun now calmed the surface of the lagoon. During the days of rain the water had been too turbid for Neil to fish, and Inger and Trudi sat morosely under the dripping rattan of the beach hut he had built for them. They fiddled with their coral beads and refused to meet Neil's eyes when he served them their ration of fried plantain and sweet potato.

Now the water had cleared, and the fish rose to the surface of the lagoon, ready to attend a banquet. Dr Barbara had even allocated a jug of the coconut wine that Kimo brewed to Professor Saito's recipe. Convinced that the sexual auguries were in the right sphere, Dr Barbara allowed them to take Gubby from the clinic, as if the infant might remind Neil of his expected duties.

Despite the sun and the drowsy, groin-stirring pleasures of the sweet wine, Neil doubted that Dr Barbara's hopes would be fulfilled. He had been too tired, first by the task of building the hut, and then by the far greater effort needed to catch enough fish for the four of them, and had strained his lungs while trawling for the bulldozed oxygen cylinders that had rolled into the deep trench beside the reef.

Once he found the cylinders a steady supply of fish reached the charcoal spit, and Trudi and Inger soon rediscovered his attractions, but they still saw Neil as little more than a mascot and older brother of Gubby. Both women had begun to put on weight. Cut off from their amphetamines, acid and pot, they were transforming themselves into a pair of robust and strong-chinned Bavarian *Hausfrauen*. Years of experience in the bars outside the American air-bases made them more than a match for a sixteen-year-old, especially one as guileless as Neil.

Dr Barbara insisted that the baby be weaned, and Trudi reluctantly left Gubby at the clinic. She and Inger had both been pregnant when they joined Werner and Wolfgang, and gave birth together in Vancouver. Too feckless to care for her own child, a baby girl with a black American father, Inger abandoned it to the care of a Catholic adoption agency. Free of responsibility now, she and Trudi spent their time sunbathing outside the hut and waiting for the next meal.

'You've done wonders, Neil,' Dr Barbara had complimented him after the first month of this new regime, as she watched the two women saunter back to their tent. 'They do look splendid.'

'It's hard work, doctor.' Neil sat beside her desk in the clinic, gazing at his latest urine sample. 'Is this what marriage is like?'

'Not exactly. In marriage it's women who do the work and the men who take it easy – it's called going to the office.' She stared at the plant laboratory, from which Professor Saito rarely emerged, and at the radio-cabin that Carline had begun to rebuild. 'Rather like Saint-Esprit, in a way.'

'Are there any office jobs here, Dr Barbara?'

'No, and a good thing too.' She turned to face Neil with one of the intense smiles that always prefigured, he had noticed, a sudden swerve of policy. 'As it happens, though, I do have a job for Inger and Trudi.'

'Great.' The prospect cheered Neil. 'They could work on the farm.'

'Not the farm. I'm thinking of something more suited to their talents.'

'Talents?' Neil pondered this abyss. 'They're only good at lying on their backs.'

'Precisely.' Dr Barbara took the urine sample from Neil and returned it to the rack. 'Something along those lines had occurred to me.'

'What about the kitchen? They could help Monique.'

'They're overweight as it is. No, Neil, I think they should each have a baby.'

Neil turned to see how Gubby greeted this, as he sat in his baby-chair beside the window, eyes following Dr Barbara's imperious gestures. 'Well, Inger left her baby in Vancouver. And Trudi already has Gubby.'

'Yes, but he's . . . not very well.' She allowed Gubby to play with her fingers, though Neil was aware that she never looked the swollen-headed child in the eye. She touched Neil's still-warm urine sample, as if drawing inspiration from it. 'They need a fresh start, with a new husband. It would mark a true beginning, and really send a signal to the world.'

'If you spoke to them, doctor . . . I know they're both interested in sex. But who would be the fathers?'

'I'm thinking of only one father, in point of fact.'

'Wolfgang? He's their partner. Sometimes Werner slept with Trudi, if she was feeling edgy . . . '

'No!' Dr Barbara ruled this out. 'You can't breed thorough-breds from damaged blood-lines. Their DNA must look like used ticker-tape.'

'What about Kimo?'

'He's saving his semen for the new Hawaiian kingdom.'

'Or David?'

'Too old. And anyway he's already married.' Dr Barbara pressed the urine sample to Neil's forehead, like an archbishop crowning an adolescent king. 'Neil, I was thinking of you.'

'Doctor . . . ?' Startled, Neil tried to evade her advancing smile, approaching him like a tsunami. 'I don't think they would – '

'You're young, in the peak of health, and ready for responsibility. Why do you think I've been testing your blood and urine all this time? You do like them, don't you?' Dr Barbara seemed suddenly anxious for Neil. 'Or is Trudi too petite for you? Inger is a lot more sturdy, but those heavy breasts might be a little suffocating . . . '

'I like them both. They're – '

Dr Barbara had always been matter-of-fact about sex, noting in her diary how often he masturbated, but now her frankness unnerved him. He watched her stride up and down the floor, counting the chairs and medical vials with the distracted manner of a caged mathematician. For reasons of her own she had begun to neglect herself, no longer bothering to comb her hair, another sign that she hungered for change.

Dr Barbara had become bored with the sanctuary. Work filled every hour of their lives, and there was an unending struggle to maintain the animals and find enough food for themselves. She reluctantly accepted a consignment of animal feed that a Japanese whaler delivered to the island, but this respite merely allowed Kimo and Carline to laze in their tents. As the men weakened, more and more of the work now fell to the women, and in Dr Barbara's eyes the sanctuary had begun to imitate the worst kind of bourgeois life that she had known during her bleak Scottish childhood, with all of the chores and no conveniences.

Watching her as she stared severely at Gubby, Neil guessed that she was eager to let another radical dimension into the sanctuary, a disruptive element that would first unsettle and then steel them. All along she had tested them, exposing them to the French guns and the media glare, then rejecting the watching world and its aid. They had coped with these challenges, but by laying duckboards and digging deeper latrines, and Dr Barbara was now looking for another means of provoking them. Their sexuality, dormant since their arrival at Saint-Esprit, offered a potent weapon of self-disruption. The absurd confrontation over the powdered milk had left her angry with Neil, but now she realized that his urgent hormones could soon quicken the plodding pace of sanctuary life. Even the slightest hint that Neil was sexually involved with Trudi and Inger, and the father of their expected children, would light a touch-paper inside the minds of Monique and Mrs Saito.

Lying by the beach fire, and playing with the fish-tail in Gubby's hand, Neil gazed at the two women asleep beside him. The pearls of needle-scarred tissue on their thighs and arms had almost vanished. The listless hippies with their waxy and toneless skins who had limped ashore from the leaking yacht had been transformed by the diet of fish and Dr Barbara's vitamin injections. Without a second thought both had turned their backs on Werner and Wolfgang, who remained in the ruins of their shack encampment, trying to ready the *Parsifal* for sea. Frequently separated from her baby, Trudi was still unsettled by life in the sanctuary. Small and sharp-featured, she was the more astute of the pair, but neither she nor Inger had any idea of the plan that Dr Barbara had devised for them.

'Gubby, Gubby . . . ' Neil circled the child's head with the fish-tail, tickling his nose as Gubby followed his hand with a wondrous stare, eyes like camera windows under the bunker-like mass of his forehead. 'It's a flying fish, Gubby . . . '

'You like children, Neil,' Trudi remarked. The women had woken and leaned on their elbows, exposing their breasts to the sun. 'Did you have a young brother in England?'

'No. But Gubby's fun. And he's very intelligent.'

'Of course. He'll play games forever.' She pinched the child's nose, laughing when he emitted a trumpet-like roar. 'He loves you, Neil. You must be a natural father.'

'Well . . . ' Neil replied cautiously, aware that Dr Barbara was standing among the trees above the beach, a latter-day Margaret Mead watching the courtship rituals of an island tribe. 'I might be . . . I won't know until I've tried.'

'So you should try.' Inger lay on her side, inspecting Neil with a practised eye. She noted his long, swimmer's thighs and muscled shoulders, and mentally weighed his sand-covered scrotum. She touched his leg, running her forefinger across the hard tendon above his knee-cap that gathered his thigh muscles together like the clasped reins of a charioteer. 'Neil, did Dr Barbara talk to you?'

'Talk? What about?'

'Imporant things, of course.' Inger sipped from the wine jug. 'Dr Barbara only talks about important matters. Life and death, her precious animals.'

'The albatross,' Trudi reminded her.

'Naturally. Never forget the albatross.' Inger brushed the sand from Neil's nipple. 'One day they'll fly away and there will be no more sky.'

'No more life and death. Dr Barbara is too serious for life and death.' Trudi lay with her back to Neil, elbow resting on his hip. 'Now we must do what Dr Barbara tells us – fish and dream and make peace in the afternoon.'

Inger searched Neil's hair for any fleas. Lying between the two women, as the surf hissed against the sand and Gubby chuntered to himself, Neil felt the wine dim his brain, a haze of soft flesh and guttural endearments.

'Inger . . . ?'

'Yes, Neil?'

'Dr Barbara has a new idea. For you and Trudi.'

'Of course. We always follow Dr Barbara's ideas.'

'She explained it to me.' Neil searched for a delicate phrasing. 'She wants another baby.'

'That's nice. But she has you. You're her baby.'

'What she means is, she wants you to have a baby. You and Trudi.'

'But how?' Trudi seemed genuinely puzzled as she turned to face him. 'We can't do it ourselves, even for Dr Barbara.'

'Well, you wouldn't do it yourselves . . . '

'Show us, Neil.' Inger sat up, her breasts brushing Neil's chin. 'Can you show us, please? There must be some special equipment. Is it here? Or down here, maybe? Trudi, I think it's disappeared!'

'Poor Neil! Take him to the clinic and tell Dr Barbara . . . '

The two women were kneeling astride him, hooting with laughter as they poured sand over his groin. Realizing that they had been teasing him, and thumbing their noses at Dr Barbara, he tried to sit up, but Inger swore and pushed him down. Carline's angry voice sounded through the trees. There was a threatening rattle of bamboo clubs striking the palm trunks. Werner and Wolfgang had crossed the runway and were insolently lolling against the bulldozer. As Carline thrust at Wolfgang's tattooed chest, feinting with the straw hat in his left hand, Werner side-stepped the American and sprinted towards the beach. There was a shout from Kimo, who set off after him and raced down the sandy slope. Scarcely breaking his stride, he hurled Werner into the surf. Wolfgang, meanwhile, had already given up and was walking back to the shanties, kicking the coral surface of the runway into clouds of acrid dust.

'Neil, we leave you now.' Upset by the violence, Trudi gathered Gubby in her arms.

'We'll see you, Neil.' Inger brushed the sand from her arms. 'It's not nice today . . . '

They reached for their clothes, dressed quickly to hide themselves from Kimo and Carline, and hurried to the safety of their tent.

Mottled by the sunlight, the bed of the lagoon lay below Neil, the timeless floor of an embalmed garden. Giant sponges sat like ornamental shrubs among the anemones and sea-cucumbers, and groves of kelp waved their pennants at the undulating surface of the mirror floating fifty feet above them, through which Neil's face and arms protruded as if he were waking from a deep sleep.

Sliding over the side of the Andersons' dinghy, Neil let the cool water embrace him. He released the canvas sea-anchor and lifted the concrete flagstone resting on the stern seat. Filling his lungs, he held the heavy sink-weight to his chest and began his rapid descent towards the lagoon floor. Shoals of coral trout and blue-fish sped from his plunging feet, and a large sea-turtle approached to inspect him before rolling away like a top-heavy galleon.

After borrowing the dinghy, Neil had loaded it with heavy stones from the beach, though Kimo had often warned him that the pearl-fishermen's inertial diving might damage his lungs. But he was too tired to wear the oxygen cylinders and mask, and the sudden descents gave him a brief but clearer look at the lagoon deeps.

He had rowed two miles from the shore, to a point where the lines of sight from the camera-towers seemed to intersect. For some reason he had convinced himself that a caisson designed to hold an atomic weapon, or a device for anchoring nuclear mines, lay on the lagoon floor. If not the weapon itself, he would have found the core site of Saint-Esprit, the epicentre of all his dreams of Mururoa, Bikini and Eniwetok.

His feet touched the smooth sand, the momentum of his descent carrying him onto his knees. Still clutching the stone slab, he watched the pressure bubbles from his goggles race towards the surface. Speckled sea-snakes haunted the cliffs of dead coral that rose like encoded palaces through the dim water. The confrontation on the beach had unsettled him, exposing the many rivalries at the sanctuary, but here in the quiet deeps he felt at peace, on the dark edge where the volcanic crater shelved into the abyssal chill.

Twenty feet from him, sitting in a small glade of sponges, was the barnacled shell of a French patrol boat, its torpedo tubes like the claws of a giant lobster. The craft had assumed a coralline life of its own, its rails and ladders transformed into encrusted versions of themselves. Beyond it the fuselage of a drowned aircraft lay between its broken wings, the rear turret presiding over the lagoon, a deserted observation cage.

Curious to see the aircraft more closely, Neil released the flagstone and rose towards the surface, shedding the spangled air from his lungs into the startled faces of the watching fish. He climbed into the dinghy and rested for half an hour among the heavy stones, then shipped the sea-anchor and rowed the few oar-lengths to the aircraft's position.

His second descent carried him down to the plane, a two-engined bomber of unfamiliar design. Fending off a small reef-shark, Neil watched the fuselage rise towards him. Through the open canopy he could see the pilot's barnacled seat and controls. It occurred to him that the French might have called off their nuclear tests after the bomber's crash, and that the aircraft was in some way implicated in the programme of atomic trials.

Neil released the cement building block and seized the tail-plane above his head, pulling himself to the empty turret. Lying on the seat in this steel bower were the remnants of an armoured vest and flying suit, seams unravelled by generations of searching fish. Whether the suit's owner had escaped from the bomber with the rest of the crew he could only guess, but as his bursting lungs swept him towards the surface he seemed to glimpse a clutch of bones lying below the seat. A few vertebrae or detached ribs, they resembled the remnants of a meal laid out for Neil, one course in that banquet of death that had filled his boyish mind. He broke the surface and clung to the bows of the dinghy, realizing that all the waters of the lagoon had passed through the filter of those bones.

Soon after Neil's discovery of the drowned bomber the members of the expedition fell ill with a recurrent dysenteric fever. Kimo was the first to succumb. Cutting palm logs on the hillside above the plant terraces, he collapsed over his axe, racked by cramp. He rested and returned to work, but fell to his knees again and was helped to his tent by Neil and Carline. He lay there shivering for three days, barely able to hold Dr Barbara's thermometer between his teeth.

Professor Saito and Monique were next to be affected. Mrs Saito found her husband lying among the seedling orchids in the plant laboratory. After a feverish night he ate a bowl of tepid tapioca, which set off another bout of vomiting and diarrhoea. By then Monique had failed to cook the expedition's breakfasts, and Dr Barbara found her in the cemetery beside the prayer-shack, calling for her father and rambling to herself over his soiled grave.

Trudi and Inger set about boiling all the pans and utensils in the kitchen. Dr Barbara ordered Neil to destroy any eggs that the hens might lay, and for the next days they lived on the few fish that Neil could catch and the dwindling stocks of canned food in the storage tent.

Neil was impressed by the way in which Dr Barbara rose to the challenge of this mysterious fever, even when displaying the first symptoms. She insisted on doing her rounds of the sick, as the sweat greased the cold wax of her forehead, and supervised the digging of new latrines.

Fearing that in some way all the fish in the lagoon had been poisoned by his dreams of nuclear explosions, Neil felt a growing guilt that he had brought on the sickness. He tried to tell Dr Barbara of the bones he had glimpsed in the drowned bomber, but she was too exhausted to listen to him.

'Ask David to keep an eye on Trudi and Inger – they may have brought something nasty with them from the Marquesas. Then help Mrs Saito to wash her husband. You'll have to boil the sheets. Thank God, you're the strongest of us, Neil.'

'Dr Barbara – the skeleton I saw . . . part of a skeleton, any-way. The lagoon may be poisoned.'

'Nonsense. If there is a skeleton the poor man's bones were picked clean twenty years ago. This isn't a time for superstition, Neil.'

Fortunately, Professor Saito soon discovered the source of the fever. As they all suspected, the hippies had infected the sanctuary. Rousing himself from his sick-bed, the botanist tested samples from the water-purifier beside the reservoir. A huge concentration of coliform bacteria had overwhelmed the filters, and his further analysis of the liquid in the aqueduct confirmed that the camp's water supply was contaminated by faecal matter.

Neil remained sceptical, but everyone agreed that Werner and Wolfgang had taken a perverted revenge for what they saw as the abduction of their womenfolk. A last punitive expedition was set for the following night when Carline and Mrs Saito would lead a raiding party that would drive the Germans forever from Saint-Esprit.

Still exhausted by his fever, Professor Saito assembled a temporary distillation system that provided a small but secure supply of sterile drinking-water. Dr Barbara, pierced by a deep chill and irritated by the fractious cries of the baby, lay inside her

mosquito net at the clinic as Carline planned the assault with
Kimo and Mrs Saito. The Andersons were too old to join the
raiding party, but protested when they visited the camp to care
for Dr Barbara and found Carline draining the fuel from the
bulldozer's donkey engine.

'David . . . ' Major Anderson tried to stop him filling a wine
bottle with the gasoline. 'Isn't this against the whole spirit of the
sanctuary? We can't be sure the pollution was deliberate.'

'Major, people have been saying that for a hundred years.'
Carline tore the lapel from his cotton shirt and stuffed it into the
bottle's neck. 'But what do we see? All over the world chemicals
are pouring into rivers, effluents are fouling our beaches and
poisoning our children. Just for once, let's assume it *was* deliberate.'

'Why not talk to them?' Mrs Anderson suggested, squinting at the bomb as if trying to read its vintage. 'We can
compromise . . . '

'Too late, Mrs Anderson. We came here to save life, and I
won't allow us to be destroyed . . . '

Carline seemed shaky but determined, as if seizing this last
chance to prove himself. The endless doubts that had dogged his
life, the lack of self-confidence that had nagged at his well-shod
heels, were about to be dispelled. Like Dr Barbara, he thrived on
tension. All the well-bred certainties of his upbringing had
conspired to devalue him, and now he could redeem himself in
the simplest way. Neil had noticed that he was one of the few
members of the expedition not to fall ill. Had Carline poisoned
the water supply, drawn the obscene graffiti on the camera-
tower, strangled the chicken? All were juvenile acts, the revenge
of a perpetual child against the overbearing nanny within himself.

Wanting no part of the assault on the peaceable Germans, Neil
waited by the airstrip. Kimo and Mrs Saito set off through the
forest, but Carline commandeered the Andersons' dinghy, in-
tending to mount what he clearly saw as a surprise landing from
the sea in the style of General MacArthur. Neil listened to

Gubby's wearying cries from the clinic, as the American rowed strongly through the dark surf, eager to seize the beach and burn down the modest shacks.

But Carline was after a more tempting target. Neil watched the waves beyond the beach, where a canopy of flame enveloped the sinking sloop. Exploding gasoline drenched the hull of the *Parsifal*, crazing the psychedelic patterns. The rigging fell from the mast, ropes coiling like catherine wheels.

Wolfgang leapt naked from his shack and sprinted down the beach into the water, but the yacht was already capsizing, its cabin glowing like an incandescent lantern. As they watched from the shore even Kimo and Mrs Saito seemed startled by the craft's destruction. Carline rowed through the burning waves, his oars scooping up pockets of flame, grinning owlishly to himself like a drunken parent at a deranged children's party.

Turning his back on them all, Neil crossed the runway and set off for the lagoon. Below the beach hut the surf sluiced across the ashy sand, overrunning the remains of the barbecue where he had fed the two women and played with Gubby. The last of the grouper's bones were withdrawing into the deep, eager to join the sleeping eminence of the lagoon.

When he returned to the camp an hour later the embers of the burning yacht had faded as the gutted hulk settled to the ocean floor. Saint-Esprit was dark again, lit only by the albatross circling the alarmed sky and by the sea rinsing the black shores like a tireless washerwoman of the night.

'Monique! Trudi!'

Torch-beams flared from the windows of the clinic. Inger was sobbing on the steps, comforted by Mrs Anderson, while Kimo paced around the door, calming himself like a compassionate policeman at a tragic roadside accident. Roused by the noise, Professor Saito stepped from the plant laboratory, buttoning his shirt around his narrow shoulders.

Had Dr Barbara died? Neil felt the runway slip beneath his feet. He imagined her body borne in state along the pale coral to the cemetery beside the prayer-shack. Saint-Esprit, its fluted cliffs and its albatross seemed to slide into the lagoon as he ran towards the clinic and stepped past the weeping Inger, trying to read Kimo's solemn face in the swerving torch-beams.

Major Anderson stood beside Dr Barbara's bed, his hand raising the mosquito net as if releasing the death-spring of a trap. He shone his torch into the white bower where Dr Barbara rested on her sweat-swollen pillow, blonde hair caked to a damp peruke. Her eyes rolled in the torch-beam, and for a moment she seemd to be far out to sea in the burning *Parsifal*.

'Dr Barbara . . .' Neil pushed past Major Anderson and knelt beside the bed. 'It's Neil, Dr Barbara. Don't die . . .'

Monique drew him away, refusing to meet Dr Barbara's gaze. When she embraced Neil he could feel her heart beating through her breasts.

'Dr Barbara is not dead,' she assured him. 'Her fever is down. Sadly, there is a death . . .'

Mrs Anderson stood beside the baby's cot, and lifted the large pillow that covered Gubby's face. The child lay still, hands forced behind his back, pupils unmoving in the veering lights. Mrs Anderson placed her hand under Gubby's stony head, lifting it so that everyone could see the vacant gaze.

But Neil was staring at the pillow. The damp cotton was marked with vomit, like Monsieur Didier's pillow-slip after his death, and stained with the same bloody imprint of a mouth.

12

Fever in the Blood

WRINGING A CRY from the air, an albatross soared past the summit, its black wing-tips outstretched as if trying to strike Neil's face. He rested against the plinth of the radio mast and waved at the solitary creature restlessly hunting the wind. Bored by the sky, the sea-birds sat at the cliff's edge like passengers delayed forever at an unknown terminal, a nomadic tribe misplaced by time.

Thousands of albatross now gathered at Saint-Esprit, the one undoubted success of Dr Barbara's sanctuary dream. While Neil roamed the island, searching the forest paths and swimming to the outlying sand-bars of the atoll, he would hear their monotonous voices crying to the white-haired woman who had abandoned them.

Neil walked along the cliff, scanning the wooded slopes above the plant terraces. Viewed from the summit, all seemed at peace in the camp beside the runway, an impression taken back to Papeete by the few light aircraft that photographed the island. Smoke rose from the kitchen fire, where Monique was preparing breakfast. Inger and Trudi had already spent an hour at the washing tub, and a line of sheets hung between the trees. In the pantry behind the plant laboratory Mrs Saito was curing fish and pickling the sea-fruit she found in the rock-pools below the cliff.

None of the men had stirred. It was past ten in the morning, but Kimo and Carline still lay in their tents, already tired by the prospect of a day spent pounding taro and hunting for yams. Later, Carline would amble over to the burnt-out radio-cabin and tinker with the dials and microphone as he mused upon the fate of his marooned airport. Kimo, even more disoriented than Neil by Dr Barbara's absence, found companionship of a kind among the endangered inmates of the animal enclosures, though he had allowed several of the rare birds to escape. In the afternoon Professor Saito would emerge from the plant laboratory, blinking at the sun, and join Mrs Anderson for an hour's work, weeding and watering the overgrown plant terraces while Major Anderson sat stern-faced in the cockpit of the sloop, reluctant to step onto Saint-Esprit's blighted sand.

All seemed well, but without Dr Barbara the sanctuary had lost its compass-bearing. Neil missed her keenly, and even now, three weeks after her disappearance, found it difficult to grasp that she no longer stood on the steps of the clinic, scolding him as he dawdled around Inger and Trudi before setting off to fish. He assumed that she had fled the island, accepting a lift from a passing yacht, aware that the French authorities would soon be investigating the child's death.

No-one was certain that Dr Barbara had killed the baby, but they all behaved as if they could still see the blood-stained pillow in her hands. Neil remembered how she ignored the expedition members as she sipped her tea the next morning, shaking off the last of her fever. Kimo had played with his callused fists, weighing and re-weighing this little death, before going off to the cemetery to dig a furious grave. Professor Saito and his wife retreated to the sanity of the plant laboratory, minds flicking at an impossible moral abacus, while Monique hunched over a photograph of her father, clearly suspecting that he too had been deliberately killed. Only Carline seemed unmoved, smiling tightly as he watched Dr Barbara with a kind of fearful admiration.

The Andersons, however, had decided to take action. Disgusted by Gubby's death, they prepared their sloop for the voyage to Tahiti, ready to sail on the first tide, and determined to report their suspicions to the prefect of police within an hour of docking. They joined Neil and the four grieving Germans as Kimo carried the baby to the cemetery in the small coffin that he had nailed together from an empty toy crate. Angry with themselves for not protecting the child, the old couple waited as Neil shovelled the black sand over the box.

'That's enough.' Major Anderson waved Neil away. 'We won't fuss over it. The lad isn't going anywhere.'

Mrs Anderson held Neil's hand when they walked from the cemetery, leaving Werner and Wolfgang to comfort the young women. The attack on the beach shacks and the destruction of the *Parsifal* had been forgotten after the discovery of the dead baby. Carline had even offered his sympathies to the two hippies, managing to turn the burning of the yacht and Gubby's death into the unhappy consequences of an over-intense collegiate game. But Mrs Anderson was well aware that Dr Barbara was playing to stricter rules.

'Neil, you'll be sure to watch yourself? Be careful of Dr Barbara. Perhaps you should come with us.'

'I'll be all right, Mrs Anderson. Dr Barbara won't hurt me.'

'Don't be certain of that. Poor Gubby, I know how much you liked him. He wasn't the first and he may not be the last.'

'Mrs Anderson . . . no-one saw Dr Barbara kill Gubby.' Trying to stem the slide of suspicion that threatened to bury Dr Barbara, Neil watched her walk head-down towards the clinic, apparently oblivious of Saint-Esprit, the sanctuary and the albatross circling above her. 'They're just making her a scapegoat because they're tired and want to blame someone. We knew the sanctuary would be hard work.'

'We didn't know that people would be killed.' Mrs Anderson listened to Trudi's crying carried on the wind. 'First Monique's father and now Gubby. Who's next, Neil?'

'Monique's father wasn't killed. He died of a stroke.'

'I'm sure he did.' Major Anderson seemed puzzled that Neil should defend Dr Barbara, as if suspecting that he had aided her. 'Suffocation can do hateful things to the brain. Dr Barbara claimed she found him the next morning. Yet we saw her inside the clinic soon after midnight, closing the mosquito net.'

'And again at two o'clock,' Mrs Anderson added. 'What was she doing, Neil? We'd like to know.'

'She was helping him to sleep,' Neil insisted stolidly.

'That's what we feared. But what kind of sleep?'

Neil tried to argue Dr Barbara's case, but the old couple were determined to take their suspicions to the French authorities. He was pushing their dinghy into the waves, resigned to seeing them sail from Saint-Esprit, when Carline caught up with them. He strode into the water, ignoring the surf that surged around his thighs, and seized the dinghy's tiller. His shirt still reeked of the gasoline that had spilled from his incendiary bomb, but for once he was resolute. The others had been confused by the events of the night, but Neil realized that for Carline the death of the child had clarified everything.

'You're leaving, Major?'

'Not soon enough. Though I dare say we'll be back. You'll be expected to give a statement.'

'I'll speak as honestly as I can.' Carline's candid smile met the Andersons' stony faces. 'Think about it, Major. If you call in the French it's all over. The sanctuary will be as dead as little Gubby. Everything you've done, every hour of hard work, will be wasted.'

Major Anderson pointed to Dr Barbara, who stood hands on hips in the doorway of the clinic, as if challenging anyone to enter her parlour. 'That woman killed the child. Even you can't ignore the fact. Now, we need to get aboard.'

Carline tried to calm the waves, his long arms steadying the dinghy. 'No-one saw her, Major. We can settle the matter ourselves, and keep the sanctuary going. Think of all the work you've done.'

'We'll live with that. It was given freely.'

'Then think of the albatross.' As Major Anderson raised his oar, ready to strike Carline in the chest, the American seized the blade. 'And think of Neil.'

'The boy will be well. She won't harm him.'

'Maybe not in an obvious way. Who knows what she has planned? You've heard the rumours, Mrs Anderson . . . '

This brutal appeal at last persuaded the reluctant Andersons to remain for the next few weeks, giving them time to question Dr Barbara and convince Neil to join them on the voyage to Tahiti.

Their decision to stay, like Carline's determination to preserve the sanctuary, brought about a curious change of heart. For all the anger, no settling of accounts with Dr Barbara took place that day. To Neil's surprise, the women were the first to come to terms with the child's death. Mrs Saito ushered her lightheaded husband back to the plant laboratory, and Mrs Anderson steered the Major to the cooler altitudes of the cultivated terraces. Everyone, even Werner and Wolfgang, realized that the survival of Saint-Esprit depended on their silence.

One by one, they returned to their tasks. They worked slowly, now and then lowering their hoes and machetes to stare at the silent camera-towers, as if sensing that their complicity in a crime was being invisibly filmed. Dr Barbara retreated to the clinic, and remained all day behind the locked door of her office.

The next morning, when the Andersons demanded to speak to her, they found that she had gone.

Were the albatross aware of their reprieve? Leaving the cliff, Neil made his way down the forest path, while the huge birds clustered shoulder to shoulder on their rocky perches, wary eyes on the changing wind. A single albatross soared along the beach, drawn to the stream where Dr Barbara had strolled with the skipper of the *Croix du Sud*. It swerved to and fro, unsettled by something it had seen beneath the forest canopy.

A line of wet footprints glistened on the black sand, and led to a narrow trail overgrown with ferns and cycads. The dewy spoor climbed the steep hillside towards an abandoned weather-station a hundred feet below the cliff. Neil had explored the trail soon after arriving at Saint-Esprit. The unmanned station, once packed with radio and barometric gear, was a dank concrete cell built into the mouth of a small cave, little more than a narrow sinus in the bony face of the cliff.

Neil left the path and made his way towards the weather-station, sliding through the scree of loose pumice that sloped from the tree-line. When he reached the trail he found the footprints were still damp, as if the forest visitor had bathed fully clothed in the stream. The cliff fell away to the rocks below, where the sea stirred ceaselessly, rearranging itself amid the volcanic rubble. Neil crouched behind the tamarinds that crowded the narrow path, listening to the demented bird. The rocky slope was strewn with bones and feathers, a gaudy copper plumage that he had last seen in the aviary beside the mammal houses.

From within the weather-station came the sounds of water pouring into a metal tin. A pale-haired woman in a damp shirt and shorts stepped into the sunlight, a collection of bloody scraps in her hand. She picked her strong nose and watched the excited bird, happy to tease it. With a coarse shout, she hurled the scraps into the air, laughing to herself as the albatross plunged towards the rocks below.

Neil stood up and climbed the stony path to the station. Only as Dr Barbara turned on him, machete in hand, did he realize that she might attack him.

'Neil . . . ?' Recognizing him, she stepped forward, warily searching the forest trail. Accepting that he was alone, she at last treated him to the barest smile. Her face was sallow and toneless, but flared with a brief rush of colour as she took his shoulders. 'I knew you'd come. How did you find me?'

'I followed the albatross.'

'I should have guessed – we've been together too long.'

Neil touched her frayed hair and scuffed forehead, nervous of the enlarged pupils that ranged across his face, and aware that she barely remembered him. She had washed herself in the stream, but he could almost taste her hands with their reek of blood and fat.

'I looked for you all over Saint-Esprit, doctor. Every day for three weeks.'

'I know. I saw you swimming between the sand-bars.' Dr Barbara was still watching him in her unsettling way, as if she had spent too much time among the albatross and was waiting for his wings to unfurl themselves. 'Have you told anyone I'm here?'

'No . . . I'll never tell them.'

'Good. It's best for them not to know. Come in – you look as if you need to sit down.'

She beckoned him into the cave behind the concrete chamber, where her sleeping bag lay on a mattress of palm fronds. There was a primus stove, a satchel filled with food cans, a canvas stool and water bucket. These modest props formed a shabby tableau, like the den of a down-at-heel sorceress.

'Sit there, Neil. I can see you're tired.'

Dr Barbara's black valise rested on the stool, a hypodermic syringe in a kidney dish beside it. She moved the syringe and lay down on the sleeping bag, adjusting her gaze to take in the long-limbed adolescent who filled the cave like a gawky animal. To Neil she seemed alternately drained and flushed, as if she had decided not to throw off the effects of her fever, incubating some reserve infection that she might put to use.

'Tell me, Neil – how is the sanctuary? Is Kimo still looking after the animals for you? I hope he's feeding them every day. And Monique . . . ?'

'They're fine, just about.' Neil moved her idle hand from his knee. 'Are you coming back, Dr Barbara? The sanctuary isn't the same any more. They really need you.'

'Do they? I'm not sure.' She stared through the open doorway at the horizon, as if expecting to see the top-masts of an approaching vessel. 'I wanted them to look ahead, to what the sanctuary might become, but I moved them too quickly.'

'You were right, doctor. They just need more time – then they'll understand.'

'Time . . . ?' Dr Barbara felt for the syringe, reminding herself of its position. 'We've wasted enough time as it is. The French will soon be here, Neil. They'll want to take me with them.'

'The French aren't coming, doctor. Everyone thinks you're still working in the clinic. You can stay at Saint-Esprit as long as you like.'

Dr Barbara roused herself, taking a closer interest in Neil. 'Didn't the Andersons leave for Papeete? Their yacht's still here, but I thought they had gone. They were so upset by that sad child . . . '

'They didn't leave. David explained everything to them. If the French take you away from Saint-Esprit all the albatross will die.

No-one's said anything about Gubby, not even Trudi and Inger.'

Dr Barbara picked at an infected mosquito bite on her hand. She rested her head on the pillow of the sleeping bag and drowsily reached out to touch Neil, reassured that her retreat to this dismal cave had proved its point.

'I'm sorry Gubby died. You were so fond of him. But he was really very handicapped.'

'I know he was, doctor.' Unsettled by her drugged calm, Neil tried to ignore the albatross that circled the weather-station, screaming over the bones. 'Trudi hoped he might get better. I was teaching him to read. Still, one day he would have grown up.'

'He would, Neil. That's what the others refused to grasp. What sort of future waited for that little chap? He was an out-of-time baby, born into a world without a future. Doctors often have to be unkind. Gubby was all they could think about – the sanctuary was turning into his crèche. You always trusted me, Neil.'

'I still trust you, Dr Barbara. Gubby couldn't read, not properly. We all trust you, even old Major Anderson.'

'The old Major . . . ?' Dr Barbara massaged the needle puncture on her left arm. 'Sometimes it's a mistake to be too old. I trust you, too, Neil – but I'm not sure if the others are strong enough. David and Kimo have worked hard, like Professor Saito, but they've started to fall ill, and soon they'll be sick all the time, just as little Gubby was.'

'We're strong enough, doctor – you and I. We'll run the sanctuary together. The others can go if they want.'

'Neil . . . ' Touched by his naïveté, Dr Barbara pinched his cheek. 'I'm too old for you, sadly. You need younger women, even younger than Trudi and Inger.'

'We can invite more people to Saint-Esprit,' Neil explained, relieved that Dr Barbara was looking to the future. 'Just announce that you want some extra volunteers – a lot of men will follow you here.'

'One man is enough, Neil. A man with the right fever in the blood.' Dr Barbara stared coolly at Neil. 'In fact we need women more than men. Women work harder and survive on less.'

'They certainly do – Monique and Mrs Saito never stop working and hardly eat at all.'

'I should have brought more women with me, but I had to make do with the men . . . '

Dr Barbara turned away from Neil. She had fallen asleep, one hand over the hypodermic syringe. Her flat voice worried Neil, and he tried not to look at the needle-marks on her arms, hoping that they were vitamin injections. She was thin and under-nourished, her pallid skin the colour of the rare arctic mush-rooms in Professor Saito's plant laboratory. Despite her welcome, a distance had opened between them that he was eager to close. As she slept, blonde hair in the sweaty hollow of her pillow, he leaned forward and whispered:

'Dr Barbara, I understand why you killed Gubby . . . '

An hour after dusk Dr Barbara woke refreshed from her sleep. She brushed the frayed hair from her forehead and tested her teeth, blue eyes taking in the darkened cave. Outside the weather-station a dozen albatross veered like flecks of flayed skin against a sky that seemed to be the back-projection of her threatening dreams. Neil had sat beside her, watching her recover her strength, heartened by her deep snores and the childlike puttering as she broke wind. He waved away the mosquitoes, and kept watch for any French patrol boat that might arrive.

'Right, Neil . . . ' Dr Barbara sat up, taking control of her modest realm. 'You must be hungry.'

Neil searched through the few cans in the satchel, squinting at the labels. 'Ravioli, frankfurters . . . I can cook for you.'

'Leave those, you need fresh meat. No time to fish now, so we'll go hunting.'

'Hunting? There's nothing to hunt.'

'There's everything to hunt, Neil. All kinds of game on Saint-Esprit, as you'll find out . . . '

Her sleep had transformed the lethargic hermit of the weather-station into the determined Dr Barbara of the *Dugong*. She waited impatiently as night settled over the island, striding up and down the parapet with the energy of a young woman. At last she hitched up her shorts, beckoned to Neil and set off along the path. Barely keeping pace with her nimble feet, Neil followed her down the steep hillside. She darted between the tamarinds, hacking at the fronds with her machete. They waded through the ferns towards the stream, following the narrow valley as it sloped through the forest to the beach. The camera-tower emerged from the restless shadows, the wind sighing through its observation slits.

Neil stood beside the blood-dark graffiti as Dr Barbara bathed her face and shoulders in the stream.

'Good, let's find our supper.' She wiped the silver moisture from her forehead and grimaced at the obscene drawing of herself on the worn cement. 'Ugly thing . . . I hope I'm a better doctor than an artist.'

She set out along the forest path below the disused aqueduct, barely visible only ten feet in front of him, strong shoulders feinting between the trees. Neil stumbled after her, glancing back at the graffiti on the tower and trying to understand Dr Barbara's motives. She had killed the chicken, smearing its entrails on the wall in an attempt to provoke him, and then poisoned the water in the aqueduct with her own excrement . . .

They stepped through the screen of palms beside the runway. Without pausing, Dr Barbara strode past the tents where the expedition members lay asleep. Steam rose from the distillation plant, a pale wraith floating on the shoulder of the wind. She paused to test the padlocked door of the clinic, and waved Neil towards the animal enclosures.

'Wait here for me. Now, Neil, cock . . . ? It's always the best.'

'What? Dr Barbara . . . ?'

'Cock or hen? Which do you want? Never mind . . . '

Machete in hand, she slipped through the wire and vanished into the darkness among the cages. Neil tried to calm the swaying fence and listened to the restive animals retreating into their lairs. He waited for a light to flare in the plant laboratory, certain that torch-beams would criss-cross the tents as Kimo roused the women.

There was a brief flurry of feathers from one of the cages, the sound of talons desperately raking a plywood wall. Dr Barbara reappeared before Neil could part the wires for her. She stepped through the fence, blood dripping from her left hand. In the other she held the trembling body of a rare Mikado pheasant which a Taiwanese surgeon had dedicated to the sanctuary. Beneath the limp coxcomb its swollen eyes stared at Dr Barbara, as if recognizing her for the first time.

13

Hunters and Lovers

AS THE LAST EMBERS of the fire faded in the evening air, Dr Barbara sat forward on the canvas stool and blew at the glowing ash. Her strong face, so ruddy in the flames, became pale and unstructured as the dying charcoal drew the light into itself. Giving up any hope of reviving the fire, she wiped the fat from her chin and tucked the hypodermic syringe into its leather wallet.

Neil sat on the floor beside her, sucking at the dark flesh of the pheasant, which reminded him of the over-ripe gamebirds he had so hated as a child. Dr Barbara had relished the meal, tearing apart the soft breast as if this was her treat of the day. Neil was still shocked by the way in which she had killed the creature, expertly wringing its neck. If the sanctuary was unable to protect the birds, what could it protect? Thinking of the hours he had spent feeding the endangered pheasant and cleaning out its pen, he realized that he had been fattening it for a midnight feast.

As he lit the fire Dr Barbara had put her dissection-room skills to work, cutting off the head, feet and wings. She briskly eviscerated the bird, whose entrails still gleamed in a heap of mucilage beside the fire. The sight of blood seemed to stimulate her, even more than the 'vitamin' shot she injected as an aperitif while Neil hunted the forest path for kindling.

When the fire died she dipped her forefinger in the entrails, searching for the pheasant's heart, and solemnly marked Neil's forehead.

'There, Neil – you'll remember me forever.' Admiring the paisley-patterned blood on her arms, she added: 'One day, who knows, you may eat me . . .'

'Wolfgang and Werner are eating the dead albatross,' Neil told her. 'What happens to the sanctuary now?'

'It's still here. More than ever. Living on my own, I've found the real sanctuary we were looking for.'

'Real?' Neil picked a shard of bone from his teeth. 'Half an hour ago this Mikado pheasant was real.'

'It wasn't real!' Dr Barbara snorted at the thought. 'Saint-Esprit was a fantasy we invented, a make-believe world we put together from all that animal rights sentimentality.'

'It wasn't just sentiment, doctor. You wanted to save the albatross.'

'I do now.' Concerned for Neil, she wiped the blood from his forehead. 'I'm sorry, Neil – first you watch me steal the pheasant and then I make you eat it.'

'It was tasty – better than grouper or blue-fish. But if we go on eating the animals there won't be a sanctuary left.'

'No, Neil . . . try to think what the sanctuary was really for. Why did we come to Saint-Esprit? It wasn't the birds – there's no shortage of albatross in the world.'

'You said they were threatened.'

'So they are, but they'll survive. Whether a few albatross or laboratory rats and beagles die isn't here or there. It's we who are threatened – Monique and myself, Mrs Saito, Inger and Trudi, even poor old Mrs Anderson, playing batman to the Major . . . I'm surprised he hasn't taught her to salute.'

'Monique and Mrs Saito? You mean the women?'

'Yes! We women!' Dr Barbara gazed triumphantly at the roof of the cave, as if welcoming a convert. 'Saint-Esprit isn't a sanctuary for the albatross, it's a sanctuary for women – or could be. We're the most endangered species of all. We came here to save the albatross and what did we do? We turned Saint-Esprit into just another cosy suburb, where we do all the work, and all the caring and carrying, all the planning and worrying.'

'Kimo works. So does David.' Neil tossed the drumstick into the ashes, uneasy with Dr Barbara's self-hating tone. 'And Professor Saito. He's catalogued thousands of rare plants.'

'They're boys, Neil, and they play their boys' games. They hunt and fish and collect their stamps while Inger and Trudi haul

170

the water and Monique bakes the bread. By God, if I see her bake another baguette I'll . . . burst!'

'She likes baking bread. Mrs Saito likes washing clothes. Inger and Trudi liked looking after Gubby.'

'Of course they did. Who were the first domesticated animals? Women! We domesticated ourselves. But I know women are made of fiercer stuff. We have spirit, passion, fire, or used to. We can be cruel and violent, even more than men. We can be killers, Neil. Be wary of us, very wary . . . '

'And what about the men?'

'Men?' Dr Barbara hesitated, as if confronting a small over-sight. 'There are too many men, Neil. We simply don't need so many men today. The biggest problem the world faces is not that there are too few whales or pandas, but too many men.'

'So what happens to them?'

'Who knows? Or cares? Their time has passed, they belong with the dugong and the manatee. Science and reason have had their day, their place is the museum. Perhaps the future belongs to magic, and it's we women who control magic. We'll always need a few men, but very few, and I'm only concerned with the women. I want Saint-Esprit to be a sanctuary for all their threatened strengths, their fire and rage and cruelty . . . '

Neil listened to the cries of the albatross in the darkness. He could hear their wings on the wind, as if they were flying through the vast spaces of Dr Barbara's icy dreams. Trying to reassure her, he began to pick the dried blood from her arm.

'Come back, Dr Barbara. We miss you at the sanctuary. Kimo and David can't survive without you.'

'Can they survive with me?' Dr Barbara laughed to herself. 'I'll make huge demands on them. Can they think like women? Are they strong enough?'

'I'll be strong, doctor.'

'I know you will. You're the only one who's understood me.' Dr Barbara shivered in the cool air that rose from the sea, chilling the damp cave. She turned towards the sleeping bag, and held Neil with a firm hand when he tried to leave.

'It's too late for you to go. We'll sleep here. I need you tonight, Neil . . . '

*　　*　　*

For the next week Neil lived with Dr Barbara, rarely moving out of her sight. By day they roved the island together, hacking pathways through the deep forest, and observing the faltering life of the sanctuary. For the first time Neil realized that he too had played a modest role in giving the expedition members their sense of purpose. His fishing, his idle but equable nature, his unsuccessful courtship of Inger and Trudi, and his obsession with swimming and nuclear weapons had provided a yardstick against which they could measure themselves.

Once he had gone, they rarely talked to each other. In many ways Neil, rather than Dr Barbara, was what they shared in common. His devotion to the sanctuary and its animals reminded them of why they had come to Saint-Esprit. An adolescent, apart from anything else, needed to be fed, even if most of his food he foraged for himself.

Now only Mrs Anderson bothered to tend the animals, the plant terraces were overgrown, and no-one hunted for yams and sweet potatoes. They had eaten the last of the chickens and were living off the reserves of canned food that Dr Barbara had bequeathed them. Mrs Saito chopped firewood for the furnace of the desalination plant, and Trudi and Inger carried water to the kitchens, where Monique served a single meal in the early afternoon.

Meanwhile Carline sat under his straw hat by the ruin of the radio-cabin, keeping watch over his runway. Kimo, befuddled by coconut wine, rested in his tent. Professor Saito rarely ventured from the plant laboratory, still recovering from his bout of fever. The sanctuary had shrunk to his trays of rare fungi and his threatened orchids, and he would sometimes stare out at the runway and the lagoon as if failing to recognize the island. Mrs Saito would lead him from the door, allowing him to exercise himself and pointing to the familiar trees with the formal manner of a psychiatric nurse.

Was Dr Barbara waiting for them to recall her to the sanctuary, or trying to provoke them into reporting her to the yacht-crews who visited the island? Major Anderson sat in the cockpit of his sloop, every detail of her misrule registered by his stern gaze, and Neil deliberately posed beside Dr Barbara, aware that the Andersons would never alert the French authorities while Neil remained with her, fearful that he might become her next victim.

By now, Neil's days as a hunter and his nights as Dr Barbara's lover had set all his doubts aside. He was ruled by the temper of this drugged and wayward woman, unnerved by the strength of her thighs when she rode him like a trainer breaking a colt, using her long breasts to bridle his mouth. Bruised by her hands, but eager to be used by her, he was obsessed by the scent of her nipples, which were scarred by ulcers as if the deranged Gubby had devoured them while she smothered him. Seizing Neil's shoulders, she knelt across him, urging him on long after he was exhausted.

At times it seemed to Neil that she was testing him against the men she remembered from her past, measuring his heart and lungs and genitals against those of the yacht-captains and life-guards who had been her lovers. Wiping the spit from his face, she stared at him with the knowing gaze of an adult abusing a child. When she urinated on him, smiling as the hot jet stung the salt-water sores on his chest, she playfully pressed her hand over his mouth and laughed through her chipped teeth as he fought and gasped for air.

At the end Neil would take her sweat-drenched head in his hands and hold it to his shoulder, embracing her while he smoothed the hair on her forehead. Trying to calm her, he caressed her cheeks, listening to the albatross bicker over the bone tip. He knew that Dr Barbara was preparing him for the task that lay ahead, satisfying herself that he was equal to whatever demands she would make on him. He waited for her to show him the affection she had displayed during the voyage from Honolulu, but affection was far from Dr Barbara's mind.

The albatross screamed through the nights, crying to the bones.

The white seaplane had landed, and was taxiing across the lagoon. As he sat on the steps of the weather-station, the charcoal ashes at his feet, Neil watched Captain Garfield manoeuvre the craft towards the pier. Plumes of spray lifted from the surface of the lagoon, like vents of steam from the drowned crater of the volcano.

Making his monthly visit despite Dr Barbara's interdiction, Captain Garfield would bring mail, a sack of children's get-well cards, fresh fruit and milk, one or two curious journalists and more donated animals for the sanctuary. Distracted by their tasks, or by the rigours of deck-chair and hammock, the expedition members scarcely noticed the seaplane mooring by the pier. Often Carline would not even leave his charred seat in the radio-cabin, and Kimo would merely flick the flap of his tent, while Monique briefly glanced at the new arrivals over her taro cake.

From a bamboo bird-cage on the pier a flash of gaudy colour caught Neil's eye, the plumage perhaps of a fire-maned bowerbird from a donor in Papua New Guinea or a rare Spix's macaw from a Peruvian sympathizer. Regrettably, as Neil and Dr Barbara had found, the glamorous birds that most appealed to the consciences of animal rights enthusiasts tended to be the stringiest in the cooking pot. The sanctuary needed more humdrum fowl, more farmyard ducks and geese.

'Dr Barbara . . . ' Neil called to her as she washed in the water he had carried from the stream, soaping her arms and shoulders under the curious gaze of the albatross.

'What is it, Neil? Have they brought us a cow? Monique will be making cheese.'

'No, but there's something strange . . . David's getting up. And Kimo.'

Carline had taken off his straw hat and was walking towards the pier, saluting the seaplane's disembarking passengers like a district commissioner greeting a consular delegation. Kimo had rolled from his hammock and tossed aside the grass crown he was weaving. Major Anderson was rowing ashore in the dinghy, while his wife had left the kitchen and hurried across the runway. Monique dusted her floury elbows and abandoned the bread-board. She stood behind Mrs Saito under the flapping bed-sheets, watching Carline greet the new arrivals. Two uniformed men with holsters on their belts were walking towards him, caps amicably raised.

'Dr Barbara – ' Neil squinted through the soaring birds. 'They're French gendarmes . . . '

Dr Barbara buttoned her shirt and stood beside Neil, looking down at the pier. For the first time she seemed unsure of herself, sniffing her clean finger-tips as if searching for the reassuring scent of dirt and blood.

'So . . . it looks as if we'll have to go, Neil. I really didn't think they'd come.'

'Why are they here, doctor? Did someone tell them about Gubby?'

'They must have done. It wasn't a secret – most of the yachts have radios.' She gave Neil a dazed smile and embraced him. 'I'll get ready.'

She dressed quickly, packed her few clothes and the hypodermic into the satchel and stood in the doorway of the weather-station, surveying the island like a distracted dreamer about to dismiss a vision from her mind. Even the albatross were deserting her. Alarmed by the seaplane, thousands of the birds had left the bone-strewn cliffs and soared out to circle the reef.

'We'll go, Neil.' Dr Barbara listened to the fading cries. 'It's best if they don't find the cave. I'll leave the sleeping bag – you can rest here when you want to be alone. You'll think of me, won't you?'

'I'll come with you to Papeete, doctor.' Neil tried to encourage her, but she had already retreated into herself, no longer the fierce lover and huntress, and once again the threadbare obstetrician he had met in Waikiki. 'I'll tell them that you didn't kill the baby.'

'But I did, Neil. I did. I want you to stay here and carry on the work. Mrs Saito knows what to do.'

Taking the satchel from her hand, Neil followed her down the pathway. On the pier the gendarmes were speaking to Carline and Monique, pointing like interested tourists to the plant laboratory and the animal enclosures, the mess-tent and clinic. Aware that Dr Barbara was about to be arrested, Neil had decided that he would leave with her in the seaplane and assure her of at least one sympathetic witness at her trial in Papeete. He tried to think of some ruse that might save her, again wondering

175

if they could marry – his mother would be shocked by her new daughter-in-law, but Colonel Stamford might well approve.

Twenty minutes later, when they emerged from the forest, everyone had returned to the pier. Neil waited for Inger and Trudi to point accusingly at Dr Barbara, but they were sitting on the beach and admiring the seaplane's graceful lines. There was still time for Dr Barbara to escape. She and Neil could swim to one of the outer islands of the atoll, trap the fish and birds and hide out forever among the hundreds of sand-bars.

'Neil – ' Dr Barbara stopped at the edge of the runway. 'Listen – that sound. What is it?'

'Engines . . . ' The satchel in Neil's hand already seemed lighter. A propeller turned and caught the sun, throwing a spear of light at the cliffs behind them. 'Dr Barbara – they're leaving . . . the gendarmes are going!'

Dr Barbara leaned against the bulldozer, her shoulders straightening as the seaplane eased away from the pier. One of the French policemen crouched in the open hatchway, saluting Monique and Mrs Saito. Already Mrs Anderson had returned to the kitchen. Her disappointed husband stood on the beach beside his dinghy, still searching the hillsides for any sign of Neil and Dr Barbara and unaware that they were waiting behind the bulldozer. Kimo ambled back to his hammock through the clouds of coral dust whipped up by the seaplane's engines, while Inger and Trudi sat on the sand and held their skirts to their knees, waving to the young crew-men aboard the plane.

'Dr Barbara . . . ' Neil raised the satchel like a battle-trophy. 'They didn't tell the police – it means you won't have to go. You can stay on Saint-Esprit.'

'It means more than that, Neil. A great deal more.' Dr Barbara was smiling modestly to herself, a hand stilling Neil when he tried to shout above the roar of the engines. In their bamboo cages on the pier three sulphur-crested cockatoos had turned their backs to the seaplane and were already eyeing the formidable figure of their new mistress.

Carline stood by the radio-cabin, holding the scorched microphone as the seaplane taxied to its take-off point. He watched Dr Barbara approach him with quiet pleasure, openly admiring her courage, and glad that he had kept the promise he had made to himself.

Shoulders square, Dr Barbara strode towards him, ready to issue her first orders of the day.

PART III

14

A New Arrival

BRUISED BY THE WAVES, the giant fish lay in the drift-net below the reef, its yellow gills streaked with blood. Thirty feet away, in the safety of the open water, Neil steadied himself against the guy-rope that ran from the stern rail of the *Dugong*. The fish was the largest he had caught, a rare species of ray that had strayed from the sea and buried itself in the snare, which he and Kimo had laboriously stitched together from the badminton nets donated to the sanctuary by a sports equipment manufacturer in Tokyo.

Leaving the creature to thrash itself towards the shore, Neil swam to the skiff where Inger and Monique rested under an awning of parachute silk. They had cheered him on during his struggle to trap the fish, aware that its flesh would provide a procession of meals. Already Neil could see them gorging themselves on the strange meat, their chins streaming with hot fat as they tore apart the barbecued flesh. For a few days they would no longer need to raid the animal enclosures. Far too many of the threatened creatures had ended their visits to Saint-Esprit in the cooking pot, though fortunately the world supply of rare and endangered mammals seemed inexhaustible.

'Well done, Neil!' Monique called to him from her cushioned sun-lounger. 'What a battle for you. And what a fish.'

'It's as large as you are, Monique.'

'Good, I'm so hungry I could eat myself.'

Neil clung to the side of the skiff, grinning through the bright water. 'I'll tell you the tastiest bits.'

'That's very cheeky. Don't you think, Inger?'

'Wait till Dr Barbara sees the fish. We'll give you the biggest helping, Neil,' Inger reminded him.

This assurance was a courtesy that would be forgotten once they sat around the table in the mess-tent. Eager to get to the kitchen and spur the weary Kimo into lighting a fire, Inger stood up and lowered the parachute canopy, air-dropped by *Médecins Sans Frontières* with the latest batch of pharmaceutical supplies.

Resting in the surf, Neil lay back to admire the women. Both were magnificently pregnant, so heavy with child that he feared the rocking motion of the skiff would send them into labour. He remembered Trudi's unhappy delivery, and Dr Barbara's 'Push . . . push . . . push' as she urged the young woman to expel the malformed foetus from her womb. The boy – he had only learned its sex from Professor Saito, unhappily drunk and indiscreet on his home-brew *sake* – had died soon after, but neither Trudi nor the other women had been too dismayed, aware that the child carried a genetic defect.

Dr Barbara had prevented Neil from seeing the infant, but once it was sealed into its coffin she allowed him to bury it beside Gubby in the cemetery. Kimo and Professor Saito attended the modest service, and the weeping botanist delivered a brief oration in garbled Japanese as Neil laid his first-born to rest.

This time, Neil vowed, there would be no unhappiness and no congenital defects. For all the vigour of the sea, thrusting at the skiff like a demented midwife, Neil found it hard to believe that either Monique or Inger would miscarry. Nothing could dim their appetite for air, sun and food. Monique stood in the bows, swimsuit rolled around her waist, exposing the large breasts that seemed to be filled by scarcely smaller pregnancies of their own. The hard-working and over-serious Air France hostess had become a sedate Juno, forever playing her earnest pranks on Neil, hiding his clothes and lipsticking obscenities on his back as he slept.

At times Neil wearied of her stolid humour, and missed the prickly and quick-handed Frenchwoman who had ruled proudly over her kitchen. But at least he had shared her tent and her bed, if not her heart, though the memory of their few nights together – a narrow window of opportunity after Monique's ovulation –

had already begun to fade. Once Neil had sired their children the women tended to forget him with dismaying speed.

Inger, like Monique and Trudi, had close-cropped her hair into a mannish trim that emphasized the heavy bones of her skull. She stood confidently in the stern, gathering the parachute silk around her like a cloudy pink crinoline. One hand rested on her belly, as if waiting for the latest bulletin from the growing baby. According to Dr Barbara, both these sleeping infants would be girls, increasing the female population of Saint-Esprit to the point where it well exceeded the number of men, but Neil was glad that there would be more women on the island. He was grateful to Inger and Trudi, and even Monique, for everything they had done to steer him to manhood. While they bore his children they had also brought the adult Neil into the world, turning him from a child into a bearded seventeen-year-old patriarch.

As soon as their babies were born, Dr Barbara would see that he slept with them again. He remembered their last nights together, now five months away, before Dr Barbara confirmed that they were pregnant. Monique had woken with surprise to motherhood and began to shed her stuffiness, though she had never relaxed with Neil even when they were in bed together, assigning him portions of her anatomy and taking him through their sex act as if demonstrating a complex piece of cabin equipment to a dimwitted passenger. Once, in an unguarded moment, she spoke almost resentfully of her father, and how the great animal rights activist had been a stern and obsessive parent, insisting that even the way in which she tied her shoe-laces was a challenge of self-discipline.

By contrast Inger and Trudi were like older sisters cheerfully committing incest with him. Neil loved their darting hands that stung his buttocks when he was clumsy or over-ardent, warning him to think more of their pleasure than his own. He loved their teeth biting his nipples, fingers gripping his testicles as if weighing the sperm he was incubating for them. Sex with Inger and Trudi was a happy version of the sex he had known with Dr Barbara, and belonged to a realm which he was certain few people on the planet had experienced.

He was surprised and hurt when they pushed him from their beds once Dr Barbara announced that they had conceived. Only Trudi had taken pity on him when she found him mooning on the beach, and took him to his tent for a last hour together, even though she was three months pregnant. When she left him he sensed that she was slipping away to join the camp of an enemy.

'Neil! Wake up!' Monique pulled his beard as he dozed over the oars. 'Inger, he's asleep again.'

'Come on, Neil . . . ' Inger crammed the parachute between her thighs and heaved on the oars. 'You can be tired later on. Trudi's coming – she must have news from Dr Barbara.'

Neil steadied the oars and pointed the skiff towards the beach. Trudi was running down the sand, her fists pummelling the air. She raced through the surf and seized the bows of the skiff, steering it onto the shore through the last of the waves. Abandoning the parachute when it ballooned over the side, Inger and Monique clambered across the seats, patted Neil and leapt into the water.

'Good news!' Monique whooped. 'Inger, did you hear? No defects!'

'Trudi! You did it this time!'

The three women were up to their thighs in the surging waves. The foam seethed around them, as if the sea was releasing its spawn in a vain attempt to impregnate them. Smiling wanly to himself, Neil waited while the women embraced and romped, celebrating another birth to come. Despite his vital contribution, they took him less seriously than he hoped. Only later, as they strode up the beach, did Trudi notice Neil and return to compliment him.

'It's wonderful, Neil!' she told him, her small face lit with pride and relief. 'You can be very happy. It's a girl for Dr Barbara – and for you.'

'That's great, Trudi.' Neil held her narrow waist as she tottered in the waves, aware that this was the last time he would embrace her. 'And no sign of any defects . . . '

'Defects?' Trudi seemed dazed. 'Of course not. It's a girl. You'll have a new Gubby to play with.'

'Gubby was a boy.'

'Never mind. A girl is even nicer – you know that, Neil.' She ran off, shouting: 'Dr Barbara wants to see you at the clinic. She has a special job for you . . .'

As Neil approached the camp the women's laughter still sounded from their tents. The noise had sent the peccaries stamping around their wire pen and set off a sympathetic screeching of cockatoos and lorikeets. All the creatures on Saint-Esprit, even those destined for the dining table, were celebrating the new addition to the sanctuary family.

In the year since their arrival on the island the sanctuary had stabilized itself. Despite the decline in media interest, the French authorities had made no attempt to re-occupy Saint-Esprit, clearly relieved to have the nuclear atoll off the world's front pages. Journalists still visited the island, reporting on the large stock of endangered birds and mammals landed by visiting ships, or brought by Captain Garfield's seaplane on its occasional visits. Saint-Esprit was now a moored ark filled with bizarre specimens – tenrecs and dwarf lemurs from Madagascar, palm civets from Java, Texan kangaroo rats and musk-shrews from Zimbabwe. Almost every corner of the globe was represented by some eccentric mating couple, and once they produced their offspring they would advance, two by two, towards the kitchen cleaver. Others languished in the unexpected heat and humidity, infertile but protected by their own inedibility.

Several of the plant terraces were now given over to kitchen gardening, but a substantial range of endangered trees and plants survived with varying success. There were dragon trees from the Canary Islands, rajah pitcher plants from Borneo, the camellia-like *Franklinia* that was a Georgia neighbour of Neil's mother, peacock moreas from Cape Town and spiral aloes from remote Lesotho. When an army friend of Colonel Stamford in Honolulu visited Saint-Esprit he was sufficiently impressed to report that Neil was thriving on the island, and had matured into a self-reliant young man displaying the kind of animal husbandry skills that would lead to a useful agri-business career. He failed to notice the one form of husbandry and stock-rearing with which Neil was most closely involved – the three pregnant women – and urged Neil's mother to let him stay a further year on Saint-Esprit. The regime, he concluded, was spartan and high-minded, qualities that Colonel Stamford admired above all.

In fact, there was something almost too idyllic about the sanctuary. Neil rested in the shade of the camera-tower beside the runway, looking at the blockhouses that ringed the lagoon. He rarely noticed them now, and his adolescent dreams of nuclear tests and their black annunciation had been vanquished by the abundant life of the sanctuary.

Yet one endangered group had not been defended by Saint-Esprit – the male sex. Now that so many of the women were pregnant much of the work on the island was done by men. Professor Saito had been forced to leave the plant laboratory and apply his botanical skills to the kitchen gardens, where he contracted a soil-borne infection. Kimo worked under Monique's direction at the cooking stove and sink, and with his sarong and long untidy hair had begun to resemble an obese transvestite. David Carline, after hours of hunting for wild yams, retired exhausted to his tent and brooded over the pistol that Dr Barbara had commandeered.

Musing on their decline, Neil climbed the steps of the clinic. He listened to Dr Barbara stalk around the sick-room, reproving Professor Saito for tearing the mosquito net. Her sharp voice and its open lack of sympathy quelled the bedridden botanist. Without thinking, Neil cupped his hands over his genitals, aware that his semen alone lay between himself and the sick-bed.

'Well done, Neil. I'm proud of you . . . ' Dr Barbara rose from her desk and embraced Neil with the formality of a general welcoming a soldier back from a dangerous war zone. 'You've come up trumps, again.'

'I did my best, doctor,' Neil told her. 'Are you sure it's a girl?'

'Absolutely. What else could it be?' Dr Barbara held him at

arm's length and brushed a single tear from her cheek, a jewel glistening like a prop placed there by a stage-hand. She wore a man's safari suit and had trimmed her hair to the bone, though at times of emotion a few filaments would spring forward as if in memory of a more feminine phase of her life. The year on Saint-Esprit had hardened her – she was too brisk with herself, Neil often felt, rationing her smallest gestures. She sat on an unpadded chair and slept on a board-like bed like the mother superior of a strict-regime convent.

'We'll drink a toast to you, Neil. You deserve it.' She opened her medicinal cabinet and drew out a bottle of communion wine left by a pious but naive priest, Father Vergnol, who had come from Papeete to re-consecrate the graveyard. Neil had wanted to tell him about the bones of the dead observer in the drowned aircraft, but the waters of the lagoon were too deep for this artless priest to ponder.

'A toast, Neil – only a small one because there's something I want you to do. Trudi tells me she's already thought of a name.'

'Gudrun? Brunnhilde?' Neil sipped slyly at the communion wine, thinking of the violent Norse heroines Trudi had described to him. He enjoyed being drunk, but Dr Barbara kept the alcohol locked away from him. 'I'd like a son one day – is it important that it's a girl?'

'It is important, Neil.' Dr Barbara nodded with deep emphasis. 'The sanctuary needs more women if it's to be secure, more sisters and daughters.' She pondered this happy prospect, and added with the arch humour that frequently unsettled Neil. 'Besides, you want any child of yours to live a long and healthy life . . . '

'I do. Won't a son be just as healthy? You've always said I'm strong.'

'You are, Neil.' Dr Barbara turned to survey him, running her eyes frankly from his shoulders to his groin. 'I knew that when I first saw you in Waikiki. Doctors have an instinct, a sixth sense. I was certain you'd make a healthy father.'

'Then my sons will be healthy too?'

'Not necessarily.' Dr Barbara helped herself to a second glass of communion wine. Already her face and neck were flushing, and she ignored the feverish ramblings of Professor Saito in his

187

mosquito net. 'The world is a hard place for men. Look at David and Kimo, and poor Professor Saito. They've all been ill. I don't think they'd survive if they were left to themselves.'

'They worked too hard,' Neil told her. 'You never let them rest.'

'They didn't work sensibly.' Dr Barbara gestured with her glass. 'They didn't pace themselves. Worst of all, they didn't work together. There were too many elaborate schemes.'

'Like David and his stockade? Or Professor Saito's fish farm?'

'Wonderful ideas, but totally impractical. Women know how to cooperate and get on together. We have our feet on the ground, we're not competing with each other all the time.' Dr Barbara frowned at the sound of Professor Saito's quavering cries. 'I only wish I'd recruited more women before we left Honolulu. Perhaps we should open the sanctuary to a new wave of volunteers. You'd be happy with that, Neil?'

'Of course. I'll have to leave eventually – like David and Kimo. You'll need more help, doctor.'

'There are so many fine young women waiting to join us.' Dr Barbara touched the pile of letters on her desk, delivered by a passing cruise liner, and shuffled through the portrait photographs. 'Strong young women, eager to help with our work here.'

'And strong men. You'd have the pick of the best.'

'No. We don't need more men, not even if they're strong. One strong and healthy male is enough, and we have you, Neil.'

Dr Barbara touched Neil's beard, running a formalin-scented finger across his lips, but he hesitated to embrace her. Starved of the women's company, he had begun to hang around the clinic, emptying Professor Saito's bed-pan and changing his blood-stained linen, in the hope that Dr Barbara might absent-mindedly take him to her bed again. When she cleaned and stitched a deep coral wound on his shoulder she caressed him with a mother's warmth for her son. But the time of sexual passion had gone.

He watched Dr Barbara laying out the photographs like a set of tarot cards, her cracked nails tapping at the friendly, open faces – a blonde dentist from Stockholm, a thirty-year-old croupier from Atlantic City, members of a lesbian cooperative in Sydney, south London schoolgirls, a Sorbonne physics graduate, a Florida cocktail waitress, two nuns.

'I'll teach them everything I know,' he assured her. 'When Inger and Trudi have their babies I'll get them to spear-fish.'

'I was thinking of something else.' Dr Barbara gathered the photographs together and tossed them into a drawer. 'Time, Neil, is the heart of the problem – the human breeding cycle is so stretched. If only nature had given us a shorter pregnancy period, I'd hot-house the future into existence and fill the sanctuary with women.'

'A sanctuary for women?' Neil reflected in an even tone. 'The sort of women who dislike men?'

'Women don't dislike men.' Dr Barbara seemed deeply shocked by the notion. 'We bring them into this world and spend the rest of our lives helping them to understand themselves. If anything, we've been too kind to them, letting them play their dangerous games. I'm not criticizing you, Neil, you've been the most loyal of all, right from the beginning. It's thanks to you that Inger and Trudi are pregnant.'

'And Monique.'

'Monique, too – and that's quite an achievement. I never thought you'd make it. We need as many daughters as we can bring into the world. Now, there's one other woman on Saint-Esprit. I want you to visit her.'

'Who?' Neil stepped forward, already noticing the narrow bed behind the desk. 'You, doctor?'

'No . . . ' Dr Barbara turned her back to Neil. 'Sadly I'm too old for child-bearing. I mean Mrs Saito.'

'Professor Saito's wife?' Neil stared through the window at the plant laboratory. Mrs Saito moved among the rare plants with her insect spray, firing punitive bursts at their tender leaves. This small, prim woman, devoted to Professor Saito's every whim but ruling him with an iron hand, would never let Neil anywhere near herself. 'Dr Barbara? Mrs Saito won't agree, not even if the professor dies. I know Mrs Saito . . . '

'I know her too.' Dr Barbara smiled down her long nose. 'We've spoken about everything together, and she accepts what she has to do.'

Neil tried to protest, and then remembered that Mrs Saito had recently spent far less time nursing her sick husband than she would have done a few months earlier. A significant change in the relationship between the two botanists had occurred, and Neil even suspected that Professor Saito had been negotiating with Captain Garfield for his return passage to Japan. He had caught the botanist in the beach hut after dark, reading his letters with a torch.

'Doctor, I still can't believe she'll – '

'Don't wake Professor Saito.' Dr Barbara unlocked her safe and withdrew a potted bonsai tree. She handed it to Neil. 'Go and see her now, and give her this. She's expecting you . . . '

15

Volunteers

TWENTY MINUTES LATER Neil stood on the steps of the plant laboratory and listened to the mosquito door snap shut behind him. Mrs Saito was already dressed and had returned to the care of her plants, her tongue clucking as she moved around them. With a wristy jerk she opened a transom window, breaching the climate-control system in order to vent any lingering trace of Neil's scent.

The briskness of the sexual act between them had startled Neil. Still breathless, he touched the bruises on his shoulders where Mrs Saito had gripped him with her strong hands. He looked out at the silent camp, disturbed only by a bleating macaque that echoed Professor Saito's moanings. An experiment with death had once been planned for Saint-Esprit, and in turn Dr Barbara was planning an equally bizarre experiment with life.

For the first time Neil sensed that the two experiments were closer than he had imagined. He felt his tender testicles, still aching from the pressure of Mrs Saito's fingers. 'Lazy boy . . . lazy . . . ' she had murmured as she manipulated him towards orgasm in the same way that she had forced the involuntary climaxes of the breeding peccaries. When he arrived with the bonsai tree – a signal, he assumed, previously agreed by Dr Barbara and Mrs Saito – she treated Neil to a smile that opened and closed with the swiftness of a camera shutter. She took the tree from his hands and directed him to the laboratory, where he lay naked on the mattress between the malignant-smelling fungi, almost expecting her to bring her battery charger and electric ejaculator.

191

Leaving the door unlocked, she undressed like a conjuror, revealing the body of a breasted child, and immediately set to work. Her white face hovered over him, hiding a world closed to the emotions. She stared at Neil as if he were a rare creature snared in the depths of the lagoon and now to be relieved of his vital spawn, as precious as the roe harvested from a royal sturgeon.

Aware that he had been ruthlessly milked, but accepting his real role on Saint-Esprit, Neil walked past the silent tents towards the runway. The ground coral was as blanched as Mrs Saito's face, and seemed to leach all pigment from the surrounding trees. The camera-towers and bunkers had withdrawn into the forest as the island reincorporated death within itself, intimidated by Dr Barbara's will to life.

A high-pitched whoop sounded from the pathway to the summit, the cry of a bird baffled by the topography of the atoll. David Carline strode through the ferns towards Neil, carrying out his ceaseless search for Werner and Wolfgang. Soon after Dr Barbara's return to her command of the sanctuary, the two German hippies had vanished, abandoning their women to Neil and taking passage to Papeete on a passing yacht. But David was convinced that they were still hiding on Saint-Esprit, waiting to wreak their revenge on the sanctuary.

Neil watched him wade through the deep ferns, tattered panama hat in one hand, an expensive walking stick in the other, striking the palm trunks as he tried to flush the lurking Germans from their secret lair. The past year had transformed the shy Bostonian and amateur missionary into the restless constable of Saint-Esprit. He was forever warning off unwelcome yachts-men, barely tolerating the Greenpeace and animal rights delega-tions who came to pay their respects to Dr Barbara.

With his long, pale hair pinned to his forehead by a red bandeau, his sleeveless French camouflage fatigues and army boots he resembled an eccentric headmistress playing a weekend war-game. Even his wife had failed to recognize him when she arrived with Captain Garfield, her skin whiter than the seaplane. Carline embraced her enthusiastically, eager to enrol her in his

one-man militia, and proudly showed her all the achievements of the sanctuary.

He promised her that he would return to Boston within three months, but Neil was sure that he had no intention of leaving Saint-Esprit as long as Dr Barbara remained. She had confiscated his chromium pistol, but Carline was committed to her, ready to accept whatever vision she chose to impose on the island. All the self-criticism and dissatisfactions of the years before his meeting with Dr Barbara had been banished by his decision to follow her to the end.

'Neil! Your eyes are sharper than mine. Did you see anything?' He stared at the summit, which the albatross were circling in a cloud of black-tipped wings. 'Someone's unsettled them.'

'It's you, David. You're banging your stick.'

'They like that. It keeps them awake.' Carline raised the walking stick and waved cheerfully at the birds. 'You look after the monkey house and I'll look after the albatross. Keep your eyes peeled for any fires.'

'They've gone, David. Wolfgang and Werner left six months ago.'

'Neil . . . ' Patiently, Carline picked the loose fibres from his panama. The hat was his sheriff's badge, which he would loan to Kimo and Neil whenever they greeted visitors. 'Let me tell you something – the Germans are here. I worked with them in the Congo. They'll go to ground and hang on as long as it takes.'

'Saint-Esprit isn't Stalingrad.'

'Well . . . in some ways it might be, more than you realize. The women are coming at us in human waves. So how is Trudi –are the ladies still keeping you busy?'

'She's expecting – Dr Barbara's confirmed it. She's having a girl.'

'Good for you, Neil. You'll soon have more daughters than I do. A girl, eh? Just what Barbara ordered. It's a pity she can't mount those little fillies herself, but I guess that's one thing we still have to offer.' He patted Neil's head in an admiring but kindly way. 'In my experience daughters can bring a lot of problems . . . '

* * *

Leaving him to continue his search, Neil walked past Kimo's hut. The Hawaiian lay asleep, exhausted by the long hours of work and troubled by the stomach ulcer that Dr Barbara had diagnosed. Neil was careful not to disturb him. The darkened tent was hung with independence banners and framed photographs of King Kalakaua and Queen Kapiolani, the last Hawaiian monarchs, decorated with lilies and frangipani. Kimo had warned him not to touch the dead blooms, a memory of his early months on Saint-Esprit when he had been the strongest member of the expedition.

Next to Kimo's tent was a bamboo chalet that he and Neil had helped the Andersons to build. Empty since their departure from Saint-Esprit, it now served as a crèche awaiting the new arrivals. While Kimo convalesced from his first heavy haemorrhages he wove a set of basket cribs for Trudi, Inger and Monique. For all his ribald leg-pulling, Kimo was proud of Neil and his swelling paternity, and his huge hands lovingly spliced the raffia that Neil brought from the forest.

The sight of the crèche, meticulously swept and disinfected every day by Dr Barbara, always unnerved Neil. He preferred to remember the happy evenings he had spent with the Andersons in their cheerful den as they brewed tea and set him his algebra and trigonometry exercises. They never mentioned Trudi or Inger, and refused to speak to Monique, disgusted by the way in which Dr Barbara was using Neil in a tasteless experiment. He was sorry when they finally decided that they could no longer remain at Saint-Esprit.

Hoping to change their minds, he worked with them to repair the sloop, which lay on the beach beside the pier, draped in its scorched rigging, the cabin open to the rain and wind. An uneasy truce had existed after Dr Barbara's descent from her hill-top exile, but someone had taken revenge on the old couple, suspecting that they had alerted the French gendarmes with a secret radio hidden aboard their little craft.

As the Andersons slept in their hut, determined to stay close to Neil and perhaps shame him out of his visits to the women's tents, a fierce blaze lit the night lagoon, rousing everyone from their sleep. Neil rowed the Andersons to the burning sloop and

helped them to extinguish the fire. They beached the craft beside the pier as the last flames curled around the mast-head. For days clouds of steam rose from the hull, staining the sky over the lagoon.

Fortunately Major Anderson had completed his makeshift repairs before falling ill with an attack of enteritis, the 'island fever' that seemed to appear at will. Mrs Anderson openly accused Dr Barbara of poisoning her husband, but Carline and Kimo calmed her and helped to rig the jury sails, floating the scarcely seaworthy sloop into the waves. Major Anderson sat fever-mouthed in the stern, one hand clinging to the tiller, while his wife embraced Neil. He guessed that they had decided not to offer him a place aboard the sloop only because they feared for the craft on the long voyage to Tahiti.

After a last look at the crèche, Neil crossed the runway and set off for the beach, eager to haul ashore the yellow ray. Already he could see the fish lying in the netting fifty yards from the skiff, where the tethered parachute sucked like a lung at the wind. The idle waves tossed the yellow carcass to and fro like restless dogs bored by a creature they had killed.

Exposed to the sunlight, the ray's underbelly was smeared with the carmine stripes of its own blood. Neil seized the slack netting and began to disentangle the sodden mesh. Trapped within it were ribbons of kelp, dead squid and blue-fish, sea-cucumbers and a rusty food can.

'Major . . .?'

The yellow fish he had glimpsed in the whirl of foam beside the reef was an inflatable life-jacket, punctured in a dozen places, stained with the red shark repellent leaking from its shoulder capsule. Neil pulled the bundle of rubber tatters from the netting and brushed aside the threads of kelp, trying to remember the yellow life-jackets that the Andersons had worn. Scores of ocean yachtsmen had died, their jackets floating the seas for years, and he could imagine the old major and his wife swimming from the sinking sloop and deciding to slip the release cords on their jackets and sink arm in arm into the Pacific deep.

*   *   *

195

He was running along the beach, impatient to tell Dr Barbara of his find, when he saw that a large, high-masted ketch had entered the lagoon, the *Petrus Christus* registered in The Hague. Sails furled, it moved towards the pier under its engine, whose rapid rhythm matched the beat of Neil's heart and sent an urgent tocsin across the water. A sun-bronzed woman in her early forties was at the helm, while her husband stood by the fore-mast, a balding man with two blonde-haired daughters of Neil's age.

Dr Barbara strode in her measured way along the pier, boots ringing against the timbers. She ignored Neil, who was waving to her from the beach and holding up the tattered jacket, and continued her appraisal of the ketch, like an excisewoman at the bar of a secret harbour.

A copper-skinned boy emerged from the cabin and stood in the cockpit beside the girls' mother. A Moluccan some three years younger than Neil, he already had the physique of a professional boxer, his trim waist carrying a deep chest and a pair of powerful shoulders. His jaw squared when he noticed the unfriendly scowl on the face of David Carline as he paced restlessly along the pier, waving his straw hat with the gestures of a tetchy traffic-master on the deck of an aircraft carrier.

Neil climbed the iron steps from the beach, waiting for Dr Barbara to ask the visitors to leave once they had filled their water tanks. Hands on hips, she continued to cast her eye over the ketch, and it occurred to Neil that she might once again be taking an interest in the sanctuary. Perhaps she hoped that this Dutch family had brought with them some valuable creature to be given pride of place among the endangered animals.

But her gaze had settled on the pretty daughters, already slyly smiling to each other over Neil, and on the handsome Moluccan. Already the youth had noticed his chief rival on Saint-Esprit and was returning Neil's level stare.

Dr Barbara silenced Carline and raised her hands, her smile of greeting so broad that it almost eclipsed the sun.

'Welcome to Saint-Esprit! We need every volunteer we can find. I hope you enjoy a long stay at our sanctuary island . . . '

On the beach behind her the pregnant women gathered, Inger, Trudi and Monique, their oceanic bellies ready to drown the Pacific.

16

A Banquet of the Fathoms

THE PATHWAY WAS STEEPER than he remembered. Fifty feet from the summit, Neil was forced to sit on the eroded steps he had helped to carve on the final approach to the radio mast. Calming his lungs, he listened to the fractious chittering of insects in the forest. Saint-Esprit seemed restless with itself. Palm fronds rasped in the wind, the notched trunks of the rare bamboos grated together, waves boomed through the wreck of the *Dugong*. Above him the albatross circled, crying mindlessly at the sky and aggravating the sharp migraine that had plagued him for days.

Even that morning's swim in the lagoon had failed to clear his head. Neil gripped his thighs, trying to steady the sweating muscles that still jumped in a fever of their own. The effort of spear-fishing in the lagoon each day had leached all the fat from his skin, and the strings of his muscles reminded him of the anatomical plates in his father's textbooks, the skin flayed back to expose the knotted cords and straps.

For the first time, despite the sun, the water in the lagoon had been almost too cold for him. He had swum out for two hundred yards, but then turned back to sit shivering on the wind-swept sand. When the van Noort sisters approached along the beach, ready to start their tiresome teasing, he left his scuba gear and set off for the summit, hoping to lose his fever in the cooler air of the high ground.

As he climbed the last steps to the radio mast, Neil could see the sisters trying on his oxygen harness, their pale hair as white as the plumage of birds. Like everyone else on the island, they were hungry all the time, and their teasing had a serious purpose, part of the campaign to irritate Neil and keep him fishing for as long as possible. The trouble with Saint-Esprit was that there were too many mouths to feed, and too many of those mouths belonged to pregnant women and adolescent girls, two groups with the voracious appetite of a great white shark.

Dr Barbara's surprising invitation to the van Noorts had now turned into an open recruitment drive. In the month since their arrival they had been joined by two New Zealand nurses, Anne Hampton and Patsy Kennedy, who were working their passage on a South African yacht sailing from Hong Kong to San Francisco. Keen environmentalists, they quickly fell under Dr Barbara's steely spell, and decided to remain on Saint-Esprit and help with the work of the sanctuary. Used to dealing with teenage patients, they soon tried to take Neil in charge, organizing every minute of his day for him, with Monique's and Mrs Saito's encouragement.

Soon after their arrival, a catamaran crewed by three Mexican ocean-racers put in for repairs. The burly trio of petroleum engineers took a keen interest in the desalination plant, whose modest performance they offered to improve, and in the drainage systems of the plant and animal enclosures.

Despite their dash and expertise, Dr Barbara was cool to them, and clearly relieved when their twin-hull slipped away through the reef. Yet only the next day a sloop sailed by an elderly Canadian couple and their grand-daughters, two school-teachers in their late twenties, arrived to a warm reception. Neil had hoped that the Mexicans would stay, evening the balance between the sexes, and tried to imagine Dr Barbara having an affair with one of the engineers.

But Dr Barbara was happiest when surrounded by women, and it occurred to Neil that he might soon be the only man left on Saint-Esprit. A series of close-knit groups had formed at the sanctuary, from which he and David Carline were excluded. At the centre of this women's republic was Dr Barbara, presiding from her office in the clinic, guarding the store of canned food and the medical supplies that had failed to save Professor Saito and Kimo from their wasting fevers. Around her were the original foursome: Mrs Saito, Monique, Inger and Trudi.

Beyond them lay an outer circle of novices, none so far pregnant, the van Noort sisters and the New Zealand nurses, now joined by the Canadian women, all committed to the success of the sanctuary.

Whenever Neil approached, bringing a large grouper to the kitchen table, or hoping to join in their easy laughter, he felt like an intruder at a private party. The women would stop their talk and stare at him, waiting for him to return to his tent with his tray of food. For all their chumminess with each other, there was a ruthlessness about them that unnerved Neil, which he had last seen displayed by his five-year-old cousins during their childhood nursery games, decapitating a loyal teddy-bear for the smallest peccadillo.

He and Carline had been left to care for the dying Kimo on their own, bathing and comforting the feverish Hawaiian, clumsily trying to ease his distress as the sweat drained from his wasting body and soaked the mattress in his tent. Only Dr Barbara had called, to give him his daily injection, and in a callous gesture she had ordered Monique to cut his food ration days before the end. Neil had hunted for taro to pulp and boil, feeding the ailing giant as his head lolled against his knees.

As the number of mouths to feed had grown, more of the animals in the sanctuary were slaughtered for the cooking stove, the rare plants plundered for edible corms and bulbs. The lucky few that survived were little more than a shop window to impress the visiting delegations. Not only had the women excluded Neil from the treats of the table, often fobbing him off with a charred fish-tail perfunctorily grilled by Inger as she chattered in German to Trudi, but he was also denied the pleasures of the bed.

Dr Barbara had assigned neither the van Noort girls nor the two nurses to his tent, perhaps fearing the fever that affected him, and which her injections did nothing to cure. Sometimes he suspected that he had completed his role for Dr Barbara, and that his successor had already been appointed.

Looking down at the camp, he could see Nihal, the fourteen-year-old Moluccan, standing under the open-air shower behind the clinic. Despite her heavy abdomen, Monique was climbing the ladder with a canvas water bucket which she tipped into the overhead tank. Trudi dropped Nihal's swimsuit to his ankles, exposing his small buttocks which she cheerfully soaped.

Dr Barbara watched from the deck-chair in her private sanctum, the wired enclosure on the higher ground above the clinic. Here she had begun to cultivate a modest garden, laying out a series of flower-beds below the overhanging trees in which she hoped to grow medicinal herbs. The garden was her retreat, to which no-one was admitted, and she sat alone in the evenings beside her large spade, surveying the sanctuary she had created.

She lay back as Nihal took his shower, but her eyes never left his sleekly muscled body. She had become almost obsessed with him, and suggested to Neil that he teach the youth how to spear-fish. But Neil was uneasy with this boyish intruder and his sly eyes, all too aware of what was going on in Dr Barbara's mind.

Besides, the lagoon was Neil's domain, the reservoir that held all the adolescent obsessions with nuclear death that had brought him to Saint-Esprit. Its deep waters seemed to merge with his own bloodstream, as he filtered through his dreams those drowned bones he had glimpsed in the submerged bomber. The camera-towers stood around the lagoon, still waiting to record a nuclear event that would now only take place within his mind. Then at last he would be free to leave Saint-Esprit and its resting dead beside the prayer-shack.

Standing on the cliff among the albatross, Neil followed the course of a single cumulus as it moved across the lagoon, mirrored by the halo of its own reflection in the glassy aquamarine. It sailed towards the north-west, cleared the reef and set off on its long sky-journey to Tahiti.

However, its white shadow remained within the lagoon, a few hundred yards from the bomber on the sea-bed, well beyond the outer limit of Neil's fishing ground. As the waves smoothed themselves in the falling wind, he saw a white triangle that resembled the bows and keel of a sunken yacht, an inverted craft hanging from the under-surface of the water as it sailed across the lagoon.

★   ★   ★

Had one of the visiting yachts foundered, only a mile from the sanctuary, as everyone slept in their tents? Refreshed by the cool summit air, Neil ran down the lower slopes of the hillside and pushed through the deep ferns towards the runway. For reasons he never understood, many of the yachts had chosen to slip away at night. The van Noorts, an amiable Amsterdam architect and his handsome wife, set sail before dawn, much to their daughters' surprise, passing a message to Dr Barbara that they would return from Tahiti by the month's end. The elderly Canadians had also sailed after dusk, without saying goodbye to their grand-daughters, and simply telling Monique and Mrs Saito that they would return after a visit to Bora Bora.

Neil, by chance, had seen the Canadians leave. Drifting through his night fever, he sat up in bed as a spectral sail crossed the dark lagoon. He heard Carline's voice, and the oars of a dinghy labouring in the water. He fell asleep but later, when he woke, all was quiet in the windless night and the Canadian couple had cleared the reef. Streaming with sweat, Neil left his bed, hoping to revive himself in the cold surf.

Carline's tent was empty, flaps open on an undisturbed sleeping bag. Neil crossed the runway to the beach and saw him hurrying between the shadowless palms. Without noticing Neil, he strode past in his drenched clothes, exhausted by his hours of rowing. He returned to his tent and roped the flaps together, sealing himself away from Dr Barbara and the sanctuary.

Remembering that uneasy night, Neil stood beside the runway, eyes spurred by the fierce coral glare. Perhaps Carline had tried to overtake the Canadians, hoping to leave the island with them? The American was wandering around the open ground by the prayer-shack, hunting for sweet potatoes that would augment the modest rations which the women allowed him. Under the straw hat his face was sallow and toneless, and despite the hunt for food his eyes forever strayed to the line of graves. So many corpses now lay in the cemetery that the contours of the headland had begun to change. Kimo was covered by a tumulus of stones and earth, decorated with his Hawaiian independence mementoes, and dwarfed the miniature grave of Professor Saito. The little botanist was so wasted by the time of his death that Neil had carried him in his arms, followed by Dr Barbara and his bad-tempered widow, pregnant with Neil's child.

'Neil? What are you doing here?' Carline struck the ground with his stick, as if hoping to rouse Wolfgang and Werner from their subterranean sleep. 'You can look for yams somewhere else.'

'I've been up to the summit,' Neil told him. 'I wanted to count the albatross.'

'Why, for Pete's sake? Save your energy. Did you see anyone?'

'No-one, David.'

'No fires or caches? A lean-to shack, maybe?'

'Nothing. Werner and Wolfgang left the island long ago.'

'That's what Barbara says. But I know better.' Carline stared at Neil's hands, almost suspecting that they held a secret message from the Germans. Neil realized that Carline was lonely, and jealous of any contact Neil might have with the two hippies. His scarecrow figure seemed about to root itself among the stunted yams. He chewed his thumb and sniffed hungrily at the blood, then wiped it on his matted hair, now grown so long that Neil suspected he was trying to resemble a woman.

'David, come fishing with me. We'll catch a small shark and cook it on the beach.'

'Barbara gets first choice.' Carline glowered at the camp, where the women were gathering around the mess-tent, ready to hold one of their endless meetings. 'There they go again. Better get out of the way, Neil, it's indoctrination time. So, you're planning to leave Saint-Esprit?'

'Not for a while. What about you, David?'

'I wouldn't try to reach Tahiti in that skiff. You might not make it out of the lagoon.'

'I don't want to leave. Why should I?'

'I can think of a few reasons. Everything's changed, Neil. Your time here is over.'

'I'll hang on.' Neil stared at Professor Saito's grave, re-membering his last anguished babble inside the mosquito net as his wife tried to calm him. The botanist had turned against the sanctuary, and had rambled to himself about the seaplane and the albatross, confusing them in his mind. 'Why do you stay, David?'

'Unfinished business . . . ' Carline raised his bleeding forefinger to the light. 'There's blood on the wind, Neil. Try not to get spattered. Even a drop can kill.'

'Then get away from the sanctuary. Go back to Boston, and your wife and daughters.'

'My wife and daughters?' Carline smiled to himself at Neil's naïveté. 'They're here on Saint-Esprit . . . you talk to them every day, you've shared your bed with them. Men are very different, Neil, each of us is an exception to the rule. Women are all the same. They may look different, but deep inside they're Barbara Rafferty. Remember that, Neil . . . '

Striking the grave, he shuffled through the cemetery, eyes on the sky as if ready to rush to the radio-cabin at the first sight of a rescue plane.

Neil watched him wander into the forest, and stood for a silent minute beside Kimo's grave. He missed the phlegmatic Hawaiian, with his moods and surliness, his hundred little kindnesses towards Neil and his earnest attempts to wean him from his dreams of nuclear weapons. During their first uneasy months on the island Kimo had regarded him as little more than a nuisance, a mascot exploited for his injured foot, but later he recognized his commitment to the sanctuary. He admired Neil's swimming and fishing skills and in a clumsy but big-brotherly way tried to protect him from the women. At the end, before he died, he had taken Neil's hands, as if hoping that he would return the favour and intercede with Dr Barbara to save him.

Neil paused at the smaller grave beside Kimo's tumulus, also aware that he had begun to miss Professor Saito. By some sleight of hand the introverted botanist had managed to be happy with his fierce and unpleasant wife, a notion that Neil found hard to grasp but which offered a curious sense of comfort. Coming so close together, the deaths had stunned everyone and prevented them from mourning the two founder-members of the expedition. Saint-Esprit's endemic fly-fever, Dr Barbara warned them, preyed on the weak and irresolute. Scarcely mourned, their graves had closed over them like the sea over two sinking stones.

Neil missed them, but at the same time he knew that he himself had been infected by Dr Barbara's demanding ethos. Neither Kimo nor Professor Saito had matched the needs of the sanctuary. They were too immersed in themselves, too prone to retreat into their private worlds, and nature had stilled them. Above all, both were men, and for Dr Barbara being a man was the greatest genetic defect of all.

The water was cold, a death-chill from which only the rubber wet-suit would save him. As he sank below the skiff the dark current reached its icy hands to seize his thighs. A parrot-fish tapped the eye-piece of his face-mask, keen to welcome Neil to its domain, but this corner of the lagoon was empty of life. The sea-snakes and squid, the fish and turtles had left for some more urgent rendezvous, leaving Neil alone in the frozen vault.

Revived by the oxygen in his mask, Neil swam through the deserted garden of the lagoon floor. The parrot-fish followed him, nosing among the mushroom corals and sea-cucumbers. Fifty feet from him, where the dark water began to seal itself into the deep, a reef-shark swam on some skittish mission of its own. The garden gave way to a veldt of black sand that sloped towards an escarpment of volcanic rock, lying across the lagoon floor like a barnacled liner.

Neil swam to the ridge, resting his flippers on the encrusted surface, and looked down at the basin below, a submerged vent of the ancient crater that had collapsed in upon itself.

A delirious convention was taking place, a deranged banquet of the fathoms. Sea-creatures were converging from all sides of the lagoon, almost obscuring the white hull of the *Petrus Christus* lying on the sandy floor. Its masts slanted through the milky light, and a Dutch ensign waved among the hundreds of jostling fish that fought frantically to dive through the open hatch into the cabin. A blizzard of animal debris drifted like dream-snow through the water, particles of tissue torn from a trapped carcass within the galley. A pennant of intestine floated on the current, hauled along by a determined blue-fish hoping to find a quiet corner of the lagoon.

A frenzied grouper blundered into Neil, striking his arms and legs. The water clouded, and a last eruption of organic matter gusted through the hatchway of the ketch. Ignored by the fish, a skein of hair attached itself to the rigging, a blonde train flowing from a plate of scalp like the streamer of a jelly-fish. It freed itself from the halyard and slipped away into the darker water, a gliding wraith that sailed towards the closing doors of the deep.

Another yacht had arrived and was dropping anchor half a mile from the shore. Neil rested over the oars, the wet-suit and oxygen cylinders at his feet. His fever had returned as he broke the surface, and seemed to draw strength from the sun. Trying to rest his head, he watched a rubber inflatable speed towards the pier, where Mrs Saito stood waiting, hands raised in greeting. Two fair-haired young women sat in the bows, while their husbands stood in the stern by the engine. One of the men was filming their arrival with a video-camera, panning from the albatross-tipped peak of Saint-Esprit to the line of tents in the camp and then to the animal pens and the aviary.

The lens rested on Mrs Saito, who smiled over-brightly at the visitors like a nightclub tout outside a tawdry bar in the Ginza. Her husband's death had scarcely touched Mrs Saito, and Neil sensed that she had mentally discarded the earnest botanist even before his illness. Professor Saito had been too blinkered for this tough little woman, hiding from the world behind his pebble lenses, trying to come to terms with life by cataloguing its endlessly multiplying varieties.

She caught the inflatable's mooring line and helped the women ashore, eyes approving their strong teeth, broad hips and rude health, the manageress of a trading house accepting a consignment of merchandise. She signalled to Dr Barbara, who was watching from the steps of the clinic and now walked at a leisurely pace towards the pier. Trudi and Inger, steering their heavy pregnancies, were already crossing the runway. The van Noort sisters and the New Zealand nurses sat at the tables in the

mess-tent, chairs drawn up like seats in a classroom. Here
Monique was addressing them, an arm around Nihal's shoulders
as if demonstrating a life-saving drill that involved the concealed
parts of the male anatomy.

Determined to warn Dr Barbara that Carline had scuttled the
Petrus Christus and drowned the older van Noorts, Neil beached
the skiff and lifted the wet-suit and cylinders through the
waves. He was exhausted by the long swim from the sunken
yacht, and fell to his knees in the ashy sand. The fever burned at
the bones of his skull, and an ugly rash covered his arms and
thighs. He tried to brush the blisters away, convinced that his
skin had already been devoured by the fish that waited for their
next banquet.

'Barbara!' Mrs Saito shouted. 'They're coming, they're
coming!'

Abandoning her visitors, Mrs Saito ran along the pier, knees
striking each other in her breathless panic. Her hands gripped the
lapels of her shirt, trying to shield her breasts from some
imminent assault. She stumbled in the soft sand as she ran past
Neil, and steadied herself against the bows of the skiff. Too
confused to recognize Neil, she stared down at him as he rested
beside his diving gear. Her mouth worked silently like the fish he
had seen devouring the van Noorts.

'They're . . . coming!'

'Who, Mrs Saito? Who's coming?'

'Neil? Why are you here?' She grimaced at him, the planes of
her face like the cards in a scattered pack. 'You fool – the French
are coming!'

Neil waited as Dr Barbara reached them and began to reassure
Mrs Saito. She embraced the little Japanese, holding her head to
her shoulder, and waved to the couples standing uncertainly on
the pier. They lowered their video-camera, in deference to the
pregnant women strolling across the runway like a party of
expecting angels who had descended from the sky.

'Barbara . . . ' Mrs Saito swallowed her nose phlegm. 'The
French . . . they're coming back . . . '

207

'Miko . . . there's nothing to fear.' Dr Barbara brushed the tears from Mrs Saito's cheeks. 'Think of the baby . . . '

'The French navy . . . ' Mrs Saito pointed to the visitors. 'They heard on the radio. Barbara . . . !'

'It's all right. Now wait for me at the clinic.' Dr Barbara steered her towards Inger and Trudi, and then turned to Neil. She seemed almost regally calm, untouched by the news that the yacht-crew had brought to Saint-Esprit, as if she had already made a crucial decision that nothing could influence. Her hands hung in front of her in a simple clasp, and the restless energy that had driven her through the first unhappy months on the island had been replaced by a serenity as measured as the sea.

'Well, Neil . . . no fish today?'

'Dr Barbara – the French are coming back . . . '

'I know, Neil. Mrs Saito told me. We'll have to arrange a proper welcome, won't we?'

'But are they really coming?'

'I can't tell if they are. They say these things from time to time just to test us . . . '

Neil stood up, trying to grip the air as his feet slipped in the sand. Through his fever he reached for the few words he needed. 'Dr Barbara, I found the van Noorts' yacht. I think David scuttled it on the far side of the lagoon. They never sailed for Tahiti.'

'Are you sure, Neil?' Dr Barbara's hands ran comfortingly across his back, smoothing away the weals left by the scuba harness. She touched his forehead and pressed his head to her palm. 'Rest for a moment, Neil. You've worked so hard.'

Neil lay against her, feeling an immense relief. He could smell her skin, the same stale, sweet scent he had inhaled as they slept together in the weather-station, surrounded by the bones and albatross droppings. When she smiled at the visiting couples he noticed the pockets of pus around her lower teeth. He realized that her breasts had shrunk like an old woman's, and that she had aged since coming to Saint-Esprit.

'Dr Barbara, you'll have to tell the Dutch girls. Their mother and father are dead.'

'Try to rest, dear . . . '

'The fish are eating them, doctor.'

'Neil, you've done so much.' Dr Barbara stroked his hair, wet with fever. 'Don't be afraid – you can stay at the clinic and I'll look after you. Think, Neil, you'll be close to your camera-towers. You'll have to tell me what they see.'

Neil listened to her calm heartbeat, its quiet rhythm overtaken by the gallop of his fever-ridden pulse.

'Dr Barbara . . . '

'Yes, Neil?'

'The camera-towers see nothing.'

17

The End of Love

BORNE BY THE WIND, the banners floated above the runway,
their painted slogans taunting the dusty trees. Neil raised the flap
of the mosquito net and squinted through the window of the
sick-room, trying to focus his eyes on the rippling messages. His
fever had subsided, as it often did in the mornings, and he could
read the familiar texts that sermonized the sky.

Life is the Last Sanctuary!
Defend Saint-Esprit Now!
Say No to Nuclear Testing!

Guided by Mrs Saito, the van Noort sisters were climbing a
ladder propped against the tallest of the trees. Neil smiled bleakly
as he watched their innocent but clumsy efforts, wondering how
they had helped their parents to sail the *Petrus Christus* on the
long voyage around the world. As they struggled with the heavy
rope the last of the banners slipped from their hands and raced
along the runway, draping itself across the bulldozer.

'Martha . . .! Helena . . .!' Mrs Saito screamed at the pair.
The girls' endless giggling had driven her into a furious temper,
and she shook her fists at them from the foot of the ladder. 'Silly
school-girls! It's not a game! Men are coming for you, brutal
men!'

'Brutal . . .?' Keeping her heels out of Mrs Saito's reach,
Helena made large eyes at her younger sister. 'Did you hear,
Martha? We like brutal men . . . '

While Mrs Saito scolded them, Monique strolled past, guiding
her large abdomen towards the chairs outside the mess-tent. She
leaned against the sun-blanched canvas and surveyed the floating

banners with little conviction, as if she had detached herself from Saint-Esprit and whatever doubtful future lay before it. Her eyes moved from the cemetery where her father lay and lingered upon Neil's face, framed by the grey shroud of the mosquito net. Neil hoped that she would smile at him, or even show a fleeting irritation, but she watched him without expression, and he sensed that she had already consigned him to the sanctuary's past along with Monsieur Didier, Kimo and Professor Saito.

Crooning to her baby, Monique waited as Mrs Saito ordered the van Noort sisters to retrieve the banner. Was Monique aware that the bones of their drowned parents lay aboard the scuttled yacht? Within days of their arrival the French soldiers would discover the *Petrus Christus*, and the deaths would be blamed on everyone in the sanctuary. When Monique brought his evening bowl of tapioca to the sick-room Neil tried to describe the sinister banquet he had witnessed, but like Dr Barbara she regarded the story as just another of his overheated ramblings.

Yet for all his sickness, he alone saw everything clearly on Saint-Esprit. A kind of collective amnesia of the future had settled over the sanctuary, a willed refusal to face the imminent French landing, as if the seizure of Saint-Esprit was irrelevant to the real life of the island. Even Dr Barbara seemed unconcerned. She sat in her deck-chair under the trees in her private garden, beside the flower-beds she had still to plant, unaware of the final challenge to her leadership that waited below the horizon.

Neil watched her lean back in the chair, idly stretching her neck as she searched the sky for any approaching aircraft. One hand held her trusty spade, while the other rested on the slim hip of the fourteen-year-old Moluccan boy, a favoured guest within her intimate enclosure. Nihal hovered beside her, unsettled by Mrs Saito's incessant shouting. Dr Barbara had prescribed for him a regime of swimming and spear-fishing, and already this had deepened his chest and hardened his thighs and stomach. Fortunately, no other duties had been assigned to him, and he slept alone in Kimo's tent.

For whatever reasons, there was a lull in Dr Barbara's breeding programme. Though confined to the sick-room, Neil had pushed his bed to the window and kept a close watch on the sanctuary. At night, when his fever was most intense and a frieze of wounded albatross paraded across the ceiling, he called to Dr Barbara as she slept in her office. Muttering to herself, she blundered into the sick-room, and seemed to spring through the trapdoor of Neil's mind like a demon queen. But at least she slept alone. The thought of the canny Moluccan lying between her breasts so disturbed Neil that jealousy alone had kept him going through the early days when he had almost succumbed to the fever.

Neil wiped his sweat onto the mosquito net, which still carried the scent of Professor Saito's hair-oil. Trying to forget the botanist, whose little body had impressed its contours into the sodden mattress beneath Neil's shoulders, he listened to his widow's tantrums as she supervised the re-hanging of the banner. This mini-drama she staged at least twice a day, as if keeping alive some archaic form of Japanese theatre with its repertoire of grunts and rages.

Of the original members of the expedition, Mrs Saito alone seemed to dread the prospect of a French return to Saint-Esprit. The two Swedish couples on the last yacht to visit the island insisted that they had not misheard the Defence Ministry broadcast, panicking Mrs Saito into a frenzy of activity. While Dr Barbara dozed in her garden, and Trudi and Inger helped Monique to prepare the evening meal in the kitchens, Mrs Saito presided over the young women with a regime of barely contained hysteria. Heaps of driftwood and damp ferns now lay at opposite ends of the runway, bonfires to be set alight once the first television crews arrived to witness the French re-occupation.

The two New Zealand nurses were Mrs Saito's loyal work-horses. Dr Barbara assured them that she could look after Neil on her own, and they devoted themselves to strengthening the sanctuary's defences, helped by the Canadian school-teachers. Together they painted the protest banners and strengthened the telephone wire around the animal enclosures, the last redoubt to which they would all retreat, defending to the end those few animals and birds which had managed to escape the cooking pot. Dedicated environmentalists and veterans of campaigns against

Norwegian and Japanese whalers, they worked through the rain squalls and enervating heat, only pausing to recharge themselves at Monsieur Didier's grave.

By contrast, the two Swedish wives took no part in the defence of Saint-Esprit, uncomfortable in the face of Mrs Saito's kamikaze zeal. They sat beside their sleeping bags in the mess-tent, still stunned by the sudden departure of their husbands, who had sailed for Tahiti to gain more accurate news and alert the world-wide network of animal rights activists. Their impulsive departure baffled their wives, who were sleeping ashore at Dr Barbara's invitation, but she assured them that they had left under cover of darkness to avoid the French reconnaissance aircraft.

No-one, however, was surprised that they had taken David Carline with them. Mrs Saito and Dr Barbara had long written off the American, sitting like a deranged air-traffic controller in his derelict radio-cabin, unable to feed himself and a burden on the work of others. Soon he would be back in Boston, intimidated by his womenfolk and preparing his next missionary flight to the Congo. Neil regretted that he had gone, missing his quirky idealism, his anger at a world that had given him everything at his birth and then, piece by piece, taken it all back from him, draining him of the last vestiges of self-respect.

Secure at last, the protest banners hung astride the runway, their slogans stamped on the sky. In a moment's silence, everyone surveyed the defiant messages, clearly visible to any low-flying aircraft. But the spectacle was too much for Mrs Saito. Giving way to an attack of anger and panic, she hid her tears behind her hands, pushed away the sympathetic embraces of Inger and Trudi and ran sobbing to the plant laboratory.

From his sick-bed Neil watched her through the glass insulation door, pacing around the trestle shelves with their trays of obscure fungi, once carefully tended by her husband as part of his quixotic attempt to taxonomize the world. Neil found it difficult to remember the hard-fisted and clear-eyed woman who had helped to build the sanctuary in its earlier days. On the rare

213

occasions that she came to the clinic she would recoil from the mosquito net, as if surprised to find Neil still lying there. He sensed that Mrs Saito understood the causes of his fever and disagreed with Dr Barbara over its treatment. Once he heard her in the office, urging Dr Barbara to increase the dosage of the medicine she prescribed. But Dr Barbara was caring for Neil in her own way.

As Mrs Saito shuffled around her overheated bower, Neil thought of his child growing in her womb. She had lost confidence in herself, and Neil searched his fuddled brain for some way of reassuring her. He had never persuaded Mrs Saito to approve of him, but perhaps the time had come when she would appreciate his friendship. As a trained botanist she understood the vast pharmacopoeia of the plant kingdom, and might brew a herbal tea that could cure his fever.

Neil pushed aside the damp mosquito net and placed his bare feet on the floor. He stood up, trying to steady the clinic around himself, but a spasm of nausea made him retch into the bucket beside the bed. He wiped his mouth on the net and tried to smooth his hair, hoping to make himself presentable to Mrs Saito. Too weak to search for his clothes in Dr Barbara's office, he took Professor Saito's silk kimono from its peg behind the mosquito door.

Neil stepped through Dr Barbara's office, past the padlocked food and medicine cabinets that surrounded her spartan bed. He opened the rear door, felt his way down the wooden staircase and set off across the dozen yards to the plant laboratory.

As the glass insulation door closed behind him he shuffled into the grey, foetid air. A scent of rotting blossoms rose from the disordered vegetation, the rancid drupes and seed-pods, a plant hell where deranged orchids grappled for the light. The acrid stench seemed to come from his own head, as if these feverish plants recognized him as one of their own.

He leaned against a trestle table, waiting for his mind to clear, when a fierce hissing emerged from the narrow arbour where he and Mrs Saito had lain together. She was kneeling among the dying fungi, her face like the mask of a demented geisha. As she stared at her husband's kimono she seemed unable to recognize

Neil, and the hissing between her bared teeth became a guttural roar, defying an intruder from the grave.

'We want you to get better, Neil,' Dr Barbara told him as she drew the sheet down to his waist. 'You've always done so much for the sanctuary. Now promise me that you won't get up again.'

'It's good for me to get up.' Neil tried to settle his aching head into the damp cavity left in the pillow by Professor Saito. 'I feel better when I'm walking around. Anyway, I wanted to help Mrs Saito.'

'You frightened her badly. Her nerves have been rather stretched recently. I worry for Mrs Saito, as I worry for all of us – I hope we're equal to the demands we'll face.'

'I am, Dr Barbara.'

'I know you are. But I want you to stay here until you're well again.'

'Will I be well again?' Neil turned to see her response, and a wave of vertigo swayed through his brain like a giddy wind. He felt both cold and feverish, as if he were swimming through the confused waters of the lagoon where the deep currents met. 'Sometimes I think – '

'Of course you'll be well again. I'll always look after you, Neil.'

She sat lightly on the bed, her head inside the mosquito net, sharing this damp bower in which two of her patients had already died. Neil liked her to sit beside him, as she had done during their days together in the weather-station, surrounded by the white plumage shed by the albatross. The threat of the French return and the prospect of the sanctuary's end had drained the colour from her skin, exposing the insect bites that stared from her cheeks and forehead like semaphores of alarm. Outwardly she seemed calm and almost serene, as if she had decided to reject the possibility of failure. Her enlarged pupils worried Neil, and when she reached to the bedside table and took the syringe from the kidney basin he almost expected that she would inject herself.

'Turn over, Neil.' She spoke softly, in a voice she might have used with a docile elderly patient. 'Time for your medicine. This will make you feel better.'

Neil bared his left buttock to the needle, dreading the fierce local reaction that always followed the injections. He closed his eyes as Dr Barbara searched among the old entry points.

'Exactly what is the medicine, doctor? It usually makes me feel worse.'

'Medicines often do – the best medicines. This one will cool your blood, and make the fever go away. Now, toes curl . . . '

Neil felt the needle sink through his skin. The plunger moved under the pressure of Dr Barbara's strong fingers, but a tic jumped across the muscle in her nose, twitching her left nostril, as if she were re-calculating the dosage. Her fingers took over, forcing the plunger to its base.

'Is this the fever that Professor Saito caught?' Neil asked. He lay on his side, as the sweat ran from his face onto the pillow, and let his hand rest against her thigh. 'And Monique's father?'

'That's it. A rare fly-fever, local to Saint-Esprit. But you're much stronger than Professor Saito.'

'So the albatross might catch it?'

'Perhaps they will.' Dr Barbara returned the syringe to the kidney dish and massaged Neil's hip. 'You'll sleep soon and dream about them – I often hear you talking to the birds.'

Neil looked up at her steely but vacant eyes. She smiled in a lopsided way, like a long-term psychiatric patient, and he sensed that part of her mind had left her and gone to live on the wind with the great white birds.

'Dr Barbara – why do only men catch the fever? None of the women have been sick.'

'That's true. But in many ways men are weaker than women. They haven't our resistance. Still, Mrs Saito hasn't been very well. I think she might fall ill soon.'

'I think she might . . . and the Swedish wives.' Neil stopped himself, confused by the deviant logic that ran through their conversation. The sound of the women's voices by the mess-tent warned him that he was now the only adult male on the island. 'What about the French, doctor? They'll land soon, won't they?'

'I'm afraid so. This is their place of death. The sanctuary is too much of a rival for them.'

'And David?' He decided not to mention the scuttled yacht, reluctant to undermine Dr Barbara's calm resolve. 'He might come back to help us.'

'I doubt it, Neil – he'd done all he could here.'

'He was very tired. Like Kimo and Professor Saito.'

'Exactly. It was a kindness to let him go.'

'They were all very tired.' He waited as an attack of nausea rolled by like the waves washing through the wreck of the *Dugong*. When it passed, he asked: 'Why do the men get so tired?'

'It's . . . hard to explain. Men do tire easily. I've been a doctor for a long time, Neil, and as a whole men aren't very well.'

'Can't you make them better? Treat them with your medicine?'

'I have tried. But men carry a weakness they've borne with them from the past. Their genes have been poisoned by all that aggression and competition, so they're like soldiers who have seen too much of battle. We need to let them rest.'

'Where, doctor?' Neil tried to address his mind to this vast recreational problem. 'There are an awful lot of men around.'

'We can always find somewhere for them.' Dr Barbara was watching Neil in her kindliest way, as if mentally assigning him some quiet sward where he could convalesce forever. 'Men exhausted themselves building the world. Like tired children they're always fighting each other, and they can't see how they hurt themselves. It's the women's turn to take over now – we're the only ones with the strength to go on. Think of all-women cities, Neil, parks and streets filled with women . . .'

'Like Saint-Esprit, doctor?'

'Yes, like Saint-Esprit. A sanctuary isn't a place for the weak, it's a place for the strong. I've tried to set an example here, but I'm not sure now. Perhaps even women aren't strong enough. We've given too much, too much of everything, and especially too much love. Now it's the end of love.'

Despite his fever, Neil gripped her hand, wanting to reassure her. 'I'll stay with you, Dr Barbara. I won't ever leave.'

'No, Neil. You'll stay here.' Her hand touched his forehead. 'You'll stay on Saint-Esprit forever.'

Another air-raid alert was taking place. Supervised by Mrs Saito, the women ran from the mess-tent and took up their positions at fifty-yard intervals down the runway, striking the empty fuel drums with their machetes. Too tired to think in the clamour, Neil stood in the crushing sunlight outside the door of Dr Barbara's office. Scarcely able to breathe, he held his rib-cage between his hands, trying to force the air into his lungs. He could hear his erratic heart pounding against his breast-bone, its rhythm confused by the drum-beating women. Sweat streamed down his thighs, and he felt more ill than at any time since the start of the fever. He wanted to call Dr Barbara, but she was striding towards the runway, arms raised proudly to the banners.

Determined to leave his sick-bed for as long as he had the strength to stand, Neil fastened the kimono around himself and shuffled to the nearest of the animal enclosures. Almost all the creatures had gone, but two lemurs cowered among the debris in their den. Once Neil's pride, the spectral creatures backed away from him, as if aware that they were only a few steps from the evening's menu.

In the next enclosure a solitary peccary snuffled up to Neil, hungry for its feed. The hog-like beast danced around him, snout jabbing his ankles, trotters scattering its calcified droppings. In its search for food it had attacked the wire fence, beyond which Dr Barbara's private garden sloped upwards to the forest wall.

Neil leaned against the fence, pressing his inflamed forehead to the wooden post. Despite the excitements of the past days, Dr Barbara had been busy in the garden, digging more beds for the flowers she hoped to plant, apparently confident that she would remain on Saint-Esprit. One of the beds had been completed that morning, the broken soil still dark with the night's rain. Her spade rested against the canvas chair, a straw hat over its handle.

The peccary nudged Neil's legs, fretting to be let into the garden, nostrils scenting a treasure of insects in the damp earth. Neil ignored the creature and stared at the straw hat, a man's expensive panama that he had never seen Dr Barbara wear. The rotting brim had been patched with strips of raffia, and he remembered David Carline sitting beside the radio-cabin, threading the fibres into the scarecrow bonnet.

Had he bequeathed Dr Barbara this tattered relic before leaving with the two Swedish husbands? As his fever ebbed for a brief moment, Neil parted the barbed wire and stepped through the fence. The peccary squealed past him, ripping its coarse pelt on the wire, and raced towards the flower-beds.

Neil paused by the deck-chair, recognizing David's hat. Beside the newest of the flower-beds a shallow grave had been excavated. On its damp floor, two feet below the surface, lay a parcel of Neil's clothing, a faded shirt and cotton shorts, and the leather belt with the royal Hawaiian crest that Kimo had given to him.

Curious why Dr Barbara had decided that he would never need his clothes again, Neil drew the kimono around his chest. He assumed that she intended to destroy the germ-laden fabric, though she had allowed Neil to wear the garments until he had collapsed under the mosquito net in the clinic.

Lilies grew from the flower-beds in the garden, trampled by the peccary as it rooted in the soft soil, dragging at the tags of cloth that its snout had uncovered. Excited by its finds, it raced back to Neil and licked the salty sweat from his knees, then scuttled away to tug at a rubber-cleated boot that emerged from the ground.

All over the garden the disturbed flower-beds were waking their secret sleepers. Neil gripped the spade and began to loosen the soil around the boot. Its pair emerged, followed by a man's linen trousers, the calves stained with blood. Neil brushed away the sandy earth, still hoping that Dr Barbara had chosen to bury this contaminated clothing rather than burn it in the clinic's incinerator.

But the boots and trousers contained a man's legs, blond hairs stiffening in the sunlight. Scattering the soil across the bemused peccary, Neil uncovered the arms and face of the younger of the Swedish yachtsmen. He lay back on the corpse of the older husband, whose hands gripped his waist, as if hitching a ride into the grave.

A long-limbed man lay in the adjacent flower-bed, wearing the camouflage trousers and French combat boots that had once made Carline a figure of ridicule. The American's eyes were closed in a frown, nervous of the soil that covered his cheeks, and his hands were clasped around the Swedes' video-camera. Neil could imagine him standing by the graves, unsure whether to film the macabre scene for Dr Barbara and never realizing that he was about to become part of it.

Seizing the spade, Neil heaped the soil into Carline's face, covering his last grimace. As he swayed among the dead men he was aware of the camera-towers watching him across the lagoon. The old bunkers had been denied their nuclear finale, but were making do with these few small deaths and another yet to come.

The albatross sailed over the banners proclaiming their safety on Saint-Esprit. The women struck the steel drums with their machetes, but Dr Barbara was trying to silence them. She stood on the steps of the clinic, the kidney dish in one hand, searching the plant laboratory and the animal enclosures for any sign of Neil.

Neil threw the spade into Carline's grave and climbed the slope to the trees that formed the rear wall of the garden. While he forced the loose wire from its posts the peccary was dragging a human hand from the soil. The muddy fingers rose through the trampled lilies, trying to clasp the sky. As the fever flooded his brain Neil stripped the kimono from his shoulders and ran naked into the safety of the forest.

18

A Gift to a Death

THE BIRDS WERE STARTING TO DIE. While Neil lay in the deep ferns beside the runway he counted three of the dead albatross on the landing pier, their dishevelled wings hanging through the wooden slats. A fourth bird tottered past them, flat eyes staring at the lagoon. Too exhausted to take to the air, it sat glumly on the iron railing, unable to read the sky. A dozen of the creatures lay on the bonfire beside the radio-cabin, their wilting plumage like flowers on a funeral pyre.

Could he eat the albatross? Thinking of their oily flesh, and the cruel malady that now swept the colony, Neil fixed his eyes on the trestle table outside the kitchen. Three freshly baked loaves of coarse white bread steamed on an oven tray where Inger had left them to cool. Already a small, crimson-hooded honeyeater which had escaped from the aviary was watching from a nearby tree, as hungry as Neil.

Inger moved cumbersomely around the kitchen, hefting her abdomen as if already pushing a pram, and washed her arms in a canvas bucket. The camp was silent, and few of the women had stirred from their sleeping bags. Neil stepped from the ferns and slipped through the screen of palms, ready to launch himself at the baguettes once Inger settled down to her morning doze. Anne Hampton, the older of the New Zealand nurses, emerged from her tent with a towel around her shoulders and stared frowzily at the protest banners across the runway.

The signal bonfires with their freight of dead birds waited to be lit, and the protest banners flaunted their slogans at the empty sky. A line of chairs stood outside the mess-tent, ready for the press conference that would never be held if the French, as Neil assumed, failed to arrive. He waited for Dr Barbara to appear on the steps of the clinic, but she slept late, rarely stirring until noon. By then Mrs Saito would have roused the younger women and set them their tasks for the day, collecting driftwood for the fires, painting placards to be nailed to the trees and keeping an exhausting watch on the horizon.

The honeyeater flitted to an empty table, eager to make its assault on the bread. Neil whistled at the bird, holding its attention until Anne plodded away to the showers. As yet no-one had reported these early-morning thefts of the bread, and Neil hoped that the food was left for him deliberately, one of the few vestigial memories of the sanctuary's happier days. Despite Dr Barbara's attempt to poison him, he liked to think that Inger and Trudi retained a small core of affection for the young man who had been their lover and fathered the children they carried within their wombs.

Inger slouched in a kitchen chair, large and unkempt, feet on the stove to rest her swollen legs. A kettle rumbled towards its boiling-point, but she was lost in her thoughts of the child waiting to be born during the coming week, the first of Dr Barbara's babies to be allowed to greet the sanctuary. Soon after, Monique was due to give birth, followed by Trudi and Mrs Saito, and a unique generation of infant girls would begin the repopulation of the women's republic of Saint-Esprit.

Neil silenced the honeyeater with a raised forefinger. Inger's head lolled against her pillow as she crooned a Bavarian lullaby. He stepped across the open ground to the mess-tent, waved the flies from the trestle table and selected the largest of the loaves, placing his grimy hand on the warm crust.

'Salaud . . .!'

'Lazy shit . . . ! Get the bastard . . .!'

'Inger, we have him . . .!'

The steel blade of a carving knife stabbed his left forearm. Too shocked to feel the pain, Neil turned as Monique lunged at him from the side-door of the kitchen. She was almost cross-eyed with anger, a streak of white flour like an arrow through her black crew-cut hair. Facing him was Trudi, who had been hiding behind the water-butt, a meat cleaver in her small hand. Waving it to and fro, she was calmly sizing him up as if he were a pig about to be slaughtered.

'Monique, the other arm . . .! Little shit, he won't steal again . . .!'

'Inger, cut him now . . .!'

As the blood streamed down his arm, Neil stepped back and tried to defend himself with the baguette. The women had been waiting for him, and the unguarded bread of the previous mornings had been a decoy. What dismayed him was the open contempt in their eyes. He side-stepped Monique when she lunged at him again, hissing as if he were a mongrel dog with a vile disease that might infect her baby or her precious bears.

'Monique, it's me!' he shouted. 'We sailed on the *Dugong* together. We came to save the albatross . . .!'

'You came to save yourself!' Monique tried to slash his arm again, still nimble despite her pregnancy, eager to avenge herself on all the passengers whose seat-belts she had tightened. 'Go and live with the fish! Find another island – we rule Saint-Esprit!'

Inger strode from the kitchen, brandishing a shovel-blade filled with hot charcoal. Cursing Neil, she scattered the blazing ash across his bare feet.

'Trudi, make him dance for his bread! On the table, Neil, you can dance for us . . .!'

Trudi darted forward and sank the cleaver into the table-top. Neil feinted at her face with the bloody baguette and leapt across the stinging cinders. Pursued by the foul-mouthed women, he ran across the runway towards the trees. As he passed the clinic he noticed Dr Barbara standing behind the mosquito door, an arm around Nihal's shoulders. Chin raised, she surveyed the scene without expression, as if disturbed by a game in a children's playground.

Sucking his blood from the bread, Neil squatted in the door of the weather-station and shielded his wounded arm from the eyes of the ailing albatross on the cliff above him. The women's anger had startled him, and he felt too disturbed to eat the grimy bread.

He knew that Mrs Saito had disliked him from the start, perhaps seeing in Neil the toughness and self-confidence so lacking in her husband. Monique had always been wary of him, suspecting his motives for coming to Saint-Esprit, but he was sure that Inger and Trudi had been fond of him.

Now they had turned against Neil, partly because Dr Barbara's contempt for men had infected their minds, but also because he knew the truth about Dr Barbara and all the deaths of the sanctuary, a truth that they still hid from themselves and of which he reminded them.

Despite the sun, Neil shivered inside Dr Barbara's blanket. He pressed the worn fabric to his face and inhaled the faint odour of her body, thinking of the sweat that had once bathed his skin, a sea more potent than any through which he had swum. He wrapped his wounded arm in his shirt, remembering how he would stand naked beside Dr Barbara as she washed his clothes in the water he carried from the stream. He found it difficult to accept that she wanted to kill him, as she had killed Professor Saito, Kimo and David Carline.

But he knew now that Dr Barbara was demented, and that he had to escape from Saint-Esprit and report everything he had learned about her to the French authorities at Papeete. Her sanctuary for threatened animals had turned into an extermination camp for the male race. She had killed not only her fellow expedition members but the visiting yacht-crews who stood in her way, the parents of the young women she had seized for her breeding programme and intended to mate with Nihal. And she had killed Gubby and Neil's male first-born, forcing Trudi to abort the child.

All the men had died, but Dr Barbara remained a danger to everyone on Saint-Esprit, and would kill again when it suited her. Neil was shocked that he had tolerated her for so long, mesmerized by this strong-willed woman who had played on his childish infatuation with nuclear death and the vacuum in his life left by his depressed and passive mother.

Thinking of the robust affection that Dr Barbara had once shown him, Neil tried to find some way of excusing her. He could imagine her despairing at the sanctuary's failure and the imminent return of the French military. In some deranged way she had seen Neil as part of the male world and its death-games that threatened everything she had worked for on Saint-Esprit.

Yet as he ran naked from the burial garden he knew that his return to the weather-station was an act of faith in Dr Barbara – part of him still believed in her and wanted her to need him. At night, as he lay in the sleeping bag, comforting himself with the scent of her urine, he was aware that she could easily track him to the cave and ensure that Mrs Saito added his bones to those on the slope below the pathway. Somehow he would manage to report her to the French authorities, and see that she was arrested and brought to trial, but he hoped that she would always remember the weather-station, one of the secret places of the heart where Neil would forever wait for her.

These confused reveries of Dr Barbara had sustained him when he first reached the refuge. Exhausted by the climb, he had slept in the cave and dreamed of the lagoon as he seemed to swim through the shallows of his own death. On the fourth day his fever at last began to fade. His head and eyes soon cleared, and the blurred image of the hillside grew sharper as the world refocused itself. He tasted the salty wind stained by the albatross droppings, and could smell the bonfire that Mrs Saito had lit during a false alarm and then doused with sea-water, releasing a vast steam-cloud that capped the island for days.

For three weeks Neil rested in the weather-station, dozing in Dr Barbara's sleeping bag and recovering his strength as his body rid itself of the toxins that had poisoned him. Ravenous, he stole eggs from the nests on the cliff and gorged himself on the greasy yolks. Still naked, he crept down the forest slopes and searched the beaches for crabs and sea-snails. One dusk, among the rock-pools, he trapped a small turtle, severed its head with a flint blade and drank its blood.

The next day he explored the derelict hippie camp on the beach. Among the collapsed hovels and half-buried netting he found a ragged, hand-printed shirt and a pair of wave-washed jeans which he fastened around his waist with a length of electric cable. Already he took for granted that Wolfgang and Werner had never left Saint-Esprit, but lay in the deepest graves in Dr

Barbara's garden. David Carline had been right to believe that they were hiding somewhere on the island, certain that the Germans would not have abandoned Inger and Trudi to Dr Barbara.

But was Carline aware that Dr Barbara had poisoned them? Neil assumed that the insecure and unhappy American had been drawn into her scheme to recruit more women to Saint-Esprit, and rid the sanctuary of its male population, without realizing how she proposed to achieve this goal. Perhaps she claimed that the van Noorts had died of a mysterious fever brought to the island by one of the donated animals, a virus that soon became endemic within the sanctuary, and persuaded him to scuttle the yacht and dispose of their bodies for fear of alerting the French authorities.

Thinking of their meeting beside the prayer-shack, Neil guessed that Carline had been searching, not for yams and sweet potatoes, but for any sign of the Germans' burial place, suspecting by then that he himself would soon be Dr Barbara's victim. Carline had lacked the will to challenge her or warn any visitors to the island, while Neil had been all too ready to submit to Dr Barbara's ruthless ambition.

Neil had known that she was poisoning him, but dying at her hands at least brought him close to her and made him the centre of her attention. He had closed his eyes to the murders she had carried out, and by the end had been ready to be killed by her. For reasons of her own she had relented, perhaps testing him to see if he was the first of the men on Saint-Esprit with the strength to survive her.

And despite the deaths, Dr Barbara had been right – the men were weak, and the women strong. Kimo, Carline and Professor Saito had failed her and failed the sanctuary. Even now, after everything he had endured, Neil felt guilty that he had let Dr Barbara down. Secretly, he wanted to stay on Saint-Esprit until he had proved himself to her again.

Still wary of Dr Barbara, however, he only left the weather-station after dusk. When night had settled over the island he

226

made his way down to the runway and waited among the trees beside the aqueduct. Usually the women sat by the camera-tower, where they lit a fire after their meal, chanting a French round-song that Monique had taught them. Mrs Saito's preparations for the French naval landings had brought everyone together, and even the Swedish wives took part in the monotonous singing. Since the alarm first raised by their husbands, who now lay in each other's arms in Dr Barbara's garden, only two high-altitude aircraft had circled Saint-Esprit. Few sea-borne visitors ever called at the island, deterred by the grudging welcome and the rumours of a grim-faced animal rights sect in their Calvinist haven.

A passing multi-hull crewed by midshipmen in the Colombian navy anchored in the lagoon for no longer than it took them to refill their water tanks, watched by the intimidating group of pregant women. The Colombians brought with them a breeding pair of rare spider monkeys, but one sight of the abandoned cages in the animal enclosures and the fearsome knives hanging from the kitchen walls was enough for them to decide on another sanctuary for the threatened creatures. They thankfully raised anchor and sailed away to the fierce rhythm of beaten fuel drums. Mrs Saito had rung the loudest clamour from the dented metal, her small back turned defiantly to the nervous cadets, her raised fists threatening the van Noort sisters and the Swedish women when they were tempted to leave with the Colombians.

By now they were locked into Mrs Saito's mounting delusions. The ceremonial slaughter and roasting of the peccary, which Neil watched from his hide beside the runway, was an almost eucharistic rite, with the cowed Nihal served the first bloody haunch of flesh. Surrounded by the pregnant women, he uneasily sank his teeth into the meat and returned their approving smiles, aware that his real part in this intense drama had yet to be assigned to him.

Meanwhile, Dr Barbara worked in her garden among the graves, re-interring the feet and hands which the mischievous peccary had dragged into the light. She stirred the soil with care, singing to herself as she patted the earth with her spade, not wishing to disturb the reveries of sleeping men.

* * *

A glutinous mist rose through the forest, an oily wraith that lingered among the dusty tamarinds and eucalyptus, as if conjured by the waves from the ruptured fuel tanks of the *Dugong*. Secure in his sky-island, Neil watched the sickly albatross totter along the cliff, shaking the heavy vapour from their wings. A virulent plague had broken out among them, transmitted by some infected bird released from the sanctuary, and the healthier albatross had begun to leave Saint-Esprit.

Neil finished the blood-stained baguette and let the blood trickle from his arm onto the last crust. He threw his shirt onto the steps of the weather-station and lay back in the sun, already thinking about his next meal. Once he was strong enough, he would steal the scuba gear from Nihal's tent and fish for grouper in the lagoon. When Dr Barbara saw him with his spear-gun and wet-suit, ready to take his place again as the sanctuary's hunter, she would appoint him her deputy while she served her long prison sentence. In time, Monique and Mrs Saito would respect him, and Inger and Trudi would defer to him as the father of their children.

The mist coiled into the cave, a cloud of acrid dust tinged with fuel oil. Neil roused himself and stepped onto the parapet. Streamers of smoke wove through the trees on either side of the path, and a blizzard of unsettled insects swept the cliff face. The albatross rose from their rocky perches, soaring out to sea as the grey billows enveloped the summit.

Thrashing the smoke with his bloodied shirt, Neil made his way to the path. Rivulets of flame ran down the hillside like miniature lava flows, igniting the dry undergrowth and devouring the copper parasols of the dead palms. Drops of oily rain struck his chest and face, carrying with them the stench of diesel fuel.

Monique and Inger stood on the cliff above him, each holding a jerry can taken from the bulldozer's fuel store. Both were tired after the long climb from the camp, but they vigorously sprayed the diesel oil onto the forested slope, and then snatched the burning tapers from the tinder fire at their feet and hurled them into the air.

'Monique, Inger . . .!' Neil wiped the oil from his mouth and shouted up to the women. 'You'll kill the albatross . . .!'

Monique pointed to him and shook the jerry can. Looking up at her bared teeth, he realized that she had been eager to kill more than the birds when she set out to climb to the summit.

Hands over his face, Neil searched for the pathway in the seething smoke. Mrs Saito stood by the door of the weather-station, a pruning knife in one hand. She held Neil's shirt to the sky, a child's daub of her national flag, and drove the knife through the sodden fabric, slashing it into bloody strips.

Neil slid down the bone-strewn slope, trying to escape from these violent women who pursued him through the forest. Each carried his child like a gift to a death. Seeing him below her, Mrs Saito threw aside his tattered shirt and seized her jerry can. She showered the fuel into the air, drenching Neil in the volatile oil, and urged Monique to aim a burning taper at him as he lay among the sun-baked skulls and drumsticks of the endangered birds.

But Monique and Inger were staring at the sky, arms raised to follow an intruder into the island's air-space. A light helicopter that Neil had last seen on the landing deck of the *Sagittaire* was approaching Saint-Esprit from the north-west. It flew over the distant sand-bars of the atoll, circled the scuttled *Petrus Christus*, which the pilot had noticed in the clear waters of the lagoon, and set course for the main island.

Already Monique and Inger had dropped their fuel cans and were hurrying down the hillside. When Neil climbed the slope to the pathway Mrs Saito sprang through the smoke towards him, her eyes sharper than the pruning knife in her hand. She slashed at his oily hands, her voice lost in the steel band below and the beat of the helicopter's fans as they cuffed the air. Shouting at the flames, she ran down the path, following the burning forest as it rushed headlong to the sea.

'Man . . .! Lazy man . . .!'

19

Lilies of the Sanctuary

SILENCE, STARTLING ITSELF, had returned to Saint-Esprit. Neil stood in the centre of the runway, surrounded by the dead birds, and surveyed the empty and unguarded camp. Tent flaps stirred in the pale wind, and flies feasted on the unwashed oven dishes in the kitchen. Had Dr Barbara and the women abandoned the island, taking passage on a visiting whaler? Blackened by the bonfires, the protest banners hung askew between the charred palms. Everything that might conceivably burn had been hurled onto the pyres, and glowing embers still skittered across the runway. Sections of duckboarding and chairs from the mess-tent, cartons of animal feed and plywood placards lay in the mounds of sodden ash, their cores still smouldering after the night's rain.

No-one, however, had seen these signals of despair. Neil squatted beside one of the fires, warming his hands at a glowing cave, in which a dead booby had been roasted to its bones. He picked at the carbonized skin and tasted the oily flesh with its tang of kerosene.

For three days Saint-Esprit had been on fire. After escaping from Mrs Saito and her attempt to burn him alive, Neil had lived among the secret rock-pools below the cliff. Watched by the dying albatross, he trapped the fish and crabs as an immense anvil of dark smoke rose above the island, readying Saint-Esprit for the hammer that would split it to its core. For the first time since landing on the atoll he watched the horizon and willed the French navy to arrive, but the reconnaissance helicopter had not returned. At night he slept in the camera-tower beside the stream, guarded by Dr Barbara's obscene cartoon, while the flames leapt ever higher from the bonfires and set alight the trees beside the runway.

He was still numbed by the hatred he had seen in the eyes of Monique and Mrs Saito, and his infected arm-wound and the diesel oil that clung to his skin warned him that only death awaited his return to the sanctuary. From the forest above the plant terraces he saw them sitting with Dr Barbara in her burial garden. As they rested, pregnant and crop-headed among the graves, he guessed that they had known all along of Dr Barbara's plan to rid Saint-Esprit of its men, but he still found it painful to accept that he had been discarded by them.

He remembered his long afternoons with Trudi and Inger, when they had played like children with each other's bodies. Sadly, their happy hours with Neil now meant nothing to the German women, let alone Monique and Mrs Saito. They had used him to sire their daughters and then rejected him as soon as Nihal arrived with his younger and fresher blood.

Wiping the booby's fat from his lips, Neil walked along the runway towards the camp. The charred banners hung from their overhead ropes like the tails of fighting kites shot down in combat. A gust of wind sent a flurry of hot ash across the ground from a smouldering fire, as if the sanctuary was still venting its anger on the world.

Neil climbed the steps of the clinic and pushed back the open door. His unmade bed stood where he had left it in the sick-room, the impress of his shoulders in the damp mattress, dried blood streaking the grey shroud of the mosquito net.

Dr Barbara had ransacked the medical cabinets in her office, pulling back the drawers of her desk in a last frantic search. Phials and syringes lay scattered across the floor, as if she had inoculated a fleeing garrison in the final hours of Saint-Esprit. Neil sat on her narrow bed, avoiding the unwashed underwear between his feet, and raised the pillow to his face. He imagined Dr Barbara forcing it over his mouth and nose, and waiting until his breath fell silent. Somewhere among the ampoules on the desk, among the sedatives and abortifacts, was the poison she had concocted to kill Kimo, Carline and Professor Saito.

The botanist's silk kimono hung from the sick-room door. Neil touched the worn fabric, and then stepped from the clinic into the open air. Nursing his wounded arm, he walked through the drifting ash to the women's quarters. Outside Monique's tent lay Mrs Saito's wooden clogs, the only sign of tidiness in the disordered landscape. Neil raised the canvas flap and peered into the dim interior. A bitter scent rose through the swarming flies, a medley of mouth-wash, antiseptic fluid and a cloying Japanese perfume that evaporated from an open jar among the novels on the bamboo table.

Mrs Saito and Monique lay together on the small bed, hands clasped around their waists. Flies festered on their bruised lips, drinking the tears that filled their eyes. Their naked shoulders were speckled with soot that had blown from the bonfires, scattered over them like confetti at a sapphic wedding. Monique's strong mouth was drawn across her teeth in a last grimace, her gaze fixed sternly on the green roof. Mrs Saito rested beside her, small hips dwarfed by the Frenchwoman's heavy thighs, her face collapsed upon itself like a papier mâché mask. Her nose had swollen and darkened, and her thickened forehead resembled her husband's, as if she had already assumed his identity, determined to dominate him even in death.

Neil closed the perfume jar, trying to comprehend the strange pride that had led the two women to scent their dying-space for those who discovered them. Spitting a fly from his mouth, he stepped from the tent and steadied himself against the white geometry of the runway.

In the next tent, as he guessed, Inger and Trudi lay beside each other, Inger's strong arm around Trudi's slender shoulders. The dark had entered their faces and drained the flesh to the waiting bones, and flies fought among the open needle-marks on their arms. Already they resembled the pair of shabby hippies who had lived with Wolfgang and Werner on the beach.

Neil drew the cotton sheet across the women, trying not to look at their abdomens, where his daughters lay in their flooded wombs. But his head rang again with the warning pain that had sent him racing from Dr Barbara's garden.

'Neil . . .? You've come back . . . '

Blood smiled. Dr Barbara stood beside him, spade in hand, beaming at him with surprise and pleasure, as if interrupted while gardening by an unexpected friend. Her shirt was stained with the yellow craw-fluid of albatross, but she seemed unaware of the destruction around her, the exhausted bonfires and the dead women in the tents.

'Neil . . . ' Proudly she touched his beard. 'I hoped that I'd see you again. Mrs Saito said – '

'She's dead, doctor.' Neil stepped back, aware of the soil freshly caked across the polished blade in her hand. He feared the spade, which Dr Barbara might still use to bury him. 'They're all dead – Inger, Trudi and Monique.'

'I'm sorry, Neil.' Dr Barbara managed a contrite smile. 'They knew it was time to go. They asked me to put them to sleep. Now you can help me take them to the garden. The French won't find them there.'

'Dr Barbara – Monique isn't pregnant any more. What happened to the baby? Is she in the crèche?'

'No, Neil. We couldn't leave her to die inside her mother. The other babies were younger, they would have known nothing when sleep came.' Dr Barbara gestured with her spade, as if blessing the island. 'She's resting now in the garden, waiting for Monique to join her. We'll grow lilies over them. Lilies of the sanctuary . . . '

'Doctor . . . ' Neil turned angrily to the silent tents beyond the crèche. He counted the idling flaps, aware that the Canadian teachers, the two nurses and the Swedish women would be lying on the cold beds. 'What about Nihal? And Martha and Helena?'

'They've gone, too. They've all left together. They didn't want to go, so I helped them on their way.'

'Why? Dr Barbara, why?' Neil shouted at her, but she seemed suddenly deaf. He stepped forward and kicked the blade from her hand. 'Why did you kill them? They loved the sanctuary!'

'They needed to rest, Neil. All of them – even little Nihal.' Dr Barbara rubbed her jarred hand, smiling at the sky. 'They were never really happy at the sanctuary. Saint-Esprit asked too much of them.'

'You killed the men . . . ' Neil realized that he accepted the deaths of Kimo, Professor Saito and Carline, but the women's deaths were meaningless. 'Why kill the women?'

'They weren't strong enough. In a sanctuary only the strong can survive. You and I, Neil. We've earned the right to live.'

A faint cry, like a cat's plaint, came from the tent behind the crèche. Rousing himself, Neil seized the spade and held Dr Barbara away when she tried to embrace him. Blood leaked onto her teeth from an open ulcer on her lip. He hurled the spade at her feet and ran past her towards the crèche.

The New Zealand nurses lay on the floor of their tent, clothes and bedding strewn around them as they fought to save themselves. Patsy was barely conscious, and too exhausted to recognize Neil, but Anne raised one hand to him.

'Neil, find the children . . . be careful . . . Dr Barbara . . . '

Neil sat her against the bed and forced her to vomit. She retched into her hands, wiping the bloody phlegm onto her tunic, then leaned on his shoulder and gasped at the air. Satisfied that she was awake, he turned to Patsy, slapping her cheeks when she fell asleep. He knelt across her knees, massaging her thighs and driving the blood towards her heart as the Waikiki lifeguards had taught him. Both the nurses were dressed in their working clothes. He remembered the syringes and ampoules on Dr Barbara's desk, and all too easily could see her giving a promised vitamin booster to the younger women, helped by the trusting New Zealanders, the last to bare their arms to the lethal needle.

'The children, Neil. And Nihal . . . ' Anne sucked the air through her teeth. 'Don't let Dr Barbara touch them . . . '

Neil clasped her hands, waving the flies from her face, but she pushed him away and sat herself on the bed. Leaving her to care for Patsy, he backed into the open air, uncertain how to force Dr Barbara to revive the women.

She stood in the centre of the runway, smiling at a sickly albatross that tottered towards her from the beach.

'Dr Barbara!' he shouted. 'Anne and Patsy are strong enough! They can share the sanctuary with us . . . ' He waited for her to reply, but he could see that she had lost interest in Neil and Nihal and the young women she had poisoned. She wandered across the runway, the glowing embers of the bonfires flitting around her feet, too distracted by the demons of her tilting world to hear the sounds of an approaching aircraft.

A mile away, a French twin-rotor naval helicopter swept across the lagoon. Dr Barbara frowned as the craft scudded over the sand-bars, sending a froth of wavelets onto the black beaches. She pointed to the grey silhouette of the *Sagittaire* waiting beyond the reef. The corvette's raked prow and flashing signal lights emerged from the haze of smoke that drifted from the island.

'Neil . . . it's time, Neil!'

Dr Barbara strode up to him. After a moment of indecision, when she seemed unwilling to recognize the approaching warship, all her energy had returned. The insect bites glared from her bony forehead, and she was as committed and strong-willed as the woman Neil had first seen outside the hotel in Honolulu. In her hand she held the chromium pistol she had taken from David Carline.

'The French are here, Neil.'

'Dr Barbara, they'll shoot you – '

'Listen to me . . . there's still time.' She raised the pistol, as if ready to fire at Neil. When he stepped back, hands trying to catch the bullet, she pointed to the dying bird on the runway. 'Neil, we must kill all the albatross.'

20

The Secret Door

LOWERED FROM THE HELICOPTER, the last of the stretchers settled itself onto the after-deck of the *Sagittaire*. Neil shielded his face from the downdraught of the propeller blades, and followed the French medical orderlies onto the landing platform. Spray spangled Patsy Kennedy's cheeks and forehead like ice-beads on a frozen fish, but beneath the damp fringe her eyes seemed to recognize Neil. Passive and troubled, they stared at his freshly shaven face, as if afraid that he would hurt her. When he tried to touch her chin she flinched and turned her head from him.

Nihal, the Canadian teachers and the other women were safely below, being treated by the emergency medical team flown out to the corvette. All had survived – Martha and Helena van Noort, and the two Swedish wives – though none was yet aware of the fate that had overtaken their parents and husbands. Even the French officers who interrogated Neil had scarcely grasped the scale of the year-long massacre they had interrupted. Fortunately for Neil, a still shaky but lucid Anne Hampton had assured them of his role in saving the women's lives.

Major Anderson and his wife stood by the starboard rail with their binoculars, surveying the smoke-stained foliage of the forest slopes above the runway. Patsy Kennedy was carried past on her stretcher, and they broke off their search for Dr Barbara to pat her shoulder. Neil waited for them to approach him, but like everyone else they were wary of him, as if he were one of the survivors of a tragedy at sea who had turned to cannibalism. Neil suspected that for all their concern they still regarded him as Dr Barbara's principal accomplice.

Neil could feel the bruises that the Andersons had left on his arms when they stepped from the helicopter onto the runway, almost ready to assault Neil in their anger and relief. As he stood, drenched in blood, among the slaughtered albatross Mrs Anderson cupped her small hands over his eyes, trying to shut out forever everything he had seen on Saint-Esprit.

The stains of the birds' blood clung to their weather-jackets, and reminded Neil of the carmine streamers of shark repellent that had leaked from the jacket he found trapped beside the reef. Close to death from exposure, the Andersons had survived their intended death-voyage to alert the French authorities on Tahiti. As Dr Barbara expected, their fire-damaged sloop sank in the first rain-squall. After losing almost all their equipment, including the major's jacket, they drifted in their dinghy until seen by a Japanese whaler.

Whatever the Andersons assumed, Neil had killed none of the birds. He remembered his last sight of Dr Barbara, covered in blood as she slashed with her machete at the albatross, firing dementedly at the dying birds with Carline's pistol while the helicopter hovered over the runway, its loudspeaker blaring through the carnage. Dr Barbara had been poisoning the birds for weeks, setting out infected fish for them, saving them from a fate worse than their own extinction. Death, for Dr Barbara, was a secret door through which the threatened and the weary could slip to safety.

Almost to the end, Neil had believed her. Without ever admitting the truth to himself, he had known from the start that she had killed Gubby and Monsieur Didier, that she had poisoned the unwanted members of the yacht-crews and murdered Kimo, Carline and Professor Saito. But had he tried to warn the French, passing a message to a visiting craft, he would soon have found himself in the cemetery by the prayer-shack, or lying beside Dr Barbara's deck-chair in the burial garden.

He had accepted Dr Barbara's deranged logic, aware that he was only secure when he was with her and doing whatever he was told. From their first meeting in Honolulu she had played on his dreams of death, his senseless guilt over his father's cancer and the fantasies of nuclear apocalypse that presided over

Saint-Esprit. She had known, long before Neil, that he was sexually obsessed by her and unable to resist her ruthless determination to build her sanctuary.

The real sanctuary Dr Barbara had sought had been for herself, and for the cruel and dangerous strengths that no humane order could tolerate. Despite all she had done, part of him still believed that Dr Barbara was right. He searched the fire-blackened slopes of the island, hoping that she would evade the French landing party. He guessed that she had prepared for the end, laying down a cache of emergency supplies on an outlying sand-bar of the atoll, and was now hiding in one of the remote camera-towers, at last fulfilling Neil's dream for him. Had the Andersons died at sea, she would soon have been alone on Saint-Esprit, free to make her escape on a passing yacht and reappear with her protest banners on the streets of Manila, Cape Town or Hong Kong.

Even now, Neil found himself unable to betray her. He told the Andersons and the captain of the *Sagittaire* that she had become deranged after the helicopter's arrival and had drowned herself near the reef, in despair that the sanctuary would become a nuclear testing-ground.

As steam pumped from the corvette's funnel Neil counted the camera-towers for the last time. Dr Barbara had shown him a dream of death more real than any fantasies of nuclear war. He could still see her on the runway, spattered with the entrails of the dead albatross. She had thrown away the pistol and smiled a last bloody smile at Neil, as if regretting that she had not been able to welcome him to her realm. Then she ran towards the forest, past the clinic and the animal enclosures and her private garden, where the French landing party were now disinterring the first of her victims.

Signal lights flashed between the bridge and the runway. The corvette's engines drummed against the deck, impatient to begin the return voyage to Papeete. The *Sagittaire*'s captain had told Neil that the French government would sign the new test-ban treaty and had no intention of resuming the programme of weapons tests. Their patience had been exhausted by the nuclear and environmental demonstrators, and they shrewdly decided to leave Dr Barbara and her party alone on Saint-Esprit, confident that this puritanical sect led by the unstable woman doctor would soon destroy itself and so help to discredit ecological movements throughout the world.

'No sign of her . . . ' Major Anderson lowered his binoculars, clearly wishing that he could direct the corvette's fire onto Dr Barbara's forest stronghold. 'They'll need weeks to search the whole atoll.'

'She walked into the sea,' Mrs Anderson reminded him. 'Neil saw her – there was nothing else for her to do.'

'I might believe it – others wouldn't. For someone obsessed with death, that woman has a knack of clinging to life . . . '

'Neil . . . ' Mrs Anderson swallowed her scruples and took Neil's arm in a show of solidarity. 'When are you speaking to your mother?'

'Tonight – they're arranging the radio-link.'

'Good, she'll be glad to hear from you. All the same, be careful what you say, especially about all those tragic babies. Poor things, she'll hear about them soon enough.' Mrs Anderson checked herself, and her small face brightened like a hopeful moon. 'Remember – whatever happens, you're free of her now.'

But was he free of her, and did he want to be? Aware that the Andersons were uneasy with him, like the entire crew of the *Sagittaire*, Neil crossed the deck to the port rail. A white-masted yacht flying the American flag had emerged from the smoke that drifted over the water in the lea of the island. Its helmsman was unlocking the door of a large wicker cage that held a pair of gaudy but timid sun-birds, ready to release them to the sanctuary sky.

The corvette pulled away from the reef, and Neil looked down for the last time at the hulk of the *Dugong*. Others would visit Saint-Esprit once the French had left. One day, perhaps, they would come across an elderly British doctor living among the sand-bars in a nuclear shelter, eager to start a new colony of threatened species. Then Neil, too, would join her, happy to be embraced again by Dr Barbara's cruel and generous heart.